Memo to earthlings from Cupid:
You don't have a *clue*. . . .

And I watched her, sitting there with Nick, talking about *nothing,* and I lost it. I was fed up to here with listening to heartfelt prayers from people like Anna, and then having to watch them screw up or chicken out. I was tired of everyone wasting my time. True love is not for the timid.

Your want true love, lady? I fumed to myself. *It's your deepest desire? Fine. I'm tired of trying to justify my low numbers to management. You want it, you got it.*

I reached into my little bag of tricks. And just like that . . . ZING . . . right when the waitress brought their salads to the table, I tightened my bow, took careful aim, and shot the biggest true-love arrow I had. Straight into the center of Anna's heart.

Also by Diane Stingley

Dress You Up in My Love

i'm with
cupid

a novel

Diane Stingley

new york   london   toronto   sydney

An *Original* Publication of POCKET BOOKS

DOWNTOWN PRESS, published by Pocket Books
1230 Avenue of the Americas
New York, NY 10020

Library of Congress Cataloging-in-Publication Data

Stingley, Diane.
     I'm with Cupid / Diane Stingley.—1st Downtown Press trade pbk. ed.
        p. cm.
     ISBN 0-7434-6492-3
        1. Love stories. gsafd I. Title.

PS3619.T565I15 2005
813'.6—dc22

2004059397

First Downtown Press trade paperback edition February 2005

10 9 8 7 6 5 4 3 2 1

Designed by Jaime Putorti

Manufactured in the United States of America

For information regarding special discounts for bulk purchases,
please contact Simon & Schuster Special Sales at 1-800-456-6798
or business@simonandschuster.com.

For the three "transformers"
who taught me some truths
(both good and bad)
about human nature

acknowledgments

Thanks to the family for always being a source of inspiration.

Lots of gratitude to Amy and Megan for your hard work and enthusiasm.

And a special thank-you to Laura Bradford for all you do and for being willing to go down new roads.

Thank you, Stephen K., for finally buying the book in spite of all the soap operas that constantly distract you. By the time this comes out maybe shrub will be replanted.

Thanks to Bo, Sita, and Thay, for showing me what's possible (but never easy).

A very heartfelt thank-you to my wonderful landlord for giving me a break when I needed it.

Thanks to "shaggy" (aka Ed and Eleanor) for all the supportive emails, and Rose and Joanne for their kind words (cousinsville lives on!).

For Dorene Podinker, thank you for all your hard work in arranging our trip, and for understanding what is truly important in life—having enough bev naps!

To Rachel and Maryah, what can I say? Not only were you willing (and qualified) to make complete fools of yourself, you were there for every wonderful minute of the WORST ROAD TRIP IN THE ENTIRE HISTORY OF ROAD TRIPS. (On behalf of all three of us, our sincere apologies to the deer population of Virginia.) Rachel, thanks for the great posters. And Brian, if you're reading this, you'll always have a special place in Maryah's heart!

Amanda, thanks for keeping me company at my first (and possibly last) book signing.

For Star and Amy, how could words suffice? What would booth forty-two be without you? You're there for the ups, the downs, the nervous breakdowns, the narrowly averted homicides, and all the joy that comes from serving the general public. All I need now to make my life complete is a washer and dryer (how's that fund-raising drive going?).

And Audrey, it only took two years, but one thing I can look back on with pride this year is finally finding you a waffle. Now it's your turn to either find me a pod or a one-way ticket to Greenland.

Love is patient,
Love is kind, and is not jealous; . . .
bears all things, believes all things,
hopes all things, endures all things.
                    —I Corinthians 13:4-7

Love stinks.
—The J. Geils Band

prologue

I have the *worst* job in the entire universe. I handle romance for Planet Thirty-Seven (better known as Earth). Call me Cupid. You couldn't pronounce my real name, and if you actually heard it you'd be vaporized into ashes. However—and I cannot emphasize this strongly enough—I'm nothing like that moron you have hawking Valentine's Day cards. The fat little cherub with the idiotic grin. I can't stand that guy, and it is just so typical of Planet Thirty-Seven to come up with something that cheesy.

What I hate most about my job is listening to you people whine and complain that you can't find true love while you do everything possible to screw up your chances. I got so fed up at one point, I put in for a transfer over to Planet Forty-Three. I love the life-forms on that planet—they operate on a completely different level than you do, and the romance guy there has it made—but the opening went to somebody else.

My job didn't used to be this bad. Your average peasant or serf was too busy trying to survive to worry about finding true love; I only had a few knights and ladies of the realm to deal with. But these days everyone thinks they deserve true love. That means *billions* of you, and the stress I have to deal with is beyond belief.

What follows is a story of true love, which I'll be narrating as we go along. The front office asked me to write this book for a lot of reasons, some of which I understand and some of which I don't. I'm only a mid-level spirit operating on a need-to-know basis.

Sometimes you'll hear me clearly; at other times I'll let the story tell itself. It's a literary device I picked up from *Literature for Idiots,* one of the books I read before taking pen to paper, since I'd never written a novel before. The characters are real, although sometimes I put thoughts into their heads to illustrate a universal truth. This is an example of literary license. All the best writers use it, but I have an advantage over them since I've been observing human nature for centuries. Many, many, long, long centuries.

I hope you get something out of my book, but a word of warning: This is a story of true love, not a romance novel. The hero's chest muscles won't ripple, the heroine's bosom won't heave, and any and all throbbing will be left strictly to the reader's imagination. And it won't be a love story like what you see in the movies, either. There isn't a wisecracking best friend or a gay neighbor. The hero and heroine don't hate each other when they first meet.

In this story our hero and heroine are just two ordinary people trying to make their way in the world, who have to overcome a lot of obstacles and their own shortcomings in order to find true love.

one

Once upon a time on Planet Thirty-Seven there lived a woman named Anna Munson and a man named Nick Wells.

Anna was twenty-nine, tall and slender. Nick, thirty-one, was two inches taller and had a lean, muscular build. Anna's hair was light brown, naturally curly, and tumbled to her shoulders; Nick had dark brown hair with a natural wave his stylist knew how to make the most of. Anna's eyes were blue; Nick's were green. They both had high cheekbones, well-cared-for teeth and gums (Anna, especially, was a fanatic about dental hygiene. She'd never gotten over the horror of seeing her grandmother take out her dentures), and the glowing skin that comes from regular workouts at the gym and lots of bottled water.

Anna and Nick met because they were employed by the same company, and since they were both attractive, healthy, and well-groomed human beings, they'd noticed each other.

At that point there were three or four guys Anna worked with whom she found attractive. But she tended to avoid office romances as a rule, since it got awkward working together if things didn't succeed.

For Nick, Anna was just one of many women who met the basic criteria on his list of people he would consider sleeping with. But he, too, tended to stay away from getting involved with someone he worked with. He didn't like any kind of mess in general, and he firmly believed in keeping his personal life separate from his career.

But one day a group of people, including Nick and Anna, were in the break room getting coffee and talking about a difficult client. One of the group did a dead-on imitation of the client's nasal voice, mimicking how the client would call and say, "I think we all have the same *conception*, it's the *execution* that still needs work."

Everyone laughed, and it was Nick's laugh that first made Anna sit up and take notice. It started off slow, so that right about the time everyone else was done laughing he was just getting started. And they all ended up laughing all over again because Nick's laugh was so infectious.

As they all stood there laughing, Anna glanced over at Nick and their eyes met. Anna felt that first spark, that moment of recognition, that unexplainable mystery—the eternal mystery—the one even I still don't understand. How some little thing about a person gets your notice, or a moment happens, and you feel this pull toward them.

You could say Anna loved laughing, and that Nick's laugh simply made her feel good. And that she loved the way his laugh seemed to make everyone else feel good, too. Or you could suppose that his laugh reminded her of someone from her childhood. A favorite teacher, a beloved grandfather. Maybe her dad laughed in a similar way. Or that Nick's laugh made her think that anyone who could laugh like that had to have a real zest for life. You could say any number of things to try and explain it, and some of your greatest minds (such as they are) have tried. And you would still know that when all is said and done, the initial spark of attraction between two people remains a mystery.

Nick felt something, too, when his eyes met Anna's. It could have been merely a response to how she was looking at him; the simple pleasure one person feels when another person they find attractive notices them, too. It could have been the way Anna's eyes crinkled at the corners when she laughed. Or how pretty her smile looked (Anna had recently completed her semiannual two-week regimen with Crest Whitening Strips). But for whatever reason, he felt an attraction toward her, an attraction stronger than the one he felt for someone he just wouldn't mind sleeping with.

By then I had arrived on the scene, as I always do when that first spark ignites, and I watched as Anna and Nick smiled at each other for a second, then looked away.

The group broke up to get back to work after they stopped laughing, and I watched as Anna and Nick made their way back to their respective cubicles.

Anna spent the next few minutes at her desk thinking about Nick. On the one hand, she felt hesitant about breaking her policy of avoiding office romances. On the other hand, she hadn't felt this attracted to anybody for a long time. And they did work in different departments. He was in finance, and she was in marketing, so they weren't competing directly with each other. And wouldn't end up working on projects together or anything like that where they'd have to be around each other for hours or days at a time.

But it could still get awkward. What if they went out a few times and she thought things were going great, but he had a fear of intimacy and commitment and suddenly ended it for no real reason she could understand? Or worse yet, started dating someone else at work? And she'd have to come in every day and see the two of them together, run into them getting a cup of coffee together, and act as if she weren't bothered by it at all. Anna hated running into old boyfriends when things hadn't ended well—especially if he was with someone new—and having to plaster on that fake smile and make small talk and pretend none of the hurt had ever happened. Having to do it five days a week at work would be even harder.

But wouldn't it be wonderful to make Nick laugh? To sit across from him at dinner and tell a funny story, and watch as he threw his head back and laughed, the way he had in the break room? And she'd start laughing again, too, because he was laughing and because it was like this unexpected reward. As if she'd pulled into first place at the last minute.

So Anna decided she'd take a wait-and-see attitude. She certainly wasn't going to pursue Nick in an obvious way and become the object of office gossip. She'd seen too much of that around this place, and her career was too important to her to do anything to screw it up. But she wouldn't write him off, either. If something was meant to happen between them, it would. For all her practicality, Anna secretly believed that true love was a destiny that nothing could prevent. She also secretly feared that you could do one wrong thing and ruin your chances for love forever, which completely contradicted her first belief. But that's a human being for you. This is what I have to deal with.

Nick returned to his cubicle, had a quick sexual fantasy about Anna as he rebooted his computer, then got right back to work.

I didn't give them much thought. Nick and Anna were just one among many millions of romantic attractions I'd witnessed that day, some of which would lead to something, more of which would not. Nothing about their interaction alerted me to the possibility that they'd cause me any more than the usual trouble I have with you people. Little did I know.

For the next few weeks, I didn't pay much attention to Nick and Anna, since nothing happened between them. They'd run into each other sometimes, but Nick's department was unusually busy, and he was preoccupied. And hardly a day went by that Nick didn't see some woman he was attracted to, so Anna didn't stay on his mind the way he stayed on hers. The fact that he'd actually felt something beyond physical attraction toward Anna wasn't a motivating factor for Nick. His feelings weren't something he paid much attention to. If he never saw her again it wouldn't have meant much to him one way or another.

The first time they'd run into each other, Anna had felt

those nervous butterflies in her stomach. But his casual smile and hello as they'd walked past each other, the complete lack of energy on his part, had made her instantly withdraw and feel a little foolish. There you go again, Anna, she'd told herself, building a whole fantasy relationship on the basis of one little smile. After a few sad days of regret, she decided it would have been a bad idea for the two of them to start dating anyway.

But one Friday night a group of people from the office decided on the spur of the moment to go out for drinks and appetizers at a local bar. It had been a really bad week. None of the clients had been happy, management had been breathing down everyone's neck, the computer system had crashed twice, and everybody was tired and irritable.

"I need a drink," Larry from accounting had groaned when the copier had jammed the report he'd been copying for the third time. "Or three or four."

"Sounds good to me," Nick had said, standing at the other copier. He was meeting someone later, but she wasn't anyone special, just someone he'd met in a bar a few days ago, and he hadn't called her back yet to set an exact time for their date. He could use a couple of drinks to recover from the past week. "You want to see if anyone wants to go to McMann's after work?"

"Sure," Larry had said. "I'll send out an email. Let me just kill this freakin' copier first."

A short time later, Larry had sent out an email to a bunch of people in the office, including Anna, inviting them to join him and Nick at McMann's for a little attitude adjustment hour.

When Anna read the email, her heart had jumped just a little when she'd seen Nick's name. She really shouldn't go. She'd told Beth, her sister, that she'd go shopping with her after work for their mother's birthday present. Anna knew this was the last chance she and her sister would have to buy a present together, since both of them were tied up on Saturday and they were due at their mother's Sunday afternoon.

But, God, it had been the week from hell. And she wasn't meeting Beth until eight. That should give her enough time for at least one drink. She could use a few good laughs with her coworkers. They didn't go out all that often.

That's why she'd told herself she was going. Yes, she knew her heart had jumped a little when she'd seen Nick's name. But she'd caught herself and told herself that even if Nick hadn't been going she'd still have said yes. And since she knew nothing was ever going to happen between the two of them—he obviously wasn't interested—it would be ridiculous to say no just because he would be there.

But I knew better. I knew that's *exactly* why she was going. Not that she wouldn't have gone otherwise. But she wouldn't have felt that new burst of energy, which, she told herself, came simply from looking forward to some laughs with her office buddies.

Twelve people from the office went to McMann's that night. Somehow, Nick and Anna ended up sitting across from each other. It wasn't planned, not in the sense of them deliberately finding a way to be near each other. The laws of attraction have a life of their own, invisible to the human eye.

To tell the truth, Anna actually felt somewhat self-conscious when she discovered that Nick was sitting right across from her. For his part, Nick didn't have much of a reaction at first, because there was a woman sitting at another table behind Anna who'd caught his eye.

For the first hour, three or four conversations were going on around the table. Anna kept her attention focused on Sara and Lindsay, who were sitting a couple of seats to the right of Nick. The three of them shared their horror stories about the client they'd all had to deal with that week.

Then the server came over to see if anyone wanted another drink, and after he left and it was quiet for a moment, Sara told Anna to tell everyone the story about what had happened with the fax machine that morning.

Anna groaned, partially at the thought of what had happened, and partially out of embarrassment. Everyone was looking at her now, including Nick, and she found herself feeling shy and flustered.

"Come on, Anna," Sara urged. "You are not going to believe this," Sara told the group as they waited expectantly.

"Well," Anna said reluctantly, "you know what the Shop Smart people have been like to deal with this week."

Everyone at the table nodded their heads and rolled their eyes.

"So they're breathing down my back, calling me every fifteen minutes wanting to see the new campaign ideas. I keep telling them I'll fax them something over within the hour, and every time I tell them that, my computer goes down. I can't access any of my files. So I call Sid and tell him I've got to have my computer working as soon as possible because I've got this client making my life a living hell. And, of course, Sid is his wonderful helpful self and tells me he'll get right on it."

Everyone at the table laughed. Once she got past her initial embarrassment and got into it, Anna was a good storyteller. And they all *hated* Sid the computer guy, who acted as if they were morons because they hadn't memorized their computer manuals. He got away with things no one else at the company did because, unfortunately, they all needed him. Which he knew. So they had to put up with him, and pretend they liked him, and they all had ongoing fantasies about strangling him with a computer cord or knocking him out cold with their keyboards.

"So I wait and I wait and Shop Smart keeps calling, and Sid is pulling his usual passive-aggressive tactics every time I call *him,* telling me he's on his way and then never showing up. So I finally decide I'll just write something out by hand that I can fax over to Shop Smart and at least get them off my back."

Anna really got into her story at that point. Her eyes were shining, and she used her hands expressively as she talked. Nick found himself paying attention and forgetting about the woman at the other table.

"I'm sitting there, writing out my presentation, and Sid finally shows up. At that point I just want to finish what I'm doing, but of course Sid wants me to give him a whole explanation of what I did to make my computer stop working. And that's when I made my fatal mistake."

"Oh, God," Nick said, drawn into the story. "You didn't say it. Tell me you didn't say it."

Nick smiled at Anna, and for a moment their eyes caught,

caught in a way that everyone at the table noticed. Anna's cheeks flushed, lighting up her face with a soft pink glow.

"I'm afraid I did," Anna said, still staring at Nick, caught up in the story she was telling, and the feeling she was feeling, and forgetting her self-consciousness. "I told Sid I didn't do *anything* to make the computer stop working."

Everyone at the table laughed. And then Nick started laughing, slowly at first until he threw his head back and laughed the way he had that morning in the break room. Anna couldn't take her eyes off him, which everyone noticed.

"Anna, Anna, Anna," Nick said, shaking his head after the laughter died down, looking at her as if she were the only person in the room. "Will you never learn?"

"I know," Anna said, hanging her head in mock shame. "I have no one but myself to blame."

Anna looked back up, and she and Nick smiled at each other, forgetting everyone else at the table. There was a moment of awkward silence, and a few exchanged glances.

"Anyway," Anna went on, telling the story now for Nick's benefit but forcing herself to look around at everyone else, "Sid explains to me in no uncertain terms that ninety-nine times out of a hundred it's the user, not the computer, that causes the problem. And I know I should be getting the presentation finished or the client is going to be calling again. But knowing that if I don't sit there and pretend that what Sid is telling me is the most fascinating thing I've ever heard I'm going to have a broken computer for days, if not weeks. So I sit there, and Sid starts asking me questions I can't answer."

"Think back, think back specifically," Nick said, imitating Sid's voice. "What did you do differently this morning to your computer that you didn't do *yesterday* morning to your computer? That, my dear computer user, is the key to solving this little mystery."

"Exactly," Anna said, laughing. "And if I've told you people this once, I've told it to you a hundred times," she went on, doing her own Sid imitation. "I believe if you would take the time to read your computer manual carefully, you could avoid most of these problems and simplify both your life and mine."

Nick and Anna both laughed again. The others laughed, too, but not quite as heartily, because they were all beginning to feel like outsiders at a private party.

"This goes on for about twenty minutes. And I nod my head as Sid lectures me, as if deep down inside I know that he's right and I'm the stupidest computer user that's ever lived. And then the client calls, and Sid stands there tapping his feet while I'm on the phone *wasting his valuable time.* And sighing loudly about every ten seconds. Anyway, I finally manage to leave Sid alone with my computer, and I go to the conference room and finish writing out the presentation, and walk over to the fax machine, thinking this nightmare might actually be coming to an end. And what do I find?"

"Sid's dead body?" Nick asked hopefully.

"Unfortunately, no," Anna said. "Coming over the fax machine is a two-thousand-page document faxed to our office by mistake that no one can figure out how to stop. A document that has already been jamming our fax machine for over two hours, and will probably take at least two hours more before it stops. And, this is the best part, do you know what this two-thousand-page document is?"

"What?" Nick asked.

"A computer manual."

"No," Nick said.

"Yes," Anna said, nodding her head. "Somebody some-where, probably one of Sid's friends or his even more evil twin brother, is faxing over to the wrong fax machine the rough draft of a new computer manual."

Anna looked around the table. Everyone else laughed po-litely, but Nick laughed louder than anyone, which made Anna laugh. The two of them laughed together for a full minute after everyone else had stopped.

"Well," Sara said after a moment, when Nick and Anna stopped laughing, "I probably need to get going."

"Me too," Lindsay said.

"Anyone feel like grabbing some dinner?" Nick asked as some of the others started agreeing that they, too, needed to leave and started gathering up their things. By "anyone" he meant Anna, and he hoped no one else tagged along.

"I would," Anna said immediately, telling herself that one or two of the others would probably tag along so it wasn't like she was being obvious.

Everyone else at the table demurred and made excuses, even though a couple of them were hungry and had no other plans, fully aware that something was starting with Nick and Anna and that they wouldn't really be welcome. People paid their tabs, and put on their coats, and said their good-byes. And then Nick and Anna were there alone with each other, and happy about it, although Anna felt a little self-conscious about how quickly she'd answered.

"So," Nick said, "I know a great little restaurant about three blocks from here."

"That sounds good," Anna said. "I just need to make a quick call and use the restroom. Why don't I meet you out front in a couple minutes?"

"Take your time," a relieved Nick said, because he had a call of his own to make.

Anna stood outside the restroom and pulled out her cell phone to call her sister.

She felt bad that she was going to cancel on Beth. But she didn't want to risk losing the momentum that had started with her and Nick. Before she'd only been attracted to him, but now she felt like they'd made a connection. They could *talk* to each other. They made each other laugh. How often did that happen, the attraction and the connection? And so quickly, as if they'd known each other for years.

Anna was afraid that love has these moments, and if you pass them up and the moment is gone, then the love never happens. Like many of you, she believed true love is the most powerful force in the world, eternal and unbreakable, but then she acted as if it could blow away in an instant. How you people ever discovered fire and invented the wheel I'll never know.

Anna took a deep breath and called her sister.

"Beth," she said. "Hi, it's me. Anna."

17

"Don't tell me, you're running late."

"Actually, Beth—"

"Oh no," Beth interrupted, knowing what her sister's tone of voice meant. "You're not going to cancel on me again."

"I'm really sorry," Anna said, "but they moved the deadline back on the project, and I'm going to have to work late tonight and all day tomorrow."

Anna felt bad about lying to her sister, and she was sorry Beth was mad. To make it up to her she'd be forced to take an hour out of her day tomorrow to buy their mother a present and put both their names on the card. Which, no matter what Anna got, her sister wasn't going to like because she'd still be mad that Anna had canceled on her.

But, Anna told herself, it was just easier this way on both of them. Her sister had been married forever and had no idea what it was like to try and meet a decent guy. And it wasn't as if it was a complete lie. The project *had* been moved back a week. She *was* going to be working on it all day Saturday. *And* going in an hour earlier now so she'd still have time to shop for a birthday present. Nick was waiting for her, and she didn't want to get into a long, drawn-out discussion with Beth. She didn't want to ruin the moment or risk having her mood spoiled.

Across the room, Nick was lying, too. He lied to the girl he'd planned on meeting later that night. But he hadn't known the girl long and she hadn't been a particularly promising girl. More like someone who'd be okay to have sex with until someone better came along. And Anna was definitely better. She had girlfriend potential. Nick could see having her in his life for a while.

He felt kind of bad canceling at the last minute. Nick always did, but it never stopped him. The way he looked at it was, sex and dating was a game where you weighed your odds and took your best shot given the circumstances. He made up a work excuse similar to Anna's for the benefit of the not-particularly-promising girl's feelings. And since he didn't know how it would go with Anna that night—you never knew, Anna could be a compulsive talker, or spend the whole time telling him about the bastard she'd just broken up with a few weeks ago—he said he *might* be able to see her Saturday night and would let her know in the morning.

As Nick and Anna made their respective phone calls, freeing up their evening so they could spend it with each other, they didn't realize (and neither did I) that they'd set into motion some major cosmic shit for themselves.

Nick was kind of an innocent bystander in this, since he didn't want true love except way deep down in the most secret part of his heart (such as it is) and was not one of the people bugging me to find it for him all day long. And Nick was so unworthy of true love that in the normal course of events it would have taken him a few more lifetimes to even find true *like*. What follows is not the normal course of events.

Anna did want true love. She wanted it with all her heart. And since one of my most important duties is deciding if and when someone is ready for true love, I tagged along on all her dates to monitor her progress. But she was nowhere near ready.

Giving the arrow of true love to someone who isn't ready is a violation of the sacred trust I was handed when they gave me this job. I took an oath to honor that trust. No one gets submitted for approval to win the arrow of true love until I'm absolutely sure they're ready.

And even if Anna had been worthy, no way in a million years would she ever have found true love with Nick.

Maybe it was the pressure I was under from the front office, since I never came close to meeting the quotas they assigned me. They acted like it was my fault so few of you are worthy of true love. I kept trying to remind them what you people are *like,* and that there's nothing much I can do about it. We were all informed from day one that the most we could do is point you in the right direction. God forbid we should interfere with your free will. But these management types don't have a clue what it's like down in the trenches.

So maybe the pressure from upstairs got to me and I reached my breaking point. Or maybe after dealing with you humans for all these centuries, I couldn't take any more. Anna was simply the straw that broke the camel's back. Or maybe I was just in a *mood* that day.

But whatever the reason, before the evening was over I'd break the number one rule governing my responsibilities and obligations as a spirit: I'd send an arrow of true love to someone who wasn't worthy.

two

The way Nick and Anna behaved while having dinner together that night, you'd swear two more courteous and considerate people had never lived. They kept smiling at their waitress and saying "please" whenever they asked for something and thanking her whenever she refilled their water glasses. And both of them did it for the same reason: to show the other person how *nice* they were. That really fries my petunias. It's okay to fake an orgasm, but don't *fake being nice.* It really pisses me and the universe off.

Things were a little awkward at the restaurant in the beginning, the way it can be sometimes after two people first connect. Anna could feel herself getting nervous, afraid the momentum had been lost when they both had gone to make their phone calls. And then, walking to the restaurant, it had been hard to talk over the noise of the traffic and the road construction that was going on for most of the way. Anna fretted and wondered if they should have stayed at the bar and had another drink and continued talking while the mood had still been there.

Because Anna was feeling nervous and was less talkative, Nick had less energy to play off, and he found himself starting to feel let down. He'd been through this before. Meeting a woman, having a great first conversation. Thinking this was a woman who would be easy to talk to, and asking to see her again. And then somehow when they met again, the conversation would start to falter, and pretty soon he'd get bored with the whole thing. Nick never understood how men could have women friends. What in the hell did they find to talk about? The only time he felt really comfortable talking to most women was when it related to work or when he was trying to seduce them.

So Anna and Nick fidgeted with their menus, neither one sure how to get a new conversation started.

"Have you had the salmon here?" Anna asked.

"Yeah," Nick replied. "It's very good. The ahi tuna is also good."

"Really? Hmmm. I had a tuna sandwich for lunch. I think I'll go with the salmon."

Anna stared at her menu for a minute.

"I'm not sure whether to get the spinach salad or the Caesar salad," she said.

"I like the Caesar better, but that's just my preference.

They're both good. If you like spinach salad, you'd probably like theirs."

"Hmmm. Well, I haven't had a spinach salad in a while. I think I'll go with that," Anna replied, feeling as if she'd turned into the most boring person in the world but unable to come up with anything interesting to say. "I really like the decor here. And the way they have the tables spaced out. I hate eating at a restaurant and feeling like the people next to you are practically in your lap."

"That is annoying."

"I can't believe I've never eaten here, with it being so close to the office."

"I like it. I've been here a number of times."

"Well, if the food is as good as it looks I'll definitely be back."

Anna thought to herself: *Oh, God, I hope that didn't sound like I expected him to bring me here again.*

Anna and Nick both continued staring at their menus even though they'd both decided what to order. Each of them dreading putting those menus down and having to face each other. Both of them prayed their waitress would show up so they could kill a few minutes talking to her. At that point they would have been willing to listen to her entire life story. But the waitress didn't show up, and after a few more minutes they were forced to put their menus down.

And as bored as I was watching this whole pitiful production, as I have to do every night of the week, I did feel a little sorry for Anna. What she desperately wanted to do was have a really great conversation with Nick. Open up, let down her guard, and show him who she was. And thirty minutes ago, that had seemed like such a possibility.

But now it was awkward and forced, and she didn't have the courage to take the plunge. What if Nick had simply been hungry and looking for someone to have dinner with? What if everything she'd been feeling, and thought he'd been feeling, too, had been completely one-sided? Anna didn't want to make a fool of herself, especially in front of someone she worked with.

Anna wanted to say *You have the greatest laugh* and have him ask her why she thought it was so great. And she'd tell him *You really laugh, right out loud, from your belly. And you always wait a few seconds, like you're really thinking about what the person just said. So that when you laugh it's like you really mean it.*

But she couldn't. Her confidence had vanished, the mood was gone, and it would have sounded forced.

"I heard your presentation to the Morganton people was great," she said instead, thinking at least they could talk about work.

That's when I first started getting in my mood. Because even though I know how hard this stuff is for you people, I felt that if I had to sit through one more dinner with two people talking about their careers, I was going to throw up.

Nick smiled modestly and thanked her.

Their waitress arrived just as Nick thanked Anna, and they spent a few stress-free minutes giving her their orders. But the waitress apparently had no interest in telling them her entire life story, and she departed to get their dinner order under way. All too soon, it was the two of them alone again.

"It's weird," Nick said then, shrugging his shoulders.

"What is?" Anna asked.

"Everyone tells me that giving presentations is one of my strong suits. But the truth is, when I'm actually giving a presentation it feels like I'm back in high school and it's the fourth quarter and I've just blown the pass that would have won us the championship."

Anna smiled at Nick, feeling a sense of gratitude and relief. He was steering the conversation back to a more personal level. She didn't want to blow it; she wanted to say just the right thing before it got awkward all over again. Should she agree and admit to a similar sense of doubt about her own abilities at times? Or tell him that her friends in finance had told her his presentations were sensational? Or would that sound too—

"That really happened to me," he continued before Anna could respond.

And then my mood really darkened, and I started to feel sick. I knew what was coming next.

"I was the quarterback on our high school football team," Nick said quietly, the way I knew he would. "Everyone thought I had it made. But what they didn't know was that my dad never came to any of my games. He was always too busy with work."

Anna nodded her head slightly, listening to him with her whole being, wanting him to keep talking, but being careful not to look too intent so that he felt uncomfortable.

"Until the last game of my senior year, the one that would clinch the division championship. We were losing by two points. I called the next play and went back. Our receiver was wide open. So I go to throw what I think will be an incredible pass, the one that will win the game, and I trip over my own two feet."

"Oh no."

"Yep. To this day I have no idea how it happened. I just remember going down and eight guys landing on top of me, and knowing I'd just blown our chances. And I have to stand up and face the rest of the team. I couldn't even look at them. So for some reason I look up in the stands. And who do I see but my dad."

Nick paused a minute for dramatic effect, the way I knew he would. Anna was hanging on every word, just the way Nick knew she would.

"And we looked at each other for a minute," Nick continued, "and he smiled. I couldn't believe it. I'd just blown the game, the only game he came to, and he smiled. It was like the worst night of my life and the best night of my life at the same time. We lost the championship, and you know how at that age you think something like that is the most important thing in the world. But it was also the night I found out my dad was really in my corner even when I screwed up."

"Wow," Anna said. They always say something like that. Anna, like the many women before her who had heard the story, was unbelievably touched and flattered that Nick would tell her such a personal story so early in their relationship.

"So that's what I do during those presentations," Nick said. "I keep smiling even if I think I've just completely blown it, and pretend my dad is sitting in the stands giving me a smile of encouragement."

And then Nick smiled. He always smiled when he finished that story.

My problem with Nick telling that story wasn't that it wasn't true. It was. It was just that the first time Nick had ever told that story to a woman (her name was Lauren), it had meant something to him and she'd meant something to him. And she'd ended up sleeping with him, which she hadn't intended to do. And he'd known that and known telling her that story was a big part of the reason. Now it's simply part of his repertoire. It had lost all its meaning a long time ago. Nick and his dad never used that moment to build on, never really talked about it, and remain distant with each other. It has, however, gotten Nick a lot of sack time—if not on the first date, usually no later than the third.

He didn't tell his story that night with the immediate intention of getting Anna into bed. Nick was a realist. He could tell Anna wasn't someone who slept with a guy on the first date, and Nick was seldom wrong about these things.

He told it because he was bored and didn't know what to say and figured it was worth a shot. Maybe it would loosen her up and get her talking again. Nick always relied on the woman he was with to do most of the talking, although he also found himself annoyed at times because the women he was with seemed to do all the talking.

Anna smiled because he was willing to take the risk she hadn't, to share part of himself with her. When he was telling his story it was as if, for a moment, she could actually see the little boy he'd once been, trying so hard to please his dad (women are total suckers for that, as Nick well knew). She felt a warm glow. He surely didn't share something so personal with just anyone. So part of that glow was really about her, what his telling of that story meant about her or what he thought about her. But part of what Anna was feeling came from the best part of herself. Genuine caring for another person. Connection. Losing herself for a moment in another human being—their history, their struggles, their complications.

So for a moment she lost some of that ever-present self-absorption you all walk around with. I saw what she felt in her heart. Anna was having this genuine moment of connection.

"That's a great story," Anna said softly, taking a second to let him know she'd *heard* him before she said anything else. She wasn't thinking about what kind of impression she might have been making, or whether she was moving too fast, or saying the wrong thing. She wasn't really thinking about herself at all.

I thought she'd actually made some progress, and I see so very little progress. I forgot momentarily all about the earlier incident with the sister. I forgot the centuries of frustration and disappointment and how even though I don't really have a physical body you people still manage to give me heartburn. I was even running through my roster to see who might have been available for Anna, someone with whom she could experience some pretty good love (it's not true love, but it's not bad).

Nick met her gaze for a second, just a second, not too long, and then shrugged his shoulders and looked down at the table. That was his signal that it was time to move on. His goal was to soften them up a little. Show them he had the *potential* of being a sensitive guy, able to share his feelings. The shoulder shrug and the lowering of the eyes let them know how hard that story had been to tell, and that he was feeling a little uncomfortable now that he'd told it.

Most women got the hint and immediately moved the conversation onto safer ground. The ones who didn't, the ones who kept pushing him to share more, never saw Nick again. The ones who responded by sharing stories about the pain and heartbreak they'd gone through with their own families, as long as they didn't spend all night going on and on about it, Nick kept seeing. Most of these women spent weeks or months coming back for more, thinking that at some point the Nick they'd seen telling that story was going to reappear.

What Anna *had* been about to say was, "Nick, let's do something really crazy tonight. Let's just be ourselves. Pretend we don't work together, forget all that stuff, and just sit here for a couple of hours and tell each other who we really are. What we really think. What we really feel. And then, even if we never see each other again, at least we've had a chance to cut the bullshit out for one night of our lives."

Anna had never in her life said that to a man on a first date, or anything even remotely like that. But for those few seconds—when she forgot to worry about herself and how she was coming off and whether or not she'd ever find love, and was Nick the one, and if he was, what was he looking for in a relationship? And would he, or anyone else for that matter, really love her if they knew what she was really like?—for those few seconds, Anna felt an incredible sense of lightness and liberation.

But then she saw the shrug, the lowered eyes, the way Nick's expression closed over, and she knew there was no way he wanted her to say that to him. And that there was no way, now, that she *could* say that to him. She felt a dreadful thud and an unbearable emptiness.

Anna wanted that feeling back more than anything. It had only lasted a few seconds, but she wanted it back. And her name for what she'd felt, that incredible sense of connection and lightness and liberation, was True Love. A taste, anyway, of true love. What true love could be. The freedom to be completely yourself and be accepted for that. Cherished for that. Loved for that and that alone.

So before she said anything to Nick, Anna sent a swift and silent prayer up to the heavens asking for true love. It was one of the most heartfelt prayers for love that I had ever heard.

And then she put a big fake smile on her face and said, "I think everyone hates doing those presentations. I tried doing that thing once where you imagine everyone in their underwear, but that just made me want to laugh. Harold Bell in his underwear is *not* a pretty sight."

Nick laughed. Not one of his great laughs, but Anna knew she'd said the right thing.

"Did you ever hear the story of my first presentation to the Shop Smart group?" she asked, knowing it was one of her best stories.

Nick shook his head.

Anna told the story, and told it well, and Nick enjoyed it and laughed in all the right places. He told her his funniest story about a presentation that had turned into a complete disaster, and she enjoyed it as well. Anna and Nick felt themselves loosening up, starting to enjoy themselves.

And I watched her, sitting there with Nick, talking about *nothing*, and I lost it. I was fed up to here with listening to heartfelt prayers from people like Anna and then having to watch them screw up or chicken out. I was tired of everyone wasting my time. True love is not for the timid.

I know fear is the common lot of mortals. And even though I'm an immortal, we've had quite a few sensitivity sessions regarding the whole mortality issue. So while I can't exactly understand, I can empathize up to a point.

What fried it for me was that Anna, like so many of you, wasn't willing to risk anything. She prayed for true love with all her heart, and ten seconds later picked the safest, most neutral topic she could find rather than risk showing even a tiny part of herself to the person she thought she could love. This is the kind of crap I constantly have to deal with from you people, which the front office refuses to understand.

I was tired of getting all the blame because you people can't manage to pull your heads out of your asses. It's not a question of me being unwilling; it's a matter of you being unable. And maybe I wasn't so much angry with Anna as disappointed, because for a moment there I thought she actually had a shot at becoming someone who might one day be worthy of what she had prayed for.

But at the time all I felt was the anger. An anger that had been building for centuries. And in that moment, I directed it all at Anna.

You want true love, lady? I fumed to myself. *It's your deepest desire? Fine. I'm tired of trying to justify my low numbers to management. You want it; you got it.*

Take it from someone who learned the hard way. Always, in these kinds of situations, take the time to count to ten. If I had, maybe I would have come to my senses and realized what I was about to do before it was too late.

But I didn't count to ten. Instead, I reached into my little bag of tricks. And just like that . . . ZING . . . right when the waitress brought their salads to the table, I tightened my bow, took careful aim, and shot the biggest true-love arrow I had. Straight into the center of Anna's heart.

three

Anna sensed a tiny quiver in her heart, a moment's palpitation, and then it was gone before it really registered in her consciousness.

She picked up her fork and tasted her salad.

"Ummm," she said, looking at Nick. "You were right. This salad is excellent."

And as she looked at him, it was as if Nick became transformed right in front of her. Suddenly, just like that, he became the most beautiful human being she had ever seen. She literally could not take her eyes off him.

To Anna's eyes, he became physically perfect. Literally. Even his imperfections were absolutely perfect. His nose, which was just a bit too large for his face, was perfect. His slightly crooked front teeth; they were perfect.

But it wasn't physical beauty that made him beautiful. Even if he'd gone completely bald and put on fifty pounds, he would still have been perfect. It was Nick himself, his being, the basic core of goodness and possibility she saw, that made how he looked physically become absolutely perfect. Anna had never seen the possibilities of another human being the way she found herself seeing the possibilities of Nick.

The four men with whom she'd fallen in love and had had serious, long-term relationships had been attractive to her. Very attractive. And their personalities had been a large part of their attraction. Even the men she'd dated casually had always been attractive to her because of their combination of looks and personality.

But this was different, beyond anything she'd ever known before. And it wasn't lust. It was desire on a whole different level that had more to do with wanting to merge with someone, to know them at the most intimate level, and very little to do with physical gratification. That almost seemed beside the point.

Anna felt as if she was seeing the real core essence of another human being for the first time in her life. He wasn't a body to her or a personality. He was just incredibly human, and the fact of him being human was beautiful and fascinating and painful and joyous and heartbreaking and breathtaking all at the same time.

She saw all his possibilities and felt an indescribable sadness that life would never live up to him, would never completely afford Nick the opportunity to be completely and totally everything he was capable of becoming.

The mere fact that he'd been a child once, and all the struggles he'd had to go through to become an adult, was almost unbearable to her. And the fact that he would grow old one day and die. And everything he would have to endure in between. Anna felt the sheer miracle of his being in a way she'd never felt it for anyone else, not even herself.

It was the most wonderful thing she'd ever felt in her life, and the most terrifying. Anna literally had to force herself to tear her eyes away from Nick and take another bite of salad. She was shocked at the strength of her feelings.

And it had happened in the blink of an eye. She was a different person from the one she'd been less than a minute ago. A minute ago she hadn't even known a feeling like this existed.

I, Cupid, was also shocked at the strength of Anna's feelings, and I sat there watching her with mounting horror. I'd never seen such a powerful experience of true love before. I wouldn't have believed Anna was capable of it, even with the help of one of my arrows.

My shock and horror turned to despair as the gravity of the situation became clear to me. How could I have lost control like that? I'd let my emotions get the better of me. I'd reacted without thinking about the consequences of my actions. I'd let the behavior of someone else turn me into an idiot and act against my own self-interest. I'd tried to take my frustrations out on someone else and had only ended up hurting myself. I'd—oh my God—I'd acted like a human being.

This was a catastrophe. If the front office got wind of this . . . I didn't even want to think about it. I was in such deep universal shit.

Anna took another bite of salad as her vision of Nick subsided. The feeling was still there, and he still seemed beautiful, but the overwhelming sensations that she had felt might engulf her had been replaced by a feeling of deep, deep calm. She was simply content to be here with him. It was enough. It was better than enough. It was a gift. She knew she'd just had an experience that was rare in this life, and she felt an incredible gratitude it had been granted to her.

She started asking Nick questions about himself, which normally drove Nick crazy. But there was something different about the way Anna kept the conversation going. He couldn't put it into words exactly, but he didn't feel as if he was being interrogated, or like there was an agenda going on. She just seemed interested, like what he had to say was enjoyable to hear.

What Nick didn't realize was that what he was experiencing for the first time in his life was complete acceptance from another human being. But he felt it, and relaxed, and opened up a little more than he usually did, and he found himself enjoying her company.

After dinner, while Nick and Anna sat sipping coffee and sharing a raspberry torte, Nick was a pretty contented guy. So far, so good. Anna was great-looking, an easy seven on a scale of one to ten, which was about as high as he'd want a girlfriend to be. Still hot, but not so hot that he'd have to feel insecure or deal with other guys coming on to her all the time. Not too needy but not pushy. Smart, but not hitting him over the head with it. And easy to talk to. The last time Nick had been with a woman he could really talk to had been in college. Her name had been Lauren, and he'd thought they'd get married after graduation.

But Lauren had met somebody else in their senior year. Nick had never really gotten over it. He didn't know he hadn't gotten over it. He thought the fact that he hated the very thought of Lauren—not that he ever really thought about her, hadn't in years—meant he was completely over her. He thought he'd proven that by the number of women he'd been with since then. He thought that planning on never letting himself feel that bad again meant he'd learned his lesson and wouldn't make the same mistake. Maybe get married one day if he decided he wanted kids, but never again let the woman get the upper hand. And until then, keep it loose and casual.

So Nick was contented, having a good time, but he wasn't sitting there thinking Anna was someone he might possibly fall in love with. He was thinking he could see the two of them together for a few months. It would be nice to have some regular, steady sex for a change.

He figured it would take a few more dates, real dates, before Anna would sleep with him. Which would mean at least two or three weeks, what with the hours they put in at work.

Nick was pretty sure the not-particularly-promising girl would sleep with him Saturday night if he took her somewhere nice for dinner and maybe showed up with flowers. She had that air of neediness and desperation about her: laughed too loudly at his jokes, repeated her phone number three times when he asked for it to make sure he'd copied it down right.

As much as he was looking forward to having steady sex with Anna—once they got to that point—Nick also knew he was going to miss the steamy, uncomplicated sex he'd been enjoying for the last few months since his previous relationship had ended.

So Nick made a series of rapid calculations as he took a bite of raspberry torte.

He decided to see the not-particularly-promising girl tomorrow night, even though he knew he wanted to see Anna again. The way he looked at it, at this point he was still *allowed* to sleep with someone else. So even if he and Anna got serious, and she somehow found out, she couldn't really make an issue of it. Nothing that couldn't be resolved with an apology, a nice steak dinner, and a solemn promise that he'd never dream of cheating on her now that they were a committed couple.

But it would take some time to get the not-particularly-promising girl into bed: a nice dinner, drinks back at his place, setting the mood, etc., etc. And if they didn't finish up until two or three, the not-particularly-promising girl would most likely expect to sleep over. Might even make a scene if he asked to call her a cab at that hour. And Nick hated scenes.

They could always go to her place. That way he could leave whenever he wanted. But Nick really preferred to have access to his own CDs and choice of wine. And he hated having to start out on a couch he wasn't familiar with.

"I had a good time tonight," Nick said.

"Me too," Anna said, smiling.

He was pretty sure that Flannery's seated for brunch until

noon. So even if he and the not-particularly-promising girl didn't finish up until late, he could still get her out of his place by ten the next morning and have time to shower and get ready and meet Anna at Flannery's by 11:30 for brunch. Yeah, with a little planning this could work out really well.

"Maybe we could do brunch on Sunday?" Nick asked.

"That sounds . . . oh, I can't. It's my mom's birthday and I'm going to be busy all day with my family. We don't all get together very often, so when we do, it's a big deal."

"Oh," Nick said, disappointed.

"I'd invite you to come along, but you probably don't like me well enough yet to want to meet my mother."

Nick smiled.

"Maybe we should give it a few more days," he joked back, "just to be sure."

And as Anna laughed, Nick found himself feeling so relaxed and comfortable that he wished he'd asked if she was busy tomorrow night.

"I wish I didn't have to work tomorrow," Nick said. "I'd ask you to lunch."

"I'm going to be in tomorrow, too."

"You want to grab some lunch?" Nick asked.

"Sure," Anna replied, even though she knew it meant going in even earlier since she'd planned on running out to the mall when she broke for lunch, grabbing a quick sandwich and shopping for her mom's present.

After they finished their coffee, Nick and Anna walked back to the office building to get their cars. They didn't talk much as they walked, and neither one of them felt compelled to make conversation. When it came time to say good night, Nick decided against kissing her. He didn't want their first kiss to be in a parking garage, although later on, as he drove home, Nick wondered if that hadn't been a mistake. He always liked to get the first kiss out of the way as quickly as possible and lay the groundwork for his next move.

Nick went home and slept like a baby. Life was good. He had lunch with Anna to look forward to the next day, and then a night of hot, steamy, guilt-free sex with the not-particularly-promising girl.

When Anna got home she was too happy and excited to sleep yet. So after throwing in a load of laundry she sat on her couch sipping a glass of wine, listening to some music and re-living every moment of her first date with Nick.

Being a spirit, I don't need any sleep, and it's a good thing. Because I wouldn't have slept a wink that night. I was a complete and total nervous wreck, and I wasn't used to feeling this way. We spirits aren't like you humans. We don't spend a lot of our time having to wonder why we do the stupid things we do. Because we don't *do* stupid things.

But I'd done about the stupidest, craziest, most dangerous thing in all of creation that it was possible for me to do. And I had absolutely no idea what to do about it.

four

The next morning, I watched every move Anna made from the moment she first woke up, hoping that maybe, since I'd violated the basic rule of true love, her feelings might have worn off. Things weren't looking good from my point of view. The first thing Anna did when she turned off her alarm clock was to lie there for a few minutes smiling to herself. Then she leaped out of bed and got into the shower, where she proceeded to sing the entire time she washed.

She smiled to herself and hummed while she dressed. While she drank her coffee. While she put on her makeup. She whistled as she walked to her car, and there was a definite bounce to her step. All the classic signs.

But there was worse to come. Because on the way to work, Anna stopped at a Starbucks and bought a pecan mocha coffee cake. Not a slice or two to take in just for her and Nick, but the entire cake, enough to share with everybody. This was bad. This meant Anna's heart was getting bigger and more generous, one of the inevitable results when someone is experiencing true love.

As luck would have it, Nick was in the break room when Anna wandered in to cut up the coffee cake for everyone. Normally, for Anna, this would have been the crucial first-time-seeing-each-other-after-our-first-date moment. She'd wonder if it would be awkward and how she should act. But all Anna felt when she saw Nick standing there in the break room was happiness at seeing him.

She was still human. She noticed how great his butt looked in those jeans he was wearing. But then again, since it was Nick's butt and therefore the most perfect butt ever created, she would have thought it looked great no matter what he was wearing.

There were a couple of other people there, and Anna offered them and Nick a piece of coffee cake. She made a point of smiling at Nick but not paying him any noticeable special attention out of consideration for his feelings, since she wasn't sure how he felt about other people knowing they were seeing each other.

As she was leaving, he asked if one o'clock would work out for lunch. Anna told him it would and walked back to her cubicle smiling to herself. He'd said it in front of Bill and Gina, two of the biggest gossips in the company. He didn't care if people knew they were a couple. Well, not officially a couple yet, but seeing each other. Starting to see each other.

Nick didn't have any real thoughts about their encounter in the break room. He appreciated the coffee cake, and he noticed how nice her ass looked in her jeans, and he looked forward to having lunch with her. But he had other stuff on his mind as well. For one thing, there was an air of tension in the finance department that morning, and it felt as if it was directed toward him. His boss was acting weird, and Mark, one of his good buddies, was acting a little weird, too. Hadn't even made his usual "Buddy, we are in serious danger of turning into workaholics" comment, a long-running joke between Mark and Nick when they came in on a Saturday.

And he was having second thoughts about spending his evening with the not-particularly-promising girl. There had been something in her voice when he'd called that morning. He couldn't put his finger on it, exactly. She'd been cool at first, and then almost giddy when he'd said he still wanted to see her that night. Little warning bells were going off in his head, but then he'd think about how hot the sex might be, and he'd put them out of his head. But then, after imagining the great sex, he'd picture what it would be like having to talk to her for an entire dinner, and what if the sex turned out to be not all that great?

Anna got a lot of work done that morning on the Shop Smart account. Thoughts of Nick would break her concentration sometimes, but she was feeling so energized that she finished everything she needed to by the time Nick called her to go to lunch. Which meant she would have plenty of time to shop for her mom's present.

"Are you sure you couldn't go to your mother's a little later on Sunday?" Nick asked Anna as they finished eating. He'd told her about the tension he'd felt in his department that morning, and

Anna had made him feel much better about things. She was right. People had all kinds of problems they were dealing with that had nothing whatsoever to do with him personally.

"I wish I could, but I've got to be on my absolute best behavior on Sunday. I'm in hot water with my sister already. Thanks to you," she added, grinning.

"Me?"

"I probably shouldn't tell you this, but I was supposed to go shopping with her on Friday night to get the birthday present. But I called and canceled because I was having such a good time with you. So going late on Sunday is out of the question."

Anna smiled at him and took a sip of iced tea.

"That's who you went to call, huh?" Nick asked, smiling himself. What was it about Anna? Why could she say things that would make him feel cornered or smothered if another woman had said them? And why was it suddenly so important for him to know that she hadn't gone out to call some other guy?

Nick and Anna made plans to meet after work on Wednesday for dinner, the earliest they could get together in the coming week, and then they went their separate ways. As far as each of them was concerned, from their very different points of view, things were going very well, although Nick wondered why he'd passed up a second opportunity to kiss Anna and get the ball rolling.

I kept a close eye on them for the rest of the weekend, clinging to any little sign that Anna's feelings would start wearing off.

I watched Anna shopping for her mom's present, a little

smile on her face, saw how she kept noticing things in the stores and wondering if Nick would like them. She wondered what the very first gift she'd buy for him would be. His birthday present? A one-month-anniversary present? Or just a little-something-I-saw-and-thought-you-might-like? She was already feeling as if she couldn't even remember what it was like not to have Nick in her life. Everything was brighter, more interesting, little things taking on a new significance.

She called one of her girlfriends when she got home late that afternoon and spent two hours endlessly dissecting every detail of her date with Nick. They both agreed that the relationship seemed promising. At the end of the call, Anna couldn't hold it in any longer. She'd always been practical, down to earth, the responsible one. But she couldn't hold it in any longer. She felt as if she was going to burst.

"I'm in love with him," she blurted out to her friend.

"What?" her friend asked, flabbergasted. "After one date?"

"I've never felt anything like this before. It's as if my whole life has been leading up to meeting Nick. I know this sounds corny, but it's like destiny. That's what it feels like. Like Nick is my destiny."

Anna's friend Nancy was pretty skeptical about the destiny thing, but she tried to sound supportive and happy for Anna. When Nancy hung up the phone, however, she shook her head. She was afraid Anna might be getting a little desperate. And then, for just a second, she had this moment of deep, incredible longing. What if what Anna said was true? What if it had really happened for her just like that?

What would it be like to meet the one person you're destined to be with and know it right from the start? To be together forever. So Anna's friend, for just a second, allowed herself to wish for that incredible kind of love.

The moment passed and she went to take a shower, but I heard it. One more prayer for true love. Great. *Just* what I needed.

On Sunday, Anna was so happy that she gave all the credit for the present to her sister, which eased the tension. She paid a lot of attention to her niece and nephew so her sister could relax, and the whole family had a nice day.

Anna didn't tell her family about Nick. There had been a couple of other guys she'd thought might be the one. Not with the sureness she felt with Nick. In fact, those relationships now seemed flimsy and colorless by comparison. How could she have thought that was love? But they hadn't worked out (of course they hadn't worked out, they weren't *Nick*), and then she'd had to break the news to her family. She didn't worry that one day she'd have to go through the same thing with Nick. But she knew how they'd react. And she kind of liked having this wonderful, delicious secret they didn't know anything about.

Nick, on the other hand, left the office feeling vaguely uneasy. He'd felt reassured while having lunch with Anna, but when he got back after lunch something just didn't feel right. It could have been his imagination. It could have had nothing to do with him. But there was definitely something wrong at work that day.

He reviewed the past few weeks in his head as he drove

home. Had he screwed up somewhere? He couldn't remember anything. His last evaluation had been glowing.

Maybe he'd stepped on someone's toes. There had been that one meeting when he'd started talking about projections for the next quarter, when technically he should have left that for Mark to bring up. But Nick remembered having made a point of directing it over to Mark before he'd gotten too far, and after the meeting he'd apologized to Mark and his boss for the blunder. And besides, that had been weeks ago.

Nick was distracted when he got ready for his date, and he thought about canceling. He didn't really feel up to pre-sex small talk, and he wished he was seeing Anna so he could talk to her about the whole situation. But when the not-particularly-promising girl opened the door, she looked hot. Really hot. Nick forgot all about his work problems and all about Anna.

The not-particularly-promising girl felt a whole lot better seeing the look on his face. She'd been really angry at Nick when he'd canceled on her at the last minute the night before. And angry at herself as well. What was it about her that made men treat her so badly? And then she'd been angry at herself all over again for being so thrilled when he'd called that morning to say he wanted to see her that night.

But she'd still found herself spending hours getting ready for their date. And now he was looking at her like she was the center of the universe, and she told herself that she had to stop being so neurotic and insecure. It was obvious from the look on his face that he liked her, so why had she wasted all that time getting down on herself?

(Note from Cupid: Always be leery of anything or anyone who makes you feel as if you're the center of the universe. You're not. If you were, you'd be doing things like creating galaxies and solar systems and new life-forms.)

The not-particularly-promising girl, unbeknownst to Nick, had some serious problems. For some very good reasons, which I won't go into here, she's a very unhappy person. Nick wined her and dined her, said wonderful things to her, and made love to her three glorious times. It was the first time in a long time that she hadn't felt absolutely miserable and alone.

So when, the next morning, Nick was vague about when they were going to get together again, she didn't take it well. She knew exactly what it meant. He'd used her, just like all the other creeps who always ended up using her. And every time it happened she couldn't figure out what had gone wrong. It made her angry.

She screamed at Nick and called him names and ended up throwing her coffee mug at him. Nick was flabbergasted, and to calm her down and end the scene and get her the hell out of his condo—God, how he hated scenes, and he'd never had one as bad as this—he told her she'd misunderstood what he said.

"I'm just swamped at work. It's really crazy this week. But I want to see you again. Maybe we can get together next weekend."

"Really?" she asked. "You're not just saying that?"

"Baby, after last night, what do you think?"

Of course he was just saying that, and of course she should have known that, but she's really miserable and she couldn't allow herself to know what, in fact, she did know. Nick managed to give her a reassuring kiss and get her out of the condo. And now he was actually relieved Anna was busy and he didn't have to meet her for brunch. He was wiped out, and he planned to spend the day watching football and forgetting what a shitty weekend it had turned out to be.

Around three-thirty his phone rang. Nick ignored it because the score was tied and the team he was rooting for was ten yards from the touchdown line. His machine clicked on, and he heard the not-particularly-promising girl's voice. Nick wasn't surprised to hear her. He'd had a feeling she'd call. They usually did. It wasn't the first scene with a woman he'd had to endure, although it had been the worst. One minute they're screaming that they never want to see you again as long as they live, and two hours later they're calling and asking for another chance.

She went on and on. Nick turned up the volume on his television to drown out the sound of her voice. As soon as a commercial came on, Nick got up from the couch, got himself another beer, and erased the message. He figured she'd probably call a couple more times before she got the hint.

That was the situation as of Sunday. The good news was that I hadn't heard from the front office yet. My hope now was that the whole experience with the not-particularly-promising girl would have Nick so rattled and put off women that he'd back off from getting involved with Anna. Her feelings would turn from true love into unrequited love (true love is always reciprocated), which is so commonplace that the front office would have no reason to notice it.

But just my luck, the opposite happened. When Nick saw

Anna on Monday morning, she seemed like a breath of fresh air. So easy to talk to and be with. So grounded and in charge of herself and her life. He could live without wild, impersonal sex if it meant he wouldn't have to endure any more scenes like the one he'd had with the not-particularly-promising girl. Nick and Anna managed to have a quick lunch on Monday, and even though things were still tense at work, Anna made him laugh and forget his problems.

On Tuesday, there was another message on Nick's machine from the not-particularly-promising girl. As soon as he heard her voice, he hit the erase button without bothering to listen.

When Nick and Anna went out to dinner on Wednesday night, it didn't start off well. Nick had been looking forward to it, but he was getting more and more worried by what was happening at work—the whole air of tension and the strange way his boss and Mark were acting.

Seeing how quiet and distant he was acting, Anna asked Nick if something was wrong. He started to say no; he hated it when women grilled him, trying to get him to explain his every mood. But she wasn't looking at him in that annoying, inquisitive way that always made him feel as if he had to justify his behavior. Something in her eyes made him suddenly want to tell her all about it.

So he did. He told her how worried he was. He outlined everything he'd gone over and over in his head, the possible ways he might have screwed up, and she listened. Didn't interrupt him once. Just let him get it off his chest.

"So," he said when he was finished, "what do you think?"

"I don't know," Anna said honestly. "I know I've always heard good things about you at work. And I haven't heard anything through the grapevine about you or your department. But it does sound like something is going on. Maybe whatever it is has to do with Mark. Maybe he's the one who's having problems. Maybe that's why your boss is so distracted and why Mark isn't acting like himself."

Nick thought about that for a minute. It made sense. He didn't know why he hadn't thought of it himself. He constantly monitored his performance at work, and he couldn't imagine how he could have made a major screwup without being aware of it.

"Yeah," he said, "that might just be it."

He looked at Anna, sitting there with one hand cupping her wineglass and the other resting on the table.

"Thank you," he said, putting his hands on top of her resting one. "I feel like a huge weight has been lifted off my shoulders."

"You're welcome," Anna said, taking her other hand from the wineglass and placing it on top of his.

They looked at each other and smiled.

"Will you come home with me tonight?" Nick asked, without any of his usual lines.

"Yes," Anna said simply, without a second's doubt or hesitation.

Neither of them had expected it to happen that night, but it felt completely right and natural. And it was good. Anna didn't feel any inhibitions, and Nick didn't even mind letting her borrow his toothbrush or lending her one of his T-shirts to sleep in. When they woke up the next morning they both knew, and I knew (to my despair), that they'd become a couple.

Anna knew she felt more for Nick than he felt for her, but she thought his feelings would grow over time. Nick knew Anna felt more for him than he felt for her, but he thought she was too sensible and levelheaded to let herself get carried away into thinking the relationship was more than it was.

When Anna got ready to leave that morning, Nick offered to walk her to her car.

"You don't have to. I know you need to get ready for work."

"I want to. Let me just throw some clothes on."

Nick took off his robe, threw on a pair of jeans, and he and Anna walked out the door. Nick put his arm around her waist as they walked toward the parking lot. Anna leaned her head into his chest, and he leaned down and playfully nibbled on her ear. They were completely absorbed in each other.

So they didn't notice that they weren't alone or that they were being watched by someone who'd been waiting for hours. Someone who'd never had a single moment of the happiness they were feeling. A short distance off, in the parking lot of Nick's condo complex, leaning against a tree, staring intently at everything Nick and Anna were doing, stood the not-particularly-promising girl.

five

After she left Nick's condo Sunday morning, the not-particularly-promising girl felt pretty okay until the afternoon. She'd overreacted a little—God, why was she always doing that!—but it had all turned out okay. He'd forgiven her and said he'd call her that week.

But by early afternoon she started to get that horrible, sinking feeling she'd had most of her life. She began to replay the morning's scene with Nick. She saw herself screaming at him, calling him names, being so *pathetic* it was unbearable, and then throwing her coffee mug at him. Why did she act that way? Every time it happened she was so embarrassed afterward that she wanted to die. Every time it happened she swore she'd never allow herself to lose her dignity like that again. Not ever. No guy was worth losing your self-respect over.

Nick wasn't going to call her. Why would he after the way she'd acted? He'd just said what she'd wanted to hear so he could get rid of her. She felt so ashamed she wanted to crawl right out of her skin. If only she'd played it cool. He would have called. A lot of guys act weird and distant the first morning after you spend the night. They get a little panicky. It wasn't anything against her, it was just the way guys were. They had to get used to you being there. They all had these mother issues, and they were afraid you were going to try and take over their lives. It was just part of the deal. All you had to do was be patient and wait it out. If she could just learn to remember that instead of overreacting all the time.

I'll call him, she thought. Apologize. Make it cute and funny and let him know I'm not usually like that.

Around three-thirty that afternoon she finally got up the nerve to call. She got his machine.

"Hey, Nick," she said, "I just wanted to apologize for freaking out on you this morning. You must think I'm some kind of psycho or something." She laughed for a second to let him know she was okay now. "I don't know what got into me. But I guess a great guy like you is used to making women go a little nuts at times." She laughed again.

"I think it was a combination of lack of sleep, thanks to you, ha-ha, plus I've been under a lot of stress. I'm not usually like that. It's not like I'm going to throw my coffee mug at you every time we have a disagreement, if that's what you're worried about.

"So to make it up to you, I was thinking that on Saturday, I know you're busy at work and everything, but I was thinking maybe I could make you dinner at my place. You have to eat, right? And I happen to be a really great cook. Give me another chance to show you I'm actually a normal human being? Call me, okay?"

Feeling a little better, the not-particularly-promising girl tried watching a movie on TV, but she had a hard time concentrating. In her mind she replayed the message she'd left Nick, thinking she'd made it sound cute and funny and light. He'd hear it and realize what he'd be missing out on if he dumped her. Not just the sex, but someone who had a great sense of humor. Could laugh at herself in spite of all the stress she was under. Maybe he'd even call today and they'd get together again tonight.

Then this commercial came on. A guy is having a business meeting with someone, and as soon as it's over, he races back to his hotel room to watch, on his computer, his wife giving their kid a bath. The kid is giggling with delight, and the husband and wife smile at each other because they love each other so much, and their kid, and the life they've made together.

As she watched the commercial, seeing how people who really loved each other acted, she knew Nick wasn't going to call. She'd sounded like an idiot on the phone, now that she thought about it. Why had she kept laughing? Why had she kept insisting she was really normal? And who in the hell was Nick that she had to prove to him that she was a normal human being? Who was he to have stood there that morning acting like she was so weird and he was so normal? How dare he have patronized her?

Any normal human being would react angrily at being used. Because that's what he'd done. He'd used her. He probably thought because they'd met in a bar she was some kind of slut. It wasn't like she'd taken him home with her. All they'd done was talk and dance and kiss a little in the parking lot.

Okay, so she'd slept with him on the first date after he'd taken her out to dinner. But after all the things he'd said to her that night, how beautiful she was and how he hadn't been able to get her out of his mind ever since he'd met her. The way he seemed to hang on her every word. He'd acted like she'd meant something to him. That's why she'd slept with him so fast. She hadn't planned on it.

She was entitled to be angry. Anger was a normal, legitimate emotion. Most women were afraid of their anger, but she wasn't. Shouldn't she get respect for being willing to show her anger instead of just burying it and then one day getting cancer or dropping dead from a heart attack?

She should call him back and tell him exactly what she thought of him and everyone like him. You can't just go around saying things to people that you don't mean, like how beautiful they are, and you can't get enough of them, when you don't really mean it. Because if you meant it you'd want to see them again. Soon. Set a time. Not give bullshit excuses about being really busy with work, and saying you're going to call when you know you aren't and they know you aren't. You're just trying to get them out of your condominium so you can go on with your life as if they never even existed.

The not-particularly-promising girl went on like this inside her head for another hour or so, then wore herself out. She turned off the television, closed all her curtains, and went to bed. When she woke up a few hours later she decided she was just getting down on herself, the way she always did, and before going off the deep end she should wait and see if Nick called, instead of blowing everything out of proportion. She was smart, pretty, had a good job, could cook, was great in bed. . . . She needed to remember these things instead of being so insecure all the time. He'd call. Probably tomorrow; the day after at the latest.

The not-particularly-promising girl called her access number all day long from work on Monday to retrieve her messages, but there weren't any. That night she watched TV, waiting for Nick to call, checking the phone every hour or so to make sure it was working, but by ten o'clock she knew he wasn't going to call her back. She should have known. Oh, well, screw him. Who needs him? There are plenty of fish in the sea. She told herself this over and over as she tossed and turned that night. She vowed she wouldn't get all depressed over someone like Nick, someone who would treat another person the way he treated her.

On Tuesday morning she decided to give him one last chance.

"Hey, Nick," she told his machine, "I know you're busy, but if you could let me know if Saturday is going to work out, that way I can start planning the incredible feast I have in store for you. Thanks." She started to hang up, then added one last little bit. "And I need to know whether or not it's worth my time to pick up that little number I saw at Victoria's Secret last week. Dessert is the most important part of the meal," she finished, trying to make her voice sound husky and sexy and tantalizing.

When she hung up, she felt sure he wouldn't be able to resist. So what if it was just about the sex? It's always about the sex at first. They all think with their dicks. It's just the way it is. But she was going to make him the best dinner he'd ever had in his life. And she'd be more than just sexy. He'd see everything she had to offer. That she was smart and nice and funny, and yes, maybe a little emotional. But who wants to be with some boring woman who only agrees with you all the time?

Tuesday went by, and then Wednesday. She told herself over and over she was better off without him. Who needed a jerk like that? She wasn't going to let an asshole like Nick Wells ruin her life. She had too much going for her. She'd learned her lesson. From now on, no guy was ever going to use her again. And maybe one day she and Nick would run into each other. She'd be with her husband, the kind of guy she deserved, the kind of guy who got to know her as a person first before trying to get her in the sack. And Nick would see how happy they were, finally see how great she was, and be sorry he was ever so stupid as to let her go.

But as Wednesday night dragged on—nothing worth seeing on TV, no new magazines to read—she decided she was letting him off too easy. She should let him know face-to-face exactly what she thought of him. Because he shouldn't be allowed to get away with this. If nothing else, she should at least get to have her say. She deserved that much. She was a human being. And maybe, just maybe, she'd get through to him. He'd see how much he'd hurt her, what an asshole he'd been.

Maybe when he saw how wrong he'd been, he'd be the one asking for another chance. Not that she'd give him one. Not anymore. But she might get him to stop acting this way, see the effect it had on the other person, save some other poor woman from going through what she was going through with Nick Wells.

At nine o'clock on Wednesday evening, the not-particularly-promising girl drove over to Nick's condominium. His car wasn't in his spot, and none of his lights were on. He wasn't home. He could be at work, she thought. It could be true that he's so stressed out right now he hasn't had time to call. No. Even if he was busy and stressed out with work, a phone call only takes a few minutes.

Who was she kidding? He wasn't at work. He was out with another woman. The not-particularly-promising girl suddenly knew this as surely as she knew what day of the week it was. She knew she was nothing to him. Not a person, not anyone. Just some slut he'd met at a bar. A one-night stand. Someone whose name he wouldn't even remember in a few months. And a year from now, if they did run into each other, he might not even recognize her.

The not-particularly-promising girl drove home. She couldn't sleep, didn't even try. Just sat and watched reruns of old TV shows and counted down the hours until she'd leave again.

Early the next morning, when she couldn't stand the waiting one more second, she left a voice message with her boss saying she was sick and wouldn't be in. She splashed some water on her face, tied her hair back with a scarf, and headed out to her car. She stopped for a large cup of coffee and drove over to Nick's. She wasn't even sure what she'd say. But something. He was going to know she existed, that she was a person with feelings, too. She wasn't going to let him get away with just forgetting about her. She parked her car in one of the guest spots and sat there sipping her coffee. It was still very early; Nick wouldn't even be up. But he was home. She'd checked his parking stall before she'd parked her car.

She sat there for two hours, sipping her coffee and watching the front door of Nick's condominium to make sure she didn't miss him if he left early for some reason. At one point, as the sun started to come up, she almost decided to leave. But then she thought about the messages she'd left, how he'd heard them, heard how much she'd wanted to see him and couldn't even have been bothered to call her back. She felt totally humiliated thinking about it, and this was all she could think to do to try and get some of her dignity back.

Finishing the last of the coffee, the not-particularly-promising girl crumpled up the cup and forced herself to open the door of the car and step outside. She closed the door quietly and took a few steps. She felt nervous and stopped next to a tree. She leaned against the trunk of the tree and took a few deep breaths to get up her courage.

She was still standing there when the porch light at Nick's

condominium came on and the front door opened. She held her breath. This was it. It would take every ounce of courage she had, but she *was* going to confront Nick Wells and let him know just what kind of person she thought he was.

The not-particularly-promising girl stepped away from the tree and headed toward Nick's condominium. She was ready—as ready as she'd ever be—to face Nick Wells.

six

I watched the three of them about to meet up with each other in the parking lot—Nick, Anna, and the not-particularly-promising girl—and I was thinking I couldn't have planned this better myself. Not that I ever get to plan anything. Don't even have a clue who's on the planning board. Just a little mid-level spirit, that's me. I fling my arrows, give it my best shot, so to speak, and then take the heat when things go wrong.

And everything *had* been going wrong. Nothing was turning out the way I'd been counting on. Nick was more open with Anna than he had been with any woman since Lauren. He wasn't experiencing true love, but he liked her enough to be on his best behavior. I knew Nick could be a pretty good boyfriend at first, long enough to keep Anna's hopes up, her feelings of true love growing strong, earning me a summons to the front office.

And Wednesday night—I didn't want to even think about it. Nick had confided in Anna, let her see him a little vulnerable. Nick! And then, back at his place, he'd been tender and considerate. And the worst part was, it hadn't all been fake. He'd been giving her what he'd been capable of, way more than he usually did. And Anna was more smitten now than ever. Nick could never survive the long haul; he'd screw the relationship up eventually. But I knew I didn't have that kind of time. (Actually, on a metaphysical level, I didn't have any time at all, since as far as the front office goes, time is just an illusion.)

So when I saw the not-particularly-promising girl waiting for Nick in the parking lot, it seemed as if my prayers had been answered. Not that spirits get to pray; we just take orders. God forbid someone in the front office should ask us our opinions or preferences. But this little scenario might just solve my problems.

I watched Nick and Anna walk out together, Anna in the clothes she'd had on the night before, Nick wearing only a hastily thrown on pair of blue jeans. He put his arm around Anna, and she leaned into his chest. They were completely into each other and oblivious to the rest of the world.

The not-particularly-promising girl stood there and leaned back into the tree trunk as her insides went cold. She'd known Nick had been out with someone else the night before. But seeing it right in front of her face, she froze. Nick wearing only a pair of jeans, his hair still tousled from sleep, so obvious they'd spent the night together. Seeing the way he had his arm around Anna and leaned down to nibble on her ear. She saw the difference, could feel it physically in the pit of her stomach. How he was being with Anna was all the ways he hadn't been with her.

She wanted to disappear into some deep, dark hole forever. If Nick hadn't noticed her, the not-particularly-promising girl would have stood there frozen, praying they didn't see her, and would never have made a sound.

But Nick saw something out of the corner of his eye. He looked, and then looked again. *Shit.* He couldn't believe it. What was *she* doing here? Oh, God. Was she going to make a scene?

Anna, being at that point completely in tune with Nick's body, felt him turning slightly, and she glanced over. She saw him looking at something a few feet off in the distance, and she followed his gaze.

A strange-looking woman was standing there, staring at them with a frightening intensity. She had on sweatpants, a stained T-shirt, and a ratty sweater. There was a scarf tied around her head, but you could tell from the chunks sticking out at the bottom that her hair was dirty and tangled. But worse than all of that was the look on her face, as if Nick and Anna had done something to her personally.

Nick and Anna both stopped in their tracks.

"Nick?" Anna asked. "Do you know that woman?"

"Kind of."

"Who is she? And why is she looking at us like that?"

"We went out once. It's a long story. She's pretty screwed up. I'll tell you about it later. Why don't you go back inside?"

"Are you sure?"

"Yeah. I don't want you to have to be a part of this. Let me handle it."

Anna let go of Nick hesitantly. And then Nick, maybe to reassure Anna, or maybe to show the not-particularly-promising girl that she was being ridiculous—that it was over, that there was no point in making a *scene*—Nick gave Anna a quick kiss and squeezed her hand. The not-particularly-promising girl might have left then. So embarrassed was she, so mortified and ashamed and hurt. What had she been thinking?

But as Anna started to turn and go back inside his condominium, Nick looked over his shoulder at the not-particularly-promising girl. The look he gave her was one of contempt, and all her anger came boiling up again, washing away the embarrassment. Who in the hell did he think he was to look at her like that, like she wasn't even worthy of a moment of his time? As if she were a piece of trash?

"So, Nick," she shouted, walking toward him. "Who's this? Your wife you conveniently forgot to mention? Your girlfriend? Or is she like me? A one-night stand dumb enough to believe all your lies? Does she know where you were Saturday night?"

Anna stopped and turned around.

"What did you tell her? That you were playing poker with the guys? Meeting a client? Or my personal favorite, visiting a sick friend in the hospital? He was with *me* Saturday!" the not-particularly-promising girl screamed, looking at Anna now. "Telling me all the same things he probably told you *last* night. Take it from me, honey, don't believe a word this son of a bitch tells you!"

"Nick?" Anna asked in a choked voice.

"Yeah, Nick, we'd both like to hear what you have to say!"

Anna felt as if she was going to be sick. She thought last night had been the most wonderful night of her life. When she'd opened her eyes that morning the first thing she'd seen had been Nick lying by her side and smiling at her. She couldn't imagine waking up to anything better. And he'd been so sweet. He'd told her to stay put, and he'd brought her orange juice and coffee and . . . and now it was all ashes. She didn't want any part of this; none at all. Fighting back tears, Anna turned and ran.

"That's right, if you're smart you'll run!" the not-particularly-promising girl yelled. "Run and never look back."

"Anna!" Nick shouted, intending to go after her, but the not-particularly-promising girl stood in front of him blocking his way, and he lost his nerve. What was he going to tell Anna? What in the hell was he going to tell her?

"You thought you could treat me like nothing! Well, I'm not nothing! Do you hear me? I'm a human being, just like you. No, not just like you. I actually have feelings! You can't say you love a person and then just toss them aside!"

"I never said I loved you," Nick said quietly. He wasn't going to yell and scream and make the situation worse. He wasn't going to take part in her scene.

"I am not a nothing! I am not nobody!"

"You're nobody to me," Nick said quietly, not intending to be cruel, having no idea how his words would affect her. He'd never felt for a moment what the not-particularly-promising girl felt almost every day of her life; even when Lauren had ended it, she'd felt really bad and had been as kind as possible. Nick thought being blunt with her was the best way. That if she saw how pointless this was, that nothing was going to change his mind, she'd see the light and get on with her life. That's exactly what he'd done with Lauren when she'd looked at him so sadly and told him she'd met someone else. Stood up from the couch, walked out of her apartment, and never looked back.

The not-particularly-promising girl looked at Nick's face and knew she was absolutely nothing to Nick Wells. If she dropped dead in front of his feet right now, he'd simply step over her body and go back inside his condominium and take a shower or have breakfast. As if she'd never existed. And at that moment, that's exactly how she felt. As if she'd never really existed, didn't exist at all.

"I hope you rot in hell!" she screamed with one last burst of anger, then turned to run to her car and get out of there before anyone, especially Nick, could see the tears streaming down her face.

Nick ran back inside his condominium, thinking that's where Anna had to be. But Anna had run past his door and gone around the other way to where her car was parked, and by the time Nick got inside she was already on her way home to change her clothes and get ready for work.

While I was very relieved that my problems seemed to be coming to an end, I felt very bad for the not-particularly-promising girl getting caught up in the middle of all this.

There are quite a few like her wandering around your planet. But since she had absolutely no ability to find the love she so desperately craved, my dealings with her up until now had been almost nonexistent.

Most likely, Stan was on the case. He's the spirit in charge of humans who have a whole lot of crap dumped on them at an early age and pay the price for the rest of their lives. I don't understand why it happens any more than you do. All I can say is what the front office told me during training: the universe knows what it's doing, and no matter how unfair something might appear, we have to trust the final outcome.

But as badly as things were going for me, I thanked my lucky stars I wasn't in Stan's shoes. Feeling the not-particularly-promising girl's heart seething with rage and vengeance and fury, I didn't envy Stan his job one little bit. And I knew she wasn't done with Nick Wells. Not by a long shot.

seven

Anna left Nick's place frantic and in a daze. She was already short on time. She needed to get home, shower and change, and be at work in less than an hour and a half.

Anna's first reaction in the parking lot had been one of shock and disbelief. She'd felt numb and hadn't even been able to take in, let alone face, what was happening. All she'd known was that she had to get out of there.

As Anna drove home and the shock wore off, she went from being a woman in love with the most wonderful man in the world to being someone who had just slept with a man who might conceivably be a complete bastard. A real creep. Probably had women all over the place. God, she should have known better than to get involved with someone she worked with. Now she was going to have to see him every day at the office, and it was going to be awkward as hell.

She felt like an idiot. Anna never slept with a guy that soon. Never. But Nick had seemed so right, she'd felt so sure about the two of them, the moment had seemed so perfect that there hadn't seemed any point in waiting. God. What if he was the kind of guy who gave out *details?*

Even though this would solve my dilemma and get me off the hook, I didn't enjoy seeing Anna suffer. I get frustrated with you people, especially your persistent illusion that the person you're in love with is the most wonderful person in the world. Has your beloved achieved complete spiritual enlightenment? Worked day and night in pursuit of world peace or a solution to one of the many ills plaguing your world? The odds are very good they are not the most wonderful person in the world, even if they do make you feel all giddy inside.

But I knew I was partially responsible for the pain she was going through. Without my interference she might still have gotten involved with Nick. But she wouldn't have loved him with her whole heart and soul. She wouldn't be feeling *this* bad.

I hoped Anna would learn from this experience. Become stronger, wiser, more compassionate, more discerning. See that maybe she had a way to go before she could have the kind of relationship she wanted. Move a little closer to being someone worthy of true love. That's what I hoped. The front office has a real thing about unnecessary suffering.

Anna arrived home and went into the bathroom to take a

shower. She couldn't take the day off; there was too much going on at work. She'd have to get through the day somehow, although the thought of having to see Nick at work filled her with dread.

Anna turned on the shower nozzle and waited for the water to heat up. As she put her hand under the shower spray, she wondered who that woman had been. His girlfriend, someone he cheated on all the time? But no one at work had mentioned he had a girlfriend. A one-night stand? An ex-girlfriend who still wasn't over him?

Anna realized she had no idea *who* that woman was to Nick or whether she had been telling the truth. She hadn't even given Nick a chance to tell his side of the story.

Could I have been that wrong about him? Anna asked herself as the shower water streamed down her back. Like most people, Anna prided herself on being a good judge of character, and like most people she was completely wrong about this. Self-awareness is *not* your strong suit.

There might be an explanation, Anna told herself. Shouldn't she at least hear him out?

I wasn't surprised when I saw a look of relief cross her face as she decided to let Nick tell her his side of the story. Avoidance of pain is built right into your wiring, and letting go of Nick was going to be hard for her. She might waver back and forth before she found the strength to end it with him once and for all.

I felt pretty confident that's how it would turn out. I knew my Anna. I knew no matter what explanation Nick gave, the scene in the parking lot would continue to haunt her. Little nagging doubts and fears would eat away at the foundation of her love for him. Even now, just moments after deciding to hear him out, she was already wondering if she could really believe what Nick told her. How would she ever know for sure?

And watching her, reading her heart, feeling the fear, the doubt, the mistrust, sensing how her liberation was gone, how she was already in that place where her relationship caused her more pain than happiness, I knew I'd been right. Even if she decided to take him back, Anna's brief taste of true love had come to an end, and we could all get on with our lives.

But then, as she applied conditioner to her hair, Anna remembered the vision she'd had in the restaurant the first night she and Nick had had dinner together, when he'd seemed to be bathed in light. She remembered how that had felt, to see another person in that way, to feel as if she herself had been lifted up to a whole other level simply by having that vision of someone else. There had been a truth to that vision that she couldn't explain in words. A basic, fundamental truth.

What if she simply decided to trust that vision? Trust its truth, and her own heart, without reservation? Because she chose to. Because it had been the best, most liberating feeling she'd ever had, which nothing else she'd ever experienced could even compare to. Because going back to being the person she'd been before felt small and confining, like closing all the windows in a room to block out the sun and air.

What if she stopped stepping back to constantly analyze the relationship and try and read signs and figure out signals, and analyze Nick and analyze herself, and how she was with Nick and how he reacted to her, and how that made her feel, and how it seemed to make him feel. And were they growing as a couple, developing, or simply standing still? Was there any future in their relationship or had they gone as far as they could go?

Were her expectations too high or too low, and were her expectations the same as Nick's expectations? And if not, was there some middle ground they could find that would still be satisfactory to both of them and meet their needs? And did they need to improve their communication skills, were things being left unsaid on both sides, assumptions being made but not fulfilled so that both parties had buried anger and resentments? Just where were they, exactly, as a couple?

God, she'd never realized how tired she was of analyzing her relationships. And what if instead of all that she just loved him?

Anna turned off the shower and reached for a towel. As she wrapped the towel around herself, she realized she'd never felt so light and free, like walking two inches off the ground. This must be what it's like to feel joy, she thought. Pure and absolute joy.

I watched her and felt hopelessness set in. This wasn't a last, desperate attempt to hang on to somebody. This wasn't about kidding herself or trying to tell herself anything to avoid the truth. This was the river that everyone on the journey of true love has to cross at some point, the fork in the road where illusion is replaced by faith.

It just wasn't possible. She wasn't capable of this even with the right person, and someone like Nick certainly shouldn't have brought it out in her. So how was this happening? She'd given no previous signs of having this kind of potential. How could I have so misjudged her? I may have the worst job in the universe, but I'm usually pretty damn good at it, considering the material I have to work with. I felt all the love pouring through her heart—all that damn stinkin' love—and even though it's my area of expertise, I was at a complete loss to explain it.

Meanwhile, Nick had his whole story worked out. It had taken him most of the drive in to work to get all the details straight, to figure out how to tell enough of the truth to sound believable but not enough to make Anna really pissed off at him. And now he had it down pat.

In Nick's opinion, he hadn't actually done anything wrong, but he knew he couldn't tell Anna the whole truth. That the not-particularly-promising girl was just someone he'd slept with. No big deal. He'd barely known her. How was he supposed to have known she was some kind of psycho?

And it wasn't like he and Anna had had any kind of commitment when he'd slept with the other girl. He'd had a great time Friday night. He'd wanted to see Anna again. And it wasn't like he was going to cheat on her if they actually got together. But you can't expect a guy to be celibate just because you had one nice dinner together. Yeah, like he could tell Anna *that*. Not when the two of them had ended up sleeping together so soon.

He knew women, and he knew sleeping with him wasn't something Anna had done lightly, and he knew she'd take it personally, like she was just another conquest. What he'd done Saturday had had nothing to do with Anna, but women never saw it that way. How was he supposed to have known she'd end up spending the night with him on Wednesday? He didn't have a crystal ball.

So he'd concocted a good cover story. Not because he wanted to lie; he had to. Women made guys lie. They said they wanted honesty, but just try it sometime and see where it got you.

When Anna got into work around eight-thirty, feeling more alive than she had since childhood, there was a voice mail waiting for her from Nick.

"Anna," Nick's voice mail said, "I am so sorry about this morning. Can we get together tonight? I want to explain what happened. I can't believe she . . . no, I don't want to try and go into it over the phone. Give me a call when you can."

Anna dialed his extension, knowing exactly what she wanted to say, but Nick was on the other line.

"Hey, Nick," she told his voice mail, "it's Anna. I'd love to get together tonight. And I think we should just forget about what happened this morning. You don't owe me any explanations. What's in the past is in the past. I'm going to be here until around seven or so. What would you think about just staying in and ordering a pizza? Let me know."

Anna smiled to herself as she played back her other messages. She felt like she'd discovered an incredible secret. All you had to do was trust and let go. She'd taken what could have been one of the worst mornings of her life and turned it around. It was really all so simple if you just had the courage to let yourself truly love someone.

Nick got off the phone a few minutes later and immediately checked his voice mail, hoping Anna had called. But when Nick finished listening to Anna's message he wasn't sure how to react. He should have been doing cartwheels. She didn't demand or even want an explanation. He wasn't going to have to go through hoops to make it up to her. He'd hit the jackpot.

He got up to get himself a cup of coffee. Walking toward the break room, he was so deep in thought (a very rare experience for Nick, let me tell you) that he barely acknowledged his boss as they crossed paths in the hallway, and he didn't even notice that his boss also barely acknowledged him.

He poured himself a cup of coffee and took a sip. He liked Anna. He liked being with her. She was good in bed; she was someone he could talk to. He liked the idea of having someone in his life to grab a pizza with after work, just kicking back instead of the constant work it took when you were with someone new. He liked her enough not to want to lose her right now, liked her enough to want her to think well of him.

So he'd put a lot of thought and energy into his story, worked it all out so she wouldn't think less of him or keep bugging him about it. He'd planned on making that very clear—that he'd explain what happened but he didn't want to go over it again and again. He'd never understood why women had to hear the same story over and over, coming up with new questions each time.

Nick had even decided it was a good thing this had happened—in a way. He'd get a chance to see what Anna was like about things. And if she turned out to be one of those women who gave him a really hard time and wouldn't let it go—refused to accept his explanation or kept digging at him about it, trying to see if she could trip him up or note inconsistencies in his story—he'd cut his losses. They'd only had a couple of dates, for Christ's sake, and if she was already going to start giving him the third degree . . .

But she hadn't given him the third degree. She hadn't yelled or cried or accused him of anything. She'd even said he didn't owe her any explanations. And it seemed just a little bit too good to be true.

Maybe she was one of those game players. He'd run into those before. At first they'd pretend that nothing was wrong, and he'd relax, and then, BAM! Out of nowhere, out of left field, the pouting started. Or: "I can't believe you really thought I wasn't upset. Of course I was upset! How could I *not* be upset? Don't you have any feelings at all?"

Was that how it was going to go? Would he and Anna get together tonight, sit eating their pizza and talking about their day, and then suddenly, just when he was feeling relaxed and enjoying himself, she'd start acting like something was wrong? He wouldn't know what was bugging her, and she'd get mad because he wouldn't know anything was wrong, and then it would all go to shit.

This nagged at him as he walked back to his office and for most of the rest of the day. So much so that he didn't notice Mark and his boss go to lunch together or that they spent a great deal of the afternoon locked up in his boss's office.

Nick was so convinced that Anna was getting ready to pull a real number on him that he picked up the phone three different times to cancel their plans for the evening. But in the end he decided he might as well see her and get it over with.

At six o'clock Anna called Nick to check in and confirm their plans.

"Hi, Nick, it's Anna."

"Oh," Nick said. "Hi."

"Did I catch you at a bad time?" Anna asked.

"No, just catching up on paperwork."

"Oh. So how does pizza sound?"

"Sounds good."

"There's a great pizza place near my apartment. You want to come to my place and I'll pick one up on the way home?"

"All right."

"Great. I do have one question I need to ask you, though."

I knew it, Nick thought to himself. Here it comes.

"What do you like on your pizza?" Anna asked.

"Uh," Nick said, "anything but anchovies."

"Me too. Thin crust okay?"

"Sure."

Anna didn't take Nick's curt answers personally. She figured he was bound to feel awkward about what had happened that morning, and it might take a little time before he felt natural around her again. He might even think she was only pretending she wasn't upset. But that was okay. When he saw she meant it, that she really wasn't going to demand to know the story, he'd relax. In the long run, this whole thing might turn out to be good for their relationship, bring them closer together.

"I'll be out of here around seven," Anna told Nick. "You want to come over around eight?"

"That'll work."

"Okay. I'll see you then." She gave him her address.

"Right. See you then."

Anna hung up the phone smiling. She loved this part. Learning what kind of pizza the other person liked, how they took their coffee, which celebrity they couldn't stand. And she loved evenings like this, staying in, throwing on your favorite pair of jeans, and doing something simple like sharing a pizza, being relaxed and natural with each other in a way that wasn't possible in a restaurant or at a movie. She could hardly wait to see him.

Nick, on the other hand, hung up the phone frowning. She was good. If he hadn't known better, he'd have sworn that she actually wasn't upset with him. But there was no way in hell that could be true. No woman was going to let something like this go without a word of explanation. He was dreading the coming night with every fiber of his being.

Meanwhile, inside her apartment, the not-particularly-promising girl, consumed with misery, grief, and anger, vowed her revenge.

eight

Nick arrived at Anna's place at eight-fifteen.

Anna gave him a big smile and let him inside. Nick took a look around. The pizza and two tossed salads were sitting on the dining room table. Anna had lit a couple of candles but hadn't done the whole candles-in-every-corner-of-the-room spectacle. He hated that. Women found it sexy, but he always felt like he was inside a cathedral.

Anna seemed happy to see him; her smile hadn't seemed forced when she'd opened the door. But that didn't mean anything. Sometimes they were happy to see you at first. It was only as the night wore on that they'd start to get angry all over again. She might have even fooled herself into believing that she was perfectly fine with things between them.

"What can I get you to drink?" Anna asked Nick. "I've got wine and beer. Soda. Iced tea. Bottled water?"

"Beer would be great," Nick said. He couldn't detect that tone in her voice. That veiled undercurrent of anger in women's voices that he'd become an expert on over the years.

"Coming right up. Do you want to look through my CDs and put on something you like?" Anna asked. "Feel free to ignore the chick music."

Nick smiled and started to relax a little. Maybe it was going to be okay. Maybe she really did mean what she'd said. Maybe he'd gotten really lucky this time, and she wouldn't make him sit through chick flicks, either. He walked over to her entertainment center and thumbed through her CDs. Yeah, lots of chick music, but some good stuff, too. He put on a Lyle Lovett CD and turned around.

Anna walked out of the kitchen and set his beer on the table.

"It's all set. I got extra anchovies."

There it was. Nick got it now, what he was dealing with. Or what he wouldn't be dealing with. She was one of the passive-aggressive ones. Passive-aggressive ones were the worst. He'd gulp down the pizza, make some excuse about having to be in early for work, and call it a night. The last thing he needed was a passive-aggressive woman in his life. The kind who would smile and get you a beer and tell you that they didn't need an explanation. But then somehow, conveniently, forget that you told her the one thing you didn't like on your pizza was anchovies. Been there, done that. No thanks.

"Hey," Anna said, "I was kidding. No anchovies. I promise."

"Oh. Sorry. I'm kind of distracted. It's been a long day."

"That's okay. Let's eat."

They sat down at the table.

"I wasn't sure what kind of salad dressing you liked," Anna said, "so I just put a bunch on the table. I hope there's one here you like."

"Ranch will be fine," Nick said, picking up the bottle. He opened it and poured some dressing onto his salad.

Anna opened the box of pizza and offered him a slice.

"Thanks," Nick said.

Each of them ate a few bites of salad, Lyle Lovett in the background, neither one of them saying a word.

Nick, for his part, simply didn't know what to say. He didn't get this. How could a woman see something like what Anna had seen that morning and not demand an explanation? It didn't make sense. He couldn't relax, didn't know how to act, and no matter how nice Anna was being, he couldn't help feeling that the second he did let himself relax, the ax would fall.

Anna, for her part, was trying to choose her words carefully. She realized from the way Nick was acting that something would have to be said. Nick was obviously uncomfortable. The tension was so thick you could cut it with a knife. Maybe he needed to hear it from her again that she didn't need an explanation. Hear it again so he'd believe it.

"Nick?" Anna said.

Nick braced himself. *Okay, this is it. I knew it was coming.*

She has that hesitant tone in her voice, the one they get right before they lower the boom. We'll get it over with and then I'm out of here.

"Look, I meant what I said. As far as I'm concerned, the whole thing that happened this morning is forgotten. There was obviously something wrong with the woman. We've all picked the wrong person at least once. I dated one guy that I look back on now, and I can't believe I ever let myself get involved with him. So I don't need to know the story, or make you give me some long explanation. Whatever went on between the two of you happened before we got together."

Nick was getting really tired of this. He'd brace himself, prepare himself to tell her the story or give her an explanation, or do whatever the hell it was she wanted. And then she'd tell him she didn't need him to tell her anything. When he knew, *knew,* that sooner or later, hell, it could be months from now, but at some point in time, she'd bring it up. He'd forget to call, or he'd have other plans, and suddenly, out of the blue, there it would be, out from the shadows and shoved up in front of his face.

"Where were you last night?" she'd shriek. "You told me you'd call. I waited by the phone all night. I tried calling you until midnight and you never answered. Were you with someone else? What's her name? Are you going to do to me what you did to her?"

"Her who?" he'd ask, like an idiot.

"Her *who?* Her who that was standing in the parking lot waiting for us that morning. The morning after our first night together. The one who you'd slept with on Saturday, one day after you'd started seeing me."

Seeing her? One casual date and plans to get together and they'd been *seeing* each other? God, how women loved to rewrite history.

Or it would be: "You're getting together with who? An old friend, huh? That's funny. I've never heard you mention him before. If you're cheating on me, just tell me now, okay? Don't make me find out two months from now that you've been lying to me all this time."

Nick got tired just thinking about it.

"Nick?" Anna asked. "Have you heard a word I said?"

Normally Nick really hated that question, but Anna's voice was soft, and the expression in her eyes wasn't angry or accusing. Either she was really different, or she just knew how to put on a better act. If he could just get his story off his chest and clear the air, then he could relax and enjoy his dinner. He'd put a lot of *thought* into his cover story.

"Yeah, I have. Anna, I think I'd feel better if I just told you about her. Why she was there in the parking lot. I know you say you don't need an explanation, but I feel as if it's just going to be hanging over our heads until we get it out in the open."

Anna smiled.

"Nick, if I sit here and make you give me an explanation, it's as if I'm saying I don't trust you. And I do trust you. It would be pointless for us to be together if I didn't. It's not going to be hanging over our heads, I promise. Hey, how are the numbers looking for Shop Smart?"

"Huh?"

"Because the Shop Smart people are driving me crazy. They're on this new kick now about how we need to market them with some real class and pizzazz instead of focusing on the discount angle. I thought we'd have the numbers from last quarter for them by now so we could show them how well the cable campaign went." ·

"I haven't gotten them yet," Nick said, not even wondering why the numbers were late, still trying to figure out what had just happened.

"Do you know they actually want the shoppers in the next commercial to be these two really glamorous model types," Anna said. "As if that's the consumer market Shop Smart is going to appeal to. Do you have any idea when the numbers might be in?"

"I'm not sure."

"Aren't they a little late?"

"Maybe a little," Nick said.

Actually, if he'd thought about it for a minute, Nick would have realized the numbers were a bit more than a little late. Which would normally have gotten major bells and whistles blowing for Nick. But he was consumed with what was happening in his relationship with Anna, and it was driving him crazy, to the exclusion of all other thoughts. It was a brand-new experience for Nick, and he didn't like it very much. He didn't like it at all.

"Listen, Anna . . . ," Nick said, just as her phone rang.

"Hold that thought."

Anna stood up and answered her phone. Nick took a bite of salad and tried to chew. It tasted like sawdust. He had no appetite whatsoever. He felt pressured, which didn't make sense considering the fact that Anna had just taken all the pressure off by telling him she trusted him. He simply didn't know what to do with the trust she'd placed in him, a trust he'd done nothing to earn.

Was this some kind of weird new test women had come up with? Nick sometimes felt there were these secret conventions men didn't know anything about, where women would get together to devise new and ingenious ways of driving men crazy.

"Hi, Joan," Anna said into her phone. "I've got someone over. Can I call you tomorrow?"

Nick watched as Anna listened for a few seconds.

"Well, as a matter of fact, it *is* a man. A very nice man. I know we agreed last week that there weren't any left, but I managed to find one and even managed to get him over to my place to share a pizza."

Nick had mixed reactions hearing Anna talk about him. He was flattered. He was baffled. He felt caught off guard. She honestly seemed okay with the whole parking lot incident. She was making jokes with her friend. She seemed completely at ease, happy to have him here, with no hidden agenda. He couldn't detect any trace of bullshit. He should feel okay about that, should be jumping up and down about that. He'd dodged the bullet. So why wasn't he jumping up and down?

Nick knew he wasn't a nice man. Not the way Anna meant it. Ten minutes ago, he might have described himself as a nice guy and probably been offended if someone had insinuated he wasn't. But hearing Anna on the phone, describing him to her friend as a nice guy, he knew he wasn't. .

"Whatever else we're sharing is none of your business," Nick heard Anna say to her friend with a laugh.

He felt weird and uncomfortable and ill at ease.

"Okay, I'll give you a call tomorrow."

He heard Anna laugh again.

"The only hot and juicy details you're getting are about the pizza," she said.

Anna said good-bye to her friend Joan and hung up the phone. Nick stuffed some salad into his mouth so he wouldn't have to say anything right away when she sat down at the table.

"That was my friend Joan," Anna said, sitting down. "She thinks we should put you on display at the Smithsonian. 'Last nice single man found alive in twenty-first-century America.' "

Nick really wanted her to stop calling him nice.

"So how was your day at work?" Anna asked.

"Boring," Nick said, after he swallowed his salad. "I spent most of the day getting caught up on paperwork."

If Nick had been thinking clearly, he'd have realized that the tension in his department had been replaced by an ominous silence. He'd literally been left alone all day, an unheard-of occurrence.

But Nick hadn't been thinking clearly that day. He'd been too consumed by what had happened that morning in the parking lot and what it meant for him and Anna.

And he wasn't thinking clearly now. He was torn between his desire to leave so he'd stop feeling so weird and uncomfortable. And his other desire to *make* Anna listen to his story. And another desire that he didn't have words for, one that was only now, very slowly, very quietly making its way into his being.

And while all of this was going on, the not-particularly-promising girl came up with the first step in her plan to make Nick Wells know how it felt to be treated like a total piece of crap.

nine

Watching Anna and Nick together at her apartment that night, everything felt wrong and out of whack. The incident in the parking lot wasn't haunting Anna at all. And Nick had me worried, too. He was filled with all his usual fears and doubts and misgivings, but a small seed had taken root in his heart. Not even a seed, really. Barely a kernel. But it was there, and he was about two or three lifetimes ahead of schedule.

I was beginning to worry that I'd put forces into motion that my limited powers wouldn't be able to fix. As soon as one thing in the universe goes out of whack, everything else can get affected, too. The butterfly-wings-causing-an-avalanche-two-continents-away principle is really true. Everything is connected (which some people find comforting, but which I, as a spirit, with the kind of responsibilities I have, often find to be a gigantic pain in the ass).

If things kept going haywire like this, causing who-knew-what kinds of possible chaos, I might be forced to have the front office intervene. And forced to admit I'd given Anna an arrow of true love, which would be major bad cosmic news for yours truly. It wasn't just that she was unworthy: I'm supposed to fill out an application form for the front office *before* I send the arrow. The rest of the romance biz they leave under my control. But true love has to go through committee and get approval. Even in the afterlife, it's the paperwork that kills you.

I'd had one bad moment after centuries of dealing with this romance crap. I thought I'd shown amazing patience and tolerance and done a hell of a job, considering what I've had to deal with. But I knew the front office wasn't going to see it that way. They've got a real attitude thing going about just who it is that runs the universe.

So I kept watching, waiting, and racking my brain, trying to come up with a solution. With my extensive knowledge of human nature, I knew I ought to be able to come up with something. But what?

Nick left Anna's apartment early that night. He managed to eat a little salad and a slice of pizza, but he didn't have much of an appetite. Despite what Anna had said, he kept trying to work the conversation back around to what had happened in the parking lot that morning. But every time he'd get his nerve up to approach the subject, Anna had already moved on to something else.

Then, just as they were finishing dinner, her sister called. Their great-aunt had suffered a mild stroke. He could tell from the bits and pieces he overheard that the aunt wasn't someone Anna and her sister were very close to, but he knew she'd be on the phone for some time, and it gave him a perfect excuse to leave.

Nick felt incredibly relieved to get out of there, but then, driving home to his empty condominium, he kind of wished he hadn't left. It had been nice, sitting there after work, eating a pizza, talking about their day. That thing about putting him in the Smithsonian was kind of cute. But it was driving him crazy that Anna wouldn't let him tell her the story about the not-particularly-promising girl, a story that had taken him forty-five minutes to perfect.

And why did she think he was so damn nice? Hell, she hardly knew him. Maybe she was one of those women who built up this whole picture of you in her mind, and at first you couldn't do anything wrong in her eyes. But then, sooner or later, when you didn't live up to it, BAM! She acted as if you've been pretending to be something you're not.

He knew what he'd do. The next time they got together, he wouldn't let her put him off. He'd insist that she let him give an explanation. And he wouldn't give her the original story, the one where he was completely not at fault, and the not-particu-larly-promising girl was just some psycho woman who wouldn't leave him alone. He'd admit he slept with her. Come clean that he'd slept with her on Saturday night even though he'd felt like something was starting to happen with him and

Anna. But that it had been *her* idea, not his. That, in fact, he'd had no plans of sleeping with her, but he'd had a little bit too much to drink and she'd been all over him. And in retrospect, he saw now it was a huge mistake.

But he'd also make it clear he hadn't made any promises or anything to the girl. That he'd been up front that he wasn't looking for anything serious with her. And that she'd acted like she'd just been looking for a good time the way he'd been.

That way Anna would see he wasn't pretending to be someone he wasn't. And if she got mad about it later, she wouldn't have a leg to stand on. He wouldn't have to sit there and take it. He'd be able to remind her he'd been straight with her about the whole thing right from the start, and it was a little late to start getting mad about it now.

Yeah, that's what he would do. Nick felt much better after making his decision.

But he didn't get a chance to talk to Anna the next day. She was in meetings most of the time, and she left him a voice mail around four o'clock that afternoon saying her parents were going to visit the great-aunt and she had to leave a little early in order to take them to the airport.

Nick was down at support services when Anna called. He was going over the quarterly reports he needed typed up and collated by the clerical supervisor, who handled the company's big projects. So he didn't get her message until around five, when he returned to his desk.

Anna's voice didn't sound any different, but she hadn't said when she'd get back that night. Or offered to call him when she got in. Was it possible that now that she'd had some more time to think about what had happened in the parking lot, she was blowing him off? Was that why she hadn't wanted to go into it with him yesterday? She hadn't wanted to be bothered until she'd decided whether or not she was going to see him again? Or was she just reacting to how distant he'd been the night before? Should he call back and leave her a voice mail? Tell her he'd be up late, ask her to give him a call when she got in?

I watched how Nick looked and acted as he listened to Anna's message. And it was written all over his face. She was *getting* to him. He's not the kind of guy who sits at his desk when he should be getting work done, wondering whether or not he should call a woman back. Not when he should be wondering where in the hell the Shop Smart numbers were and noticing that it was now three days since he'd heard from the boss. And wondering why he hadn't seen Mark all week.

I couldn't believe what I saw next. I saw him pick up his phone and dial Anna's number at home.

"Hi, Anna," he said. "It's Nick."

Nick *never* identified himself to a woman after the first date when he left her a message. He always assumed they'd be waiting for his call and know immediately who it was.

"I got your message. Hope your aunt is okay. I'm going to be up late tonight, so if you get back before midnight, give me a call."

He hung up the phone, looking distracted. Nick wasn't supposed to get distracted, not at work. He was supposed to be focused. He'd *always* been focused.

Then his intercom buzzed. His assistant was on the line. "Nick?"

"Yeah?" he asked quickly, hoping she had Anna on hold.

"Uh, the parking lot attendant just called. Someone slashed the tires on your car."

"What?"

"And they, uh, I guess they kind of trashed it, too."

"What do you mean, 'trashed it'?" Nick asked, feeling sick. He'd driven a used Toyota for five years, even though he'd started making pretty good money, so he could pay off his college loans and save up and get the kind of car he really wanted. And then he'd waited three more months until the dealer could get in the specific model he'd wanted, right down to the black midnight ebony exterior and the Sahara brown leather interior.

The day he'd driven that Lexus—the first thing he'd ever bought that had been exactly what he'd wanted—off the lot had been the day Nick had felt like he'd made something of his life. That car was a concrete symbol of everything he'd worked for.

"He says there's all kinds of stuff sprayed on your windows, and they keyed a lot of the paint off the trunk and the hood. He wants you to come down and take a look. He's already called the police. You're probably going to have to file a report. He wondered if you had any idea who might have done it."

"No," Nick said, feeling nauseated. He knew exactly who it had to have been. He remembered having driven to the restaurant the night they'd gone out and how she'd gone on and on about how nice his car was, asking him all kinds of questions about it. "Probably just a bunch of kids."

"Yeah, probably. Can you go down now? He said the police are on their way."

"Sure. Thanks."

Nick hung up the phone, feeling furious at the not-particularly-promising girl. He had insurance. He could get the car repaired, but it would never feel the same to him. She'd ruined it.

Why was she doing this to him? What had he done that was worth this kind of rage? They'd only slept together once. Hell, they'd only gone out together once. What did she think it accomplished? Was she actually crazy enough to think this would somehow make him want to be with her?

Nick wearily stood up to go down and take a look at his car. Should he tell the police the truth or pretend he had no idea who had done it? If he knew for sure this would be her last tantrum, he'd let it go. Let her get it out of her system so she'd leave him alone. The insurance would cover it, and he had a rental car rider on his policy, so he'd get over it eventually.

But what if she was one of those nutcases, a stalker type, and kept coming at him? If he didn't tell the police the real story now, how would it look if he had to contact them again?

Nick gasped when he first saw his Lexus. She'd scratched deep gouges all over the trunk and hood and sides. But the worst part was what she'd done to the windows. Sprayed a big YOU STUPID S.O.B. on the front window, and GO TO HELL, NICK on the back one. It would be obvious to anyone who saw the car that whoever had done it knew him.

A few of his coworkers walked past on their way home, and Nick felt them staring as he stood talking to the police.

He knew it would be all over the office by tomorrow. He knew what they were thinking. That things like this happen only to people with messy personal lives. He'd spent his whole adulthood deliberately avoiding any mess in his personal life.

And when Anna heard about it, she'd put two and two together, and she'd know who'd done it, too. She might have been okay before, but how would she be about something like this?

"Was this a long-term relationship?" one of the officers asked.

"No, nothing like that," Nick told him, trying to look nonchalant, feeling mortified and determined not to show it. "We only went out once."

"You only saw her one time?" the other officer asked with a hint of suspicion.

Nick didn't know if the suspicion was directed at him personally or if this was just how police officers talked to everybody they had to deal with. He'd never had to deal one-on-one with a member of the police force. Had never pictured himself dealing with a member of the police force.

"I guess you could say I saw her twice."

"Twice?"

"I met her in a bar, and we talked, I got her number. And then we went out to dinner last Saturday."

"Any idea why she'd want to do something like this to you?" the first officer asked. "Seems like a lot of hostility over one dinner. Was her steak overcooked?"

Nick saw the other officer smile to himself.

"We spent the night together," he muttered.

"Ah," the officer said, writing it down on his notepad. "And that's it?"

"Yeah. It was just one of those things. You know how it goes," he added, giving them a smile, guy to guy, trying to get them on his side.

"Was she mad when she left?" the second officer asked. "Did something happen to set her off?"

"Kind of. I guess she thought we were going to keep seeing each other, but I never called her back," Nick said. "She saw me and my new girlfriend leaving my apartment Thursday morning. She was waiting in the parking lot of my building. And she went ballistic. Started screaming at both of us and calling me names."

"Your new girlfriend," the first officer repeated. "So she was a witness. She'd be able to confirm this story?"

"Do you think I'm lying?" Nick asked, offended.

"I have no way of knowing, sir."

"She's just going to tell you the same thing I told you," Nick insisted. He didn't want Anna involved in this mess.

"Sir, in all likelihood we won't be able to prove she did this to your car. The best we can do at this point is to try and scare her off so she doesn't do anything else. And if she knows we have two witnesses to the previous incident, then she's probably going to take us more seriously. How can we get in touch with your *new* girlfriend, starting with her name?"

"It's Anna. Anna Munson. Look, her aunt just had a stroke. They were very close. She's devastated. This is the last thing she needs right now. She—"

"Sir," the first officer interrupted, "these situations can escalate. The best thing you can do is to let us handle this before it gets any worse. We're going to need the name, phone number, and address of both of these women. Let's start with the *old* girlfriend first."

"She wasn't my girlfriend, I keep telling you. And . . ."

Nick's voice trailed off.

"Yes?" the first officer asked.

"After we spent the night together I knew it had been a huge mistake. So I threw her phone number and address away."

The not-particularly-promising girl sat inside her apartment wondering if Nick had seen his car yet. His precious little Lexus that he was so proud of. He'd gone on and on about it the night they'd gone out, as if it made him special.

She thought she'd feel a lot better than this. Like maybe now he'd think about treating human beings with some of the consideration he showed his stupid little Lexus. But even picturing him, the look in his eyes when he first saw what she'd done to his car, didn't feel all that great. The truth was, wrecking his car just made her feel angrier. So he had to get his car fixed. Big deal. That paled in comparison to what he'd done to her. There probably wasn't anything she could do to him that was big enough to equal what he'd done to her. He'd never understand what it was like to be treated like you're nothing, like your feelings are nothing, like your existence doesn't even matter.

But that didn't mean she couldn't make him suffer.

ten

When they were done questioning him, the police officers asked Nick if he'd be able to find the not-particularly-promising girl's apartment, since he'd thrown her address away.

"Probably," he answered.

"Good. Let's go."

"Now?" Nick asked.

"Sir," the second police officer said, talking to Nick as if he were a misbehaving child they were having to reason with—or so it sounded to Nick—"we take these situations very seriously because they tend to get worse. If we know where she lives, we can pay her a little visit after we question Miss Munson."

"All right," Nick sighed. "Let me run upstairs and grab my briefcase."

When Nick went back inside the office, his assistant gave him a funny look as he walked past her desk.

"Everything okay?" she asked.

Nick just shook his head and kept walking. He was too upset to answer any questions. And embarrassed. Nick hadn't felt embarrassed about anything since he'd been in high school and he'd fallen asleep in chemistry to the great amusement of his classmates. God. What would it be like tomorrow when *everyone* knew? He'd be the talk of the place. The person who made everyone suddenly get quiet when he walked into the break room. And Anna? How was she going to react knowing everyone was talking about him?

But the worst embarrassment was still to come. Sitting in the backseat of the squad car, everyone staring at him whenever they were stopped at a light, thinking he was under arrest, Nick wanted to disappear. He found the apartment in twenty-five minutes, but to Nick it felt as if he'd been sitting in the back of that squad car for hours.

"That's it," Nick told the police. "On the first floor. The last one on the left."

The officers drove him back to his office building after jotting down the not-particularly-promising girl's address. Nick started to breathe a little easier as they pulled into the parking garage.

"One of our detectives will get a statement from Miss Munson and then go have a talk with the woman," the first officer told Nick as he got out of the squad car. "She'll probably deny everything, but hopefully she'll get the message."

"I'm not sure what time Anna is getting home tonight from the airport."

"The detective they assign to the case won't be able to take her statement until tomorrow morning at the earliest."

"Here?" Nick asked, starting to panic again. "At work?" This was turning into a nightmare. "That's going to be very embarrassing. For Anna, I mean."

"Don't worry. He won't be bringing the SWAT team with him. We'll be in touch."

Nick had to wait over an hour in the parking garage for the tow truck to come and get his car. He was tired and hungry, but there was no way he was going to leave his car overnight and have it sitting there the next morning for everyone to take another look at. While he waited for the tow truck to arrive, Nick called some rental companies, but the only one still open was out at the airport. So, after dealing with the tow truck guy, trying to ignore the smirk on his face, Nick had to call a cab and go out to the airport to pick up his rental car.

It wasn't until he stood waiting at the rental counter that Nick remembered Anna was at the airport, too. For a second the thought cheered him up. He'd go find her, they could grab some dinner . . . then he realized he had no idea what airline terminal she'd be at. And anyway, she'd be with her parents, and the last thing he needed after the day he'd had was to meet her parents. And how would he explain what he was doing there?

"How do you do, Mr. and Mrs. Munson," he imagined himself saying. "I'm just here getting a rental car because the psycho woman I had sex with last Saturday night is really pissed off that I haven't called here since then. So to get back at me she trashed my car in the parking garage at work."

It was the longest, most humiliating day of his life.

When he finally got back to his apartment, Nick left another message for Anna. He tried to get some work done to get his mind off things while waiting for her to call him back. She'd check for any messages when she got home, wouldn't she? Even if it was late? Yeah. A guy might not think about it. Get home beat and wait until morning to check the machine. But no woman would come home and not check to see if anyone had called. And Anna would want to know if *he'd* called. Wouldn't she?

Or maybe she'd check her messages, but there would be some others besides his. One, or maybe more than one—maybe the whole damn office had called—would be waiting for her with the juicy news. And she'd be so turned off by the situation that she wouldn't call him back, wouldn't want to have anything else to do with him.

Nick decided to leave her a third message.

"Anna," he said, "it's Nick again. I don't know if anyone else has called and told you what happened at work today. But please don't jump to any conclusions before you talk to me. Call me no matter when you get in. We've got to talk. I'll be here all night. Thanks."

Nick sat in his apartment that night, trying to work and glancing over at the phone every few minutes. What was taking Anna so long at the airport? It was what, an hour's drive round-trip? If traffic was bad, maybe an hour and a half. Even if she went in with them, saw their flight off, that was what, another hour? Maybe two if the lines were long at the check-in gate. It was almost ten.

He could try calling her again. No. He'd already left three messages. Maybe she'd stopped off somewhere on the way home. But she hadn't said anything about going anywhere other than the airport. Maybe she had to run some errands. At this time of night? He supposed she could have stopped for groceries. But how long could that take?

It did take longer now at the airport with all the new security measures. Or she could be stuck on the freeway with that new construction they were doing. But she had her cell phone with her. If she was running that late she could have called him from her car. Maybe her batteries were low.

He'd wait until eleven. Then, if she hadn't called, he'd call her. Say he'd had to go out for a couple of hours, didn't know if she'd been trying to call him. But what if she asked where he'd gone? He'd already told her he'd be at home all night waiting for her call because he needed to talk to her. What if she thought he'd been out with someone else? Why didn't she just call?

Anna was tired when she got home around ten-thirty. It had been a long drive out to the airport, and the flight had been delayed over two hours. Her parents had told her she could leave if she wanted—they knew she must be tired after a hard day at work—but she'd offered to stay with them.

"I'm hungry, anyway," she'd said. "Why don't we go get some dinner?"

Her parents had been pleasantly surprised at the offer. She was normally in such a rush, always so busy with work and her own life that they barely saw her.

After they'd ordered their meal, Anna's dad had left to check the arrivals and departures board and make sure the flight time hadn't been changed again. He tended to get nervous at airports and liked to get in line as soon as his flight was called.

"Do you need me to do anything at the house?" Anna had asked her mom.

"Your sister can take care of that," Anna's mom had said, and then she'd given Anna an appraising look. "You look different."

"I do? How?"

"I've never seen you like this before. You're glowing. And you're being much too nice to me and your father."

Anna had blushed slightly, and her mom had smiled.

"What's his name?" Anna's mom had asked.

"Who?" Anna had asked, trying not to smile but unable to stop herself.

"You know exactly who I'm talking about. So? Are you going to tell me his name or not?"

"His name is Nick."

"And?"

"I met him at work. We've only been seeing each other for a little while, but—"

"But?"

"I'm crazy about him."

Anna's mother had seen the look in Anna's eyes. She'd remembered that feeling and had felt a stab of envy. No one ever forgets that feeling. That old woman in the wheelchair, the one with almost no hair and withered skin, who looks like she could go at any minute? She remembers *exactly* how it felt to fall in love.

Anna's mom had had a million things she'd wanted to say: Don't take a minute of it for granted. As wonderful as you think it is, you still don't know how wonderful it is. You won't know until you're on the other side of it. Because you *will* get to the other side of it. And the other side is good. It's real; it's solid. But it isn't magic. You only get that for a short time.

She wanted to tell Anna: love, marriage, kids—it isn't what you think it is. I love your father. God knows there were times I didn't, but we made it. We still love each other. But, Anna, it's hard. People tell you it's hard, but you have no idea. If I had to do it all over again, would I? Yes. I got you and your sister. But if it was just your dad and me, would I do it all over again? Probably. Maybe. I don't know.

We're used to each other now, and God knows I wouldn't want to start over with somebody else. But honestly, it's not what I thought it was going to be. Some mornings I wish I could just wake up alone. Some mornings it is like I wake up alone.

And months can go by where nothing really happens between the two of you. You just live side by side, and there's no energy at all. It passes, but it's a long wait sometimes, and no matter how long you've been together, when those times hit you wonder if you're ever going to feel anything for him again. Even scarier, you wonder if he's ever going to feel anything for you again. What carries you through sometimes is simply the fact that you've made it this far.

Your sister, she's happy. But you, I think your expectations are too high. I want to see you married with children, but, Anna, at some point in the marriage you *decide* to stay. Will you be able to make that decision when he stops turning your knees into jelly?

But even if she'd found the courage to say this to Anna, she'd known Anna wouldn't have heard her. She might have listened. But she wouldn't have thought it would ever happen to her.

"Oh, honey," Anna's mom had said, "I'm so happy for you. When do we get a chance to meet him?"

Anna was tired when she got home, but it had been a good day. She was glad she'd taken the time to stay and have dinner with her parents at the airport. Telling her mom about Nick had made it seem real in a way that even telling her friends hadn't.

Anna kicked off her shoes and thumbed through her mail, then walked over to the phone to check for messages.

There was one from her sister thanking her for taking their parents to the airport.

There was one from one of her credit card companies, offering her a new disability insurance policy for only $5.95 per month, conveniently billed to her monthly statement if she decided to keep the policy after a thirty-day trial period.

There was one from Cassie, a casual friend of hers from work.

"Hi, Anna, it's Cassie. Something really weird happened at work today. Give me a call if you get a chance."

Cassie hadn't gone into details because she hadn't been sure how far along things had gone with Nick and Anna, and she hadn't quite known what approach to take.

And there were three messages from Nick.

"Anna," the second one said, "I need to talk to you. Something happened at work today. Please call me as soon as you get in. It's really important that we talk. I'll be up late, so don't worry about the time when you call."

Before she had time to react to the second message, the third one played.

"Anna," he said, "it's Nick again. I don't know if anyone else has called and told you what happened at work today. But please don't jump to any conclusions before you talk to me. Call me no matter when you get in. We've got to talk. I'll be here all night. Thanks."

Anna picked up the phone and dialed Nick's number.

I watched her get ready to make the call, but I had no idea whether the situation with Nick's car was going to work in my favor or not. I hoped it would ignite Anna's earlier suspicions about what had gone on between Nick and the not-particularly-promising girl. Then she could dump him and go back to being the afraid-to-really-risk-anything-for-love woman whose behavior in the good old days, before this whole mess got started, I could once have predicted with a 93.75 percent accuracy rate.

And I was also keeping an eye on the not-particularly-promising girl. She didn't really fall under my jurisdiction, but

I'd interfered with her life. What she was going through was partially a result of my big screwup. Unlike so many of you people, I take responsibility for my actions.

Nick had become every slight she'd ever suffered, every wound inflicted, every regret and pain, everyone and everything that had ever let her down or betrayed her. All of that, for her, had become wrapped up in the person of Nick Wells, and her anger toward him was getting worse, not better. I didn't want her to do something really stupid and ruin her life.

I knew that what she needed to do was forget all about Nick Wells and get some help. I couldn't force her to get help, but maybe I could give her a little nudge. I happened to know she had a card laying inside one of her kitchen drawers, a card she could really use, a card with the name of someone on it who could help her.

And I wouldn't be breaking any rules. Since the whole point of human existence and the whole movement of the universe are toward growth and change, any act a spirit does that nudges a human being toward personal growth or change is acceptable, even if, strictly speaking, it doesn't fall under our particular jurisdiction. As long as it's just a nudge and the ultimate choice is left up to the person involved.

But she wasn't having any of it. While Anna dialed Nick's number, I took that card out of the not-particularly-promising girl's kitchen drawer and blew it onto the table in front of her couch, but the card might as well have been invisible. She never even saw it.

eleven

Nick grabbed his phone on the first ring and said hello, desperately wanting it to be Anna and afraid it would turn out to be someone else.

"Nick. Hi. It's Anna. What's going on? Are you all right?"

"Yeah. Better now that I hear your voice," he said, sounding relieved and grateful.

This was not good. Nick feeling gratitude and relief that she'd called him back, considering what was going on in his life—that I expected. Anna liked him. She was on his side. But to come right out and tell her how happy he was to hear her voice, to sound kind of *needy*?

The Nick I knew might be feeling a little vulnerable, but he'd never have let anyone else see it, no matter what had been going on with him. Anna at least had that arrow to explain the odd way she was behaving. I hadn't sent *him* an arrow. Occasionally people can have more to them than I think. But Nick? That little kernel in his heart shouldn't have been working this quickly. I know my business, dammit. I'm an expert on romance and human nature. I may hate my job, but I am highly qualified.

The two of them were really starting to get on my nerves, Nick and Anna, especially after I watched that slow, dopey smile spread across Anna's face when she heard what Nick said. I knew she'd just fallen a little bit more in love with him. If Nick started depending on Anna for companionship, support, and maybe even—God forbid—intimacy, my ass was really in a sling.

"It's good to hear your voice, too," she said.

"Can I come over?" Nick asked. "I need to talk to you, and I'd rather do it face-to-face. And I'd really like to see you."

He'd really like to see her. Fine. Did he have to *tell* her he'd really like to see her?

Nick arrived at Anna's apartment about twenty minutes later. She'd put on the Lyle Lovett CD he'd picked the night before and thrown on a pair of jeans and a sweater.

When she opened the door and said hello, Nick felt like he'd just come in from the cold. He put his arms around her and kissed her the way he'd never kissed another woman, the way Anna had never had another man kiss her.

When they finished slobbering all over each other and making goo-goo eyes, Anna asked Nick if he wanted a beer. He said yes, and as Anna walked into the kitchen, I saw another bad sign: Nick's eyes followed her as if he never wanted to let her out of his sight.

Nick sat down on the couch feeling a hundred times better than he had half an hour earlier. He noticed that Anna had put on the same music he'd picked out the night before. Women had done that for him before. Had a glass of a wine they knew he liked waiting for him at the restaurant if he was the second one to arrive for dinner. Kept his favorite snacks at their place for when he came over. Rented a video they knew he liked. But Nick had always taken that for granted, had never appreciated it the way he did now. It made him feel really good that she'd remembered that.

Anna sat down next to him on the couch.

"Are you okay?" she asked.

"No. I'm not very okay. Something happened at work today." Nick paused, but Anna's expression didn't change. He couldn't tell if she knew anything or not. "Did someone already tell you?" Nick asked nervously.

"No. Cassie left me a message saying something happened, but she didn't say what."

"I hate like hell to have to get you involved with this," Nick said. He took a deep breath. "That woman? The one in the parking lot?"

Anna got a fearful look on her face, and I felt a new glimmer of hope. Come on, Anna. Don't stop now. Reaffirm my faith in human nature.

"What about her?" Anna asked.

"She slashed my tires and spray painted some stuff on my car. Someone saw it and reported it to the parking lot attendant. I had to file a police report, and they want to question you since you witnessed what happened outside my apartment."

"Oh, Nick."

"I know. It's awful. I am so sorry, Anna. I had no idea she was so crazy. Everyone at work is going to know by tomorrow. I can't believe this is happening. It's not like I had a relationship with her. We had one date. One."

"You only went out with her once?" Anna asked.

I heard the fear, doubt, and mistrust creeping into her voice. Hallelujah! I thought. Human nature asserts itself at last.

What had I been so worried about? These were *people*, and I know my people. She'd put on a nice show with her love and trust and loss of ego, her desire to simply love Nick out of the sheer joy of loving him. But come on. How long can the typical person keep that up?

"Anna, I swear. I didn't even want to go. I had a great time with you on Friday, and I knew I wasn't really interested in her. I wanted to cancel on her, I really did. But when I called to cancel, she sounded kind of down, and I thought, hell, it's only one dinner. Maybe it will make her feel better. And the whole time I'm thinking how much I'd rather be with you. I wanted to make it an early night. But she was having problems at work, and was upset with one of her friends, so I let her talk.

"Then, when I dropped her off she went ballistic as soon as I said I didn't want to come inside. I tried to be nice about it, but she wouldn't take no for an answer. She started getting really upset so I finally just turned around and got back in my car. I didn't even say good-bye. And, I don't know, maybe she took something I said the wrong way. But I can't see what it could have been. I've thought about it over and over, and I can't figure out where she got the idea that we were going to be together. I guess she's just crazy and there isn't any real explanation for what she's doing.

"But I am sorry as hell that you're caught in the middle of this. That's the worst part. I asked the police to leave you out of it, but they said they had to talk to you. I guess I don't know what else to say other than that I'm sorry. I'm so sorry, Anna. I can't tell you how sorry I am."

If I'd had a mouth I'd have kissed Nick right about then. He'd come through; he'd lied. Not a little white lie, but a big, fat, whopping lie that had made it sound as if he were a stand-up guy who'd had the misfortune, through no fault of his own, to have this horrible thing happen to him. Thank you, Nick! Nothing kills love quicker than lies. So from the bottom of my heart, if I'd had a heart, I, Cupid, the guy with the *worst* job in the universe, sincerely thanked you.

We had fear and mistrust coming from Anna and big, fat lies coming from Nick, which, thanks to Anna's fear and mistrust, she wasn't going to believe. Things were getting back to normal. It had been a close call, but if I knew my people, this relationship would be rapidly falling apart very soon. Before long they'd be two people who used to sleep with each other and now tried to avoid each other at work because it was so awkward and uncomfortable.

The whole experience would leave Nick feeling even more burned out about relationships than he'd been before. He'd go back to one-night stands with absolutely no desire for love, so

I wouldn't even have to bother with him. Anna would go through a grieving period and then start longing for true love again and whining that she couldn't find a decent guy. Business as usual, and for once, I was looking forward to it.

I watched anxiously as Anna and Nick sat there uncomfortably for a few seconds. The next interaction would be crucial in terms of the timing—in other words, how long I'd have to wait for the official breakup.

"You said the police are questioning me tomorrow?" Anna finally asked.

"Yeah. They thought it would be tomorrow."

"They're coming into the office?"

Nick nodded his head. "They said they'd send a detective. He won't be in uniform. They said he'd be discreet," he added, trying to sound hopeful.

But Nick didn't feel hopeful. She was going to end it. He couldn't believe how bad that felt. She knew he was lying. Maybe she could have lived with the other part, the detective coming into work, but she couldn't deal with the fact that he'd lied. Maybe he should own up right now, explain how he didn't want to risk losing her. That's why he'd lied. He hadn't realized how special their relationship was going to become. If he had, he never would have slept with another woman. But Nick couldn't find a way to get the words out.

If only she'd ask some questions. That's what a normal woman would be doing by now. Grilling him. If she'd ask, he vowed he'd break down and tell her the truth. Not right away. Let her have the satisfaction of getting it out of him, watching him squirm, then fall all over himself to apologize once she'd gotten it out of him. He was willing to do that for her. All she had to do was ask.

Anna knew he wasn't telling her the whole truth. He didn't look shocked the way a person does when something horrible happens to them for no logical reason. He looked miserable, the way a person does when they know that on some level they've brought this misfortune on themselves. She didn't know this consciously, but she knew it in her heart.

And she dreaded the idea of a detective coming into the office tomorrow to question her. It didn't matter how discreet he was. Everyone would know. Everyone always found out things like that.

What Anna did next could have been done out of fear or stupidity, but I saw the look in her eyes, and I read her heart, and I knew it wasn't. It wasn't fear of being alone, nor was she acting dumb and not seeing what was right in front of her face because she was afraid of being alone.

She moved closer to Nick and placed her hand on his cheek.

"It's going to be okay," Anna said.

She knew Nick had probably done something stupid, knew he'd probably slept with the woman from the parking lot. *Knew* he had slept with the woman from the parking lot. And it killed her.

But she thought that if she kept loving the truest part of him, the part that was more real than any blunder or screwup—the essence of him that she'd gotten a glimpse of in the restaurant that first night—he'd respond one day and that essence could come out into the light of day. And so would hers.

When Nick felt Anna's hand on his cheek and heard her say it would be okay, he was completely taken aback. He knew she didn't believe his story. And when he saw her looking at him with complete love and acceptance, it took him a minute to get it. And he didn't get it completely, but he got it a little, because I felt the kernel in his heart grow larger.

He knew she knew he'd lied. And she wasn't saying that was okay. She was saying something else. That she had faith in him and forgave him even though he couldn't bring himself to admit what he'd done. And that she believed *he* was okay even if he had screwed up.

Much to my dismay, Nick actually fought back a tear as he put his arms around Anna and held her close. And he didn't freak out or feel smothered or fight an urge to run shrieking out of her apartment, the way he usually had in the past when a woman had wanted him to hold her (or when he hadn't been able to think of anything else to do). And he actually waited almost two minutes before making the move from hugging to foreplay, a world's record of epic proportions for Nick Wells.

I left in disgust and went to keep an eye on the not-particularly-promising girl. I spent hours trying to get her to see that same card I'd tried to get her to notice earlier. I blew it in front of her over and over, but without success. She was too busy thinking about a story Nick had told her. A story she thought she could use to make him know what it was like to suffer, really suffer. All she had to do was think about it long enough until she came up with just the right idea.

twelve

Nick spent the night at Anna's, and the next morning they slept later than they'd meant to. Nick ran home to shower and change before they met at the restaurant down the street from work. They'd decided to have a good, hot breakfast before going into the office so they'd have a chance to talk and keep their spirits up and fortify themselves for the day ahead, knowing full well that because of what had happened yesterday they'd be the objects of gossip and curiosity.

Driving home, Nick vowed he'd learned his lesson. He'd never have a one-night stand again. He made a promise to himself that he would be completely faithful to Anna as long as they were together.

He felt bad about lying to her. To ease his feelings of discomfort and vulnerability, Nick convinced himself that Anna really didn't know he'd lied, that it had been his imagination. He told himself that telling Anna the whole truth at this point would only hurt her. She might have her suspicions, but she didn't *know*. And besides, if he came right out and admitted everything, then she could use it against him later. Women let these things eat away at them. Next thing he knew, she'd be keeping tabs on him and wanting him to account for his whereabouts any time he was late. And who needed that crap?

Leaving things as they were was the kindest thing he could do for Anna. He wouldn't want to know if *she'd* slept with somebody else on Saturday night. And then he thought about it again. How did he know that she *hadn't* slept with someone else on Saturday night? She'd never even brought it up or hinted around about the two of them getting together the next night, which he would have expected since things had gone so well over dinner.

For all he knew, Nick thought to himself, sitting there waiting for the light to change, Anna could have been with dozens of guys. With her looks and all she had going for her? Could have had all kinds of one-night stands. Could just as easily have had the bad luck to end up spending the night with someone who turned out to be a psycho. Because that's all it was. The luck of the draw.

Anna didn't even question my story, Nick thought to himself. It had seemed strange at the time, and now he felt really suspicious. In fact, the more he thought about it, something wasn't adding up. First she'd told him he didn't need to give her an explanation. Then, when he'd said he'd feel better about it if he could tell his side of things, she'd actually not allowed him to do so.

And then last night, as much as he'd wanted Anna to believe his story, he hadn't thought she really would. Because it had to be obvious he'd slept with the woman. He'd prepared himself for the question-and-answer period, had prepared himself to come clean if he'd had to. Still stick to his story about not really *wanting* to be with the not-particularly-promising girl but finally admit that he'd slept with her. Blame it on too much to drink, she was all over him, you and I weren't really together then, etc., etc.

Maybe she hadn't asked any questions because she had stuff in her past that she didn't want him questioning *her* about. Maybe she even had another guy in the picture. The birthday party for her mom? Taking her parents to the airport? She sure seemed to spend an awful lot of time with her family. What next? A sick grandmother?

I was delighted to see how quickly Nick dismissed the expression of love and acceptance he'd seen in Anna's eyes, and I was thrilled to feel the kernel in his heart shrivel and shrink. But of all the ways I wished and hoped Nick might screw up their relationship, jealousy and insecurity hadn't occurred to me. He'd always been the one in control in his relationships, calling all the shots. It never occurred to him that a woman he was seeing might cheat on him. And since his relationship with Lauren, he'd never cared enough to agonize about the women in his life anyway.

I knew it was the fact that he did care about Anna that was

bringing out this new side to his personality. However, it could still definitely work to my advantage. When Nick felt uncomfortable about anything in his life, he usually dealt with it by finding a new woman to seduce. And since he found it so easy to lie and cover his tracks in his relationships, he assumed other people found it easy as well. He could turn into one of those idiots who sleep around and constantly accuse their faithful partner of doing the very same thing. Yes, this new jealous and insecure Nick definitely had possibilities, I thought to myself with a renewed sense of optimism. And watched with pleasure as he spent the rest of the drive home wondering how many men Anna had slept with.

When Nick walked into the restaurant that morning, he saw Anna sitting at a table talking to a waiter. Anna was listening to whatever the waiter was saying—the young, good-looking waiter—and smiling up at him. Nick had never noticed that before, how she smiled that way at other men. What could the waiter possibly be saying that was that interesting? Look how she was gazing at him, like she'd never heard anything so interesting in all her life.

Anna spotted Nick and gave him a little wave and a smile. The same smile she'd had for the waiter, Nick thought to himself. What did she do? Practice in front of a mirror?

The waiter said something to Anna and then left for the kitchen as Nick walked up to the table.

"Hi," Anna said as Nick sat down.

"Hi," Nick said curtly.

"I got you some juice and coffee."

"So I see. Thanks," Nick said, opening his menu. "So what looks good? Did the waiter have any suggestions to make when you were so deep in conversation?"

"Yeah, he did," Anna said innocently. "There's a couple of new omelets they have that aren't on the menu yet. There's one that sounds—"

"That's okay, Anna," Nick interrupted. "I already know what I'm going to have."

Nick closed his menu, set it down, and took a sip of juice.

"Is something wrong?" Anna asked.

"No. How's your aunt doing?"

"My aunt?" Anna asked.

Aha! Nick thought.

"Oh," Anna said, "you mean my great-aunt. My parents haven't called me yet. I should probably send her a card. I barely know her, but she is family."

"Do you have your cell phone with you? Maybe you could call them now while we're waiting for our food."

"It's three hours earlier there. They're probably not even up yet."

"Oh."

"Listen, Nick, there's something I want to ask you. Have you told anyone about us?" Anna asked. "At the office, I mean?"

Nick hadn't told anyone yet. Under normal circumstances he might have told Mark, but he hadn't spoken to Mark in days.

"Not really," Nick answered, feeling slightly chilled.

She's changed her mind, Nick thought to himself. She'd had time to think about it after he left, and she didn't want the embarrassment of seeing him anymore. Probably already had something else lined up for the weekend. Made a call or two the minute he'd left that morning.

She could even use this in her favor. Make sure people knew she'd only known him a short time. Tell them that yeah, she'd gone out with Nick Wells a couple of times. But as soon as she'd found out what he was *really* like, that he had this kind of unsavory thing going on in his personal life, she'd dumped him. "I guess you can never tell about people," she'd say to the group gathered around her desk. "He seemed like such a nice guy."

Her department head would be very impressed with the way Anna had handled herself. How professional she'd been during a difficult and awkward situation. She'd be promoted at the earliest opportunity. He, on the other hand, would be held back. He might be considered for a promotion, but the other candidate would always get chosen. They wouldn't want to take a chance on someone who let his personal life get so out of control.

"I've been thinking about it," Anna continued, "and I think we should walk in this morning together, as a couple, if you're comfortable with that. I think a lot of people have an idea anyway. Maybe we should even bring it up ourselves. Just get it out in the open instead of having everyone talk behind our backs. You know how that goes.

"I don't know how you feel. I know I like to keep my personal life separate from work. But I think in this case, because of what happened to your car, and all the wild stories people are going to come up with, that the last thing we need is to give them something else to gossip about. As if you have something to hide or be embarrassed about. What do you think?" Anna asked.

Nick couldn't speak for a moment. Not only was she *not* dumping him, but she was going to stand by him. And defend him. He probably wouldn't have done it for her. For a split second Nick allowed himself to know that if the situation had been reversed, he wouldn't have risked his reputation at work, but he quickly pushed the thought away.

I felt that tiny kernel in his heart come back to life as Nick struggled with his feelings and felt all the jealous suspicions he'd had about Anna become completely forgotten and erased.

"I think," Nick said huskily, and then quickly cleared his throat. "I think I'm pretty lucky to have you in my life."

Anna had no idea that she was the first woman since Lauren that Nick had said that to outside of a bedroom, a couch, or a motel. But I, to my growing chagrin, did.

Anna smiled. "I think I'm the lucky one," she said.

And then, as if that wasn't bad enough, I listened as Anna proceeded to tell Nick a story in order to bolster his courage before going into the office that morning.

"Remember how you said that you always felt like you were in high school when you were giving a presentation?" Anna asked as he stirred the cream around in his cup over and over. "Well, I remember this guy I went to high school with. His name was Greg Irvington, and he's probably the only person I ever knew who really didn't care what other people thought of him. I was a freshman and he was a senior, and he just did his own thing, no matter what anyone thought."

Nick looked up curiously.

"Anyway, there was this one time. I'll never forget it. We were all sitting outside for lunch. It was a nice day and we were eating on the lawn. And this big, totally uncool Cadillac drives up. It stops in front of the lawn and we're all waiting to see who's going to get out. It was Greg's mother. She got out of the car and started yelling, 'Greg. Yoo-hoo! Greg!' I think she may have even called him 'Sweetie'.

"We all think this is totally hilarious. Mainly because it's one of our nightmares come true. Our *mother* coming to school and embarrassing us so much we want to die. Some people are snickering, and a few of his buddies start imitating her. She had this really high-pitched, grating voice that was easy to mimic.

"Everyone's looking over at him, wondering what he's going to do. So he stands up and really, really slowly, struts over to his mother. With this whole attitude like he doesn't give a damn. And the whole lawn is quiet. No one is saying a word. And when he reaches her, she says, 'I didn't want you to go hungry' and hands him a brown bag. He'd forgotten his lunch. Of all the worst possible reasons she could have for being there. And he takes the bag, opens it up, looks inside, and then he says, 'Roast beef sandwich. My favorite! Thanks, Mom!' and gives her a big hug. I don't know who was more surprised. Her or us. And when he gets back over to his friends, one of them makes a joke. Something like, 'Gee, Greg, it must be nice to have your *mommy* bring you your lunch.' And Greg looked him right in the eye and said, 'Yeah. It sure is. She's the greatest mom in the world.' And no one knew whether he was being serious or making fun of himself.

"And everyone started eating their lunch again. Because he just refused to be embarrassed about it. And I guess that's my long-winded way of saying I think that's what we should do. Which is probably easier for me to say than you. But you didn't do the embarrassing thing. *She* did."

"You're amazing," Nick said when Anna finished.

"And I haven't even had breakfast yet," Anna said with a smile.

"No, really. We've barely gotten started, and all this crap is happening, and most women would be giving me the third degree. Or be pretty pissed about the cops coming in to talk to them. Or figuring how to cover their butts so none of this affected them at work. But you . . . I'm blown away. You're amazing," he repeated.

Watching Nick and Anna make goo-goo eyes at each other again, all my hopes dashed once again, I told myself that much as I hated to admit it (I'd always prided myself on my ability to handle things on my own), maybe it was time I enlisted the aid of one of my fellow spirits.

thirteen

At five minutes to nine, Nick and Anna walked into the office. Everyone who was in at the time looked up when they walked past. Most people had an idea that Nick and Anna had started seeing each other, but the two had never been so obvious about it before. Nick and Anna smiled and said good morning to everyone as if they didn't have a care in the world. There were many conversations about it later, and the general consensus was that no matter how unconcerned Nick and Anna tried to act, they weren't really fooling anybody.

"Thanks for breakfast," Anna said happily as they stopped outside Nick's cubicle. She made sure to say it loudly enough to ensure that the people nearby heard her talking to Nick and being with Nick without a shred of embarrassment.

"You're welcome. Thanks for the company."

"I'll give you a call later," Anna said.

They smiled at each other, then Anna walked off toward her department. Anna felt that the first important step had been taken to diffuse the situation. Nick did, too. He thought maybe things would be okay. Anna had really come through for him. He'd take her somewhere really nice on Saturday night. Maybe even rent a luxurious hotel suite and order breakfast in bed on Sunday.

But the not-particularly-promising girl had spent the previous night thinking and thinking about it, until she'd thought she remembered every word of that conversation she'd had with Nick when they'd gone out to dinner.

She'd asked what it was like working with all that money.

"I don't actually see any real money," he'd told her. "I see printouts of numbers."

"I know that, silly. But you have access to accounts, don't you?"

"In a way."

"Don't you ever get tempted to just lift a couple million and take off for Jamaica?" she'd asked, joking, really.

"It's not that simple. There are so many safeguards and double checks built into the system. And they're always watching. A couple of big companies got burned, and no one takes chances anymore. We had one guy working there who got an inheritance so he decided to buy a new house that would normally have been way out of his price range. He figured he'd put the money in a savings account and dip into it every month to pay the mortgage. But he hadn't told anyone about the inheritance. So when the bank called for a credit reference on such a high loan, the company actually went back and checked the figures on all the accounts he handled. He was really pissed when he found out about it, but they told him it was standard procedure."

"Wow. So I guess we won't be running off to Jamaica anytime soon," she'd teased him.

"No," he'd said, and then smiled. Not at the Jamaica joke but because she'd leaned forward to give him a better view of her cleavage.

So the not-particularly-promising girl had thought about it some more as she'd sat inside her apartment, hating Nick Wells more than she'd ever hated anyone in her life. It wasn't like she could hack into his system and make it look like he'd embezzled some money. If she'd known how, she'd have done it in a split second. See how long his new cutie-pie stayed with him once he got fired. Lost his fancy new condo and his precious little Lexus. What was left of it anyway. Maybe even went to prison, and when he got out couldn't get a good job. Had to get a really crappy job frying burgers or washing cars.

No, she couldn't make it look as if Nick Wells had embezzled millions of dollars. But that didn't mean she couldn't create a little suspicion about him.

So at nine-fifteen she placed the first of two phone calls she'd make that morning.

At ten o'clock Nick finally began to work up the nerve to call his boss. He was surprised the boss hadn't called him yet so they could have a little heart-to-heart about what had happened yesterday. Nick could predict the speech he'd get about how his boss expected his employees to keep their personal lives away from the office. And did Nick think this woman was going to be causing any more trouble? Because they couldn't afford to have clients exposed to this kind of thing.

Nick had been hoping Anna would have called by now to check in with him and see how things were going, but she hadn't. Maybe the detective had shown up and she was busy talking to him. Nick hoped the cop would be as discreet as he'd promised he would be.

Nick called Anna first to give himself a few minutes' reprieve before calling his boss. He got her voice mail. He left a message asking her to call him when she could. Then he called the boss and got his assistant.

"No, Nick," she told him, "he isn't in, but as a matter of fact I was just getting ready to call you. He'd like to see you this afternoon around five."

"Oh. Okay. I'll be there at five, then."

"Great. I'll let him know."

She hung up without saying good-bye.

Nick tried calling Anna again and got her voice mail. Again. God, wasn't she ever at her desk? He tried calling Mark and got his voice mail, too. Didn't anyone ever answer their phone anymore?

Anna was, at that moment, talking to Detective Larson in the conference room. He didn't fit her preconception of a detective, the one she'd gotten from the movies. (Memo to earthlings: Movies are not real life. I know you say you know that, but secretly, you think they are. The amount of whining I have to endure from people—mostly women—unsatisfied with their love lives skyrocketed with the dawn of movies. It started with Valentino, and it's just gotten worse over time.)

Detective Larson was forty-two, balding, developing a paunch, and he could have passed for an insurance salesman. He didn't wisecrack, try to buck the system, violate the constitutional rights of his suspects, or single-handedly take on the most devious and cunning serial killer the world had ever known. He'd never reformed a hooker or dated a stripper.

He questioned people, collected evidence, testified at trials, and, in his spare time, helped coach his son's soccer team.

"So she was waiting for you?" Detective Larson asked.

"Yes," Anna said, nodding her head. "We walked out of his condo, and there she was. The minute I saw her, I knew something was wrong. She looked scary and she had this crazed look in her eyes."

"What did she do?"

"At first she just stared at us."

"Did she say anything?"

"Not at first. She just stared. I asked Nick who she was and he said she was someone he'd gone out with once. And then the next thing I knew she started screaming at him."

"Screaming what?" Detective Larson asked.

"I can't remember exactly," Anna said, which wasn't exactly true. She remembered almost word for word what the woman had said. But she didn't want to have to say it. And whether or not Nick had slept with the woman wasn't the point.

Anna knew what it was like to sleep with someone and then not hear from them again. It hadn't happened to her often. She didn't sleep with men she didn't know. But there had been a couple of times when she'd made the mistake of thinking the relationship had been more serious than the guy had, and he'd stopped calling once they'd slept together. She knew it hurt. But she'd never waited for the guy outside his home to scream at him. Or vandalized his car.

"Give me the gist of it," Detective Larson told her.

"She wanted to know who I was. Was I his wife or his girl-friend? And how dare he treat her like this. That was about all I heard. Nick said it would be better if I went inside."

"Why?"

"Nick said it would be easier to deal with her if I wasn't standing there."

"Um-hmmm. So based on what you saw, you think this woman is capable of doing what was done to his car?"

"Oh yeah. No question about it. She was furious."

"Can you think of anyone else who might have had a reason to want to get back at him?"

"What do you mean?"

"I mean other women who might have a grudge against him."

"No!"

"Are you sure?" Detective Larson asked.

"Yes!"

"Well—"

"Well, what?"

Detective Larson shrugged his shoulders. "He's got you, he's got her. Neither one of you knowing about the other. It's not a reach to think there might be others. I don't want to go accusing this woman if it might be someone else."

"He isn't like that," Anna said, starting to get angry. This detective was acting like Nick was the one on trial here.

Detective Larson nodded his head. "You know him pretty well?" he asked after a moment.

"Yes."

"How long have you two been seeing each other?"

"Not all that long, but . . . look. Even if he's sleeping with hundreds of women, only a really messed-up person would do something like that. And she was a really messed-up person. You could tell that just by looking at her."

Detective Larson nodded his head again. "Kind of makes you wonder why he went out with her, doesn't it? Okay, Ms. Munson, I think I've got enough to go on. I'll pay her a visit and see what she has to say."

"Is that it?" Anna asked with barely controlled anger. Who was he to judge Nick? He didn't know anything about him.

"For now."

Detective Larson stood up. "Thank you for your time," he said.

Anna nodded her head without replying.

At eleven-fifteen the not-particularly-promising girl placed her second call to Nick's company, being sure to disguise her voice so she wouldn't be recognized as the same person who'd made the first call.

By one o'clock Nick was starting to feel a little frantic. He kept getting everyone's voice mail. He'd dropped by Mark's desk a few times, but Mark hadn't been in. And Anna had left him a voice mail telling him she only had a minute but wanted to let him know she'd talked to the detective. She'd fill him in later, but unfortunately she had an emergency meeting with a client, which had come up out of the blue, and she'd be gone for the rest of the day.

"I'm not sure when I'll be back. I'll call you when I get out. I hope your day is going okay. Sorry I can't be there. Talk to you later. Bye."

As the day wore on, Nick grew more and more resentful. He'd gone into the break room once for some coffee, and it had been incredibly awkward. No one had even *asked* him about the car, as if it was too embarrassing to bring up.

It was all well and good for Anna to have given him that little pep talk. Easy enough for her to have told him to just hold his head high, laugh it off, refuse to be embarrassed. Especially easy since she wasn't even here to have to deal with it. She'd told him she'd stand by him, and then all of a sudden she has an emergency meeting with a client? That was pretty handy.

And Nick wasn't completely off base. Detective Larson had affected Anna more than she'd realized at the time. She'd felt so angry when he'd been questioning her, but she wondered now if she had gotten angry because he was making her see things she didn't want to see.

As she drove to her meeting she kept hearing that question he'd asked. "Kind of makes you wonder why he went out with her, doesn't it?" Not that she was excusing what the woman did, but why *had* he gone out with someone like that? She thought how the whole situation must have appeared through the eyes of Detective Larson. The way it would appear to her if she wasn't involved and had just heard about it.

Maybe the woman in the parking lot hadn't been like that when Nick had met her. Maybe she'd had a nervous breakdown or something. Maybe she was someone really fragile, and Nick had treated her really badly and she'd cracked. You read about things like that in the paper all the time. Someone who seemed normal to the people around them. And then something happens and they crack and do these really crazy things.

She'd accepted that Nick had slept with that woman. But all Anna had was Nick's word that he barely knew her. For all Anna knew, he and that woman might have been seriously involved. Might still have been involved on the night Anna had first slept with Nick.

By the time she arrived at her meeting, Anna was consumed with doubts and fears about Nick and about herself and how quickly she'd let him into her life. The vision she'd had in the restaurant could have been nothing more than her fantasies and illusions, a sign of her growing desperation that she'd never find the right man.

This wasn't like her. She was always careful in relationships and took her time. She'd seen too many of her girlfriends get involved right away with someone they barely knew. It almost never worked out.

What had she been thinking? She didn't know Nick; she didn't know him at all. They needed to have a serious talk that night. She needed to ask him some questions and get some straight answers before their relationship went any further.

Watching Anna, listening to her heart, the pain and fear and suspicion, I was so happy with Detective Larson right then that I immediately sent a lust arrow to his wife, and he had a very pleasant evening indeed.

fourteen

Nick turned off his computer, took a deep breath, and walked out of his cubicle. It was ten minutes to five. This was it. He was determined to explain the situation to his boss in a calm and rational manner. Be apologetic, even though he hadn't done anything wrong, wasn't responsible for some nutcase taking out her problems on him. He would say how bad he felt about a mess like this coming into the workplace and that he'd make sure nothing like this ever happened again.

His boss's assistant barely looked at him when he arrived. She gave him a tight smile and said the boss would be available to see him shortly. Nick sat down and picked up a magazine to read. He felt her glancing at him occasionally, but he pretended to ignore it. Screw her. And screw everyone else who was judging him. They didn't know the situation. There were a lot of nuts out there, and for the most part they looked just like everyone else. It could have happened to anyone.

As soon as he was through talking to his boss, Nick planned on going home and forgetting he'd ever met the not-particularly-promising girl. Maybe call some of his buddies and set up a poker game for later in the week. He'd gotten through the worst of it, and over time people would have other things to think about. He'd ride it out and come out back on top.

He wouldn't go to Anna's place that night or have her come over to his. He wasn't sure he'd bother to call her. She hadn't bothered to call him except for that one brief voice mail. Hell, she could have taken a minute on the drive over to the client's and used her cell to see if he was doing all right. Let him know what the detective had said. She had to know he'd be curious.

So Nick was pissed off (and also hurt, although he'd never admit it in a million years), and Anna was feeling doubts and fears, and I'm smelling a breakup in the air. I'm thinking I might send a little lust arrow to Detective Larson's wife every day for the next month and let him have the time of his life. He'd earned it.

Nick's boss came out a few minutes later.

"Hi, Nick," he said. "Come on in."

Nick set the magazine down and stood up. He followed his boss into the office, feeling the assistant glance at him again as he walked past.

"Have a seat," his boss said, shutting the door.

Nick sat down, and his boss walked around and sat down behind his desk. Nick crossed his legs, trying to get comfortable. He uncrossed them, then switched positions. Nick still wasn't comfortable. He didn't remember this chair being so awkward and uncomfortable before.

"So, Nick," his boss said, leaning back with his hands clasped behind his head, "we seem to have a little problem."

"I know, and all I can say is nothing like this has ever happened to me before. I hardly know the woman, and I have no idea why she did it, but I promise nothing like this will ever happen again. The police said they'd talk to her and we shouldn't have any more trouble."

"Well, that's not really the problem."

"It isn't?" Nick asked, surprised.

"No. We had a couple of phone calls about you this morning. It seems you're buying a house?"

"A house?"

"Yeah. A couple of different lenders called for a credit reference. And the interesting thing was that you only need a small loan. It seems you have enough cash on hand to make a large down payment. Have you come into some money lately? An inheritance, perhaps?"

"No, but there must be some mistake. I'm not buying a house."

"Hmmm. Well, the two women who called my assistant today to verify your employment and your salary seemed to think you were."

Nick felt a small chill go down his spine.

"It was her," he said.

"I beg your pardon?" his boss asked.

"It was her. The woman who vandalized my car. It has to be. I swear to you, I'm not buying a house. I haven't even looked at a house. I've only been in my condo for a couple months, and I'm certainly not in a position to buy a house."

His boss looked at Nick and furrowed his brow.

"Tell me, Nick. Haven't you wondered why the Shop Smart numbers haven't come in yet?"

"Yeah, actually, that was one of the things I was going to talk to you about today."

"The reason they haven't come in is that there are some discrepancies."

"Discrepancies?"

"Um-hmmm. Mark found them a few days ago."

"Mark?" Nick asked, feeling completely baffled. Why would Mark be looking at the Shop Smart numbers?

"He said you'd been acting kind of strange, that you seemed preoccupied and changed the subject whenever he asked you about the Shop Smart account."

Nick was genuinely puzzled. He didn't think he'd been acting any differently, and he had no recollection of Mark asking him about the Shop Smart account.

"So on a hunch he started doing some investigating, and the Shop Smart account didn't quite add up. Didn't add up to the tune of ten thousand dollars or so."

"But that's crazy. I would have noticed if they'd been off by that much."

"Nick, up until now you've done good work. So we're not going to press charges. We can move some things around and cancel the training seminar in May to cover the loss. I don't know that we could prove conclusively in court that it was you, and quite frankly, I don't want this getting out anyway. Unless we find some other discrepancies. It was just the ten thousand, wasn't it?"

"No, this is all a big misunderstanding. I didn't take ten thousand dollars. I didn't take any money and I'm not buying a house. Let me take a look at the account and figure out what's going on."

"Nick, our clients have to know they can rely on us. And between the problems you're having in your personal life and the fact that there's ten thousand dollars missing from one of your accounts, it's just a bit too much of a coincidence for me to be comfortable with. I'm afraid I'm going to have to let you go. And my decision is final."

Nick heard him but couldn't take it in. His boss waited. He hated firing people. Some cried, some screamed, and some simply sat there, the way Nick was doing. He'd learned the best thing to do was just stay quiet. They usually stood up after a few minutes and walked out the door without saying another word.

Which is what Nick finally did after about three minutes. Stood up and walked out of the office without saying another word.

Nick was in a state of shock, and I was completely confused. I knew he hadn't done it. I'd have read the guilt in his heart, and there wasn't any. Not about the Shop Smart account.

And committing a crime like this wasn't part of Nick's projected life scenario. When I say scenario, I don't want you to get the impression that you're all just a bunch of puppets with us up here pulling the strings. A scenario is a best-guess prediction of how your life will turn out, with an average 97.6 percent rate of accuracy, given a certain set of circumstances. You always have the ultimate freedom of choosing your response.

It's true I'd put a monkey wrench into the works by giving Anna the arrow of true love. But Nick wasn't guilty of taking the money. For once he was dealing with something he hadn't brought on himself.

That meant there were other forces at work, forces I knew nothing about. Great. Just what I needed. More complications. The front office always leaves us out of the loop, and just try and tell them how hard it makes our job.

If I'd heard it once, I'd heard it a million times. "The universe operates in complete harmony. You're given what you need to know to do your part. We can't tell you more than that because if you knew all the answers, then you wouldn't ever have to learn anything, would you?" They're always so *smug* about everything.

Nick getting fired changed everything. I could just picture it. If I knew Anna—the new and improved selfless wonder of an Anna who was making my life a living hell—all her doubts and fears would be forgotten the moment she heard what had happened to Nick.

But in the meantime, I needed to catch up with the not-particularly-promising girl and give her another nudge. I'd been keeping an eye on her all day. I knew she had to have made the two phone calls to Nick's office. And I also knew that after the initial high wore off, she'd feel the same way she had after she'd vandalized his car. Like it wasn't enough to make up for what he'd done to her.

But Detective Larson was due any moment (if he'd known how frisky his wife would be that night, he'd have waited until morning), and I was hoping his visit might shake her up enough to finally notice that card I kept putting in front of her.

I found her sitting in her apartment. She had the TV on but wasn't paying much attention. She hadn't been to work in two days, hadn't showered in three, and hadn't brushed her teeth that morning. She wore an old bathrobe over a torn T-shirt and wrinkled pajama bottoms, and she looked like hell. Her apartment was a mess, littered with old magazines, junk food containers, and used Kleenex.

When she heard the knock at her door, she had no intention of answering it. Whoever it was would go away. But the knocking continued, persistently, and then she heard the person at the door identify themselves as Detective Larson. She panicked.

She hadn't thought about cops getting involved, about what she'd done having consequences. (Note from Cupid: Actions have consequences. Obvious, but considering humanity's track record in the behavior department, worth repeating.)

All this over a stupid car? Did she *have* to answer the door? Was he alone, or did he have other cops with him for all her neighbors to see? Most of them would be at work, but she'd heard some music playing downstairs, so somebody was home. Would they break down her door if she didn't answer? The detective had probably heard the noise from her TV and knew she was home.

"Just a minute," she called out, and ran into her bedroom. She tied a scarf around her dirty hair, took off her robe and pajama bottoms, threw on a pair of jeans, and pulled a long sweater over her T-shirt. God, she looked awful, but it was better than answering the door in her robe.

She heard Detective Larson knocking again, and she took a few seconds to gather up some of the junk all over her living room.

"Coming," she called, picking up as many Kleenexes as she could and dumping them in the wastebasket.

She grabbed some of the magazines on her way to answer the door and threw them on top of the coffee table.

"Yes?" she asked when she opened the door, trying to look surprised to see a detective standing on her doorstep. She knew why he was here—that bastard, Nick; she should have known he'd call the cops—but he couldn't prove a thing. No one had seen her by Nick's car, she'd made sure of that. And she'd called his office from a pay phone so there wouldn't be any phone records. "Can I help you?"

"I hope so," Detective Larson said pleasantly. "May I come in?"

"Sure. Excuse the mess, but I've had a horrible flu bug for days now. This is the first time I've been out of bed in days. I think that chair's pretty clear."

Detective Larson sat down in the chair she'd indicated.

"Do you know a Mr. Nick Wells?" Detective Larson asked after he sat down.

"I did. Unfortunately." The not-particularly-promising girl

forced herself to laugh, as if Nick were old news, already forgotten. "Is this about what happened in the parking lot? I mean, I know I screamed pretty loud at him, but I didn't think screaming was against the law."

"No, ma'am, screaming isn't against the law. But slashing someone's tires is. And keying the paint off his car is. And spray painting the windows on his car is. It's called vandalism, and yes, it's against the law."

"I'm sorry, Detective, I don't know what you're talking about."

"Oh, I think you do. And I want you to think real seriously about what you've gotten yourself into. Because I'm looking around this place, and I don't think you have the flu. I think you've been sitting in here, day after day, thinking about what a louse Nick Wells is. And you want to get revenge. And the car didn't do it for you. So you're thinking about what else you can do to get back at him. And in the end, the only person's life you're going to ruin will be yours."

"I really don't know—"

"When I leave here I want you to do me a favor," Detective Larson went on. "Take a good look in the mirror at what you're doing to yourself. You're young, you're attractive, you seem intelligent, you have your whole life ahead of you. Don't screw it up. He isn't worth it."

Detective Larson stood up.

"That's all I wanted to say. We can't prove you vandalized his car. But you keep on like this and you'll get more and more reckless and end up doing something really stupid. And the odds are that we'll catch you, because you'd be the first person we'd look at. You aren't thinking clearly, and you'll end up making a mistake. A mistake that will get you caught. Please think about that before you do anything else. I'd hate to see you ruin your life over a jerk like him."

The not-particularly-promising girl looked down at the ground, her lips quivering.

"I'll show myself out," Detective Larson said, then quietly left.

I couldn't have said it better myself. I was starting to love Detective Larson. He was always so sensible, too. He never gave me a minute's trouble. All he'd ever asked was to meet a nice woman he could spend his life with, have some kids with, someone to be his companion in old age. And the more he saw on the job, the destruction that people cause in the name of love, the more grateful he was for the easy companionship he'd found with his wife. I hadn't heard from him in *years*. You could all learn a thing or two from Detective Larson.

I didn't move. I stayed right there watching, hoping his words had gotten through to her.

The not-particularly-promising girl didn't do what Detective Larson said. She didn't go take a good, long look at herself in the mirror. She didn't think she could stand it. She cried first, for about an hour. How had she turned into this? How had her life turned out like this? Why did she always, always end up feeling like this, like a piece of garbage? Why was she always in such a mess? Why?

When she finally ran out of Kleenex, she stood up and walked into her bedroom to see if she had any tissues left in the box on the table by her bed. But the box of Kleenex wasn't on the table by her bed. She looked around. She was sure she hadn't used it all up. There it was, on her dresser. Which was odd; she always left it on the table by her bed.

She picked up the box and saw a card laying next to it. Lena Grimes, Ph.D., Counseling and Therapy, the card read.

The not-particularly-promising girl picked up the card. She couldn't remember taking it out of her kitchen drawer. She'd gone to see Dr. Grimes a couple of times after her last breakup, but then she'd met a guy and had stopped going because she'd felt okay again. And it hadn't seemed as if therapy had been doing her much good anyway. Dr. Grimes just didn't understand how hard it was to meet a decent man. She didn't understand how many *jerks* there were out there.

But she looked at the card and sat down on the bed. She stared at that card a long time, and then she picked up the phone to make an appointment. She didn't know if Dr. Grimes could help her. She just knew she couldn't stand one more day of feeling like this.

Dr. Grimes answered the phone, which was unusual. But she was running late and thought it might be her husband calling.

"Dr. Grimes? I don't know if you remember me," the not-particularly-promising girl said. "I came to see you a couple times a few months ago and then I stopped because I was feeling better? Or I thought I was anyway. But I, um, I . . . I don't know if you can help me. But my life has gotten to be a big mess again. And I think maybe all these awful things that keep happening to me? I think I might be part of the problem. I think I need some help."

Did I have anything to do with Dr. Grimes's just happening to be running late and picking up the phone because she thought it might be her husband calling? Yes. I did.

We don't do miracles anymore; miracles went out with goat herding. (But look on the bright side. You don't get frogs dropping out of the sky anymore, either.) More like little coincidences. The exact book you need to read or the one person you need to talk to, and suddenly they call or the book falls out of the shelf at the library? It's probably one of us. We can't take away your ability to choose, but we can give you a little help when you're ready. You need it, believe me. Without our help you'd all still be living in caves.

So the not-particularly-promising girl got a little nudge, a little set of directions to help her find her way. But she was the one who picked up the card, and she was the one who swallowed her pride and called Dr. Grimes. All credit will go to her, naturally. God forbid someone from the front office should ever drop by to say, "Hey, Cupid, nice job. Having that card show up on her dresser was a great idea. Maybe we don't say it very often, but we want you to know we appreciate all the good work you do for us." No. As far as the front office is concerned, the job is supposed to be its own reward.

I'd also gotten some help from Detective Larson. So what was his reward? Let's just say that from that day on Detective Larson had a very stimulating and vibrant marriage. And most mornings he went into work with a smile on his face.

fifteen

I think that in the interest of fairness, I should probably take a minute here and speak up on Nick's behalf. Amateurs and hacks like to make the characters in their books either all good or all bad, but a real writer knows it's never that black and white. People are complicated.

Nick was emotionally immature, shallow, and had virtually no self-awareness, but he wasn't a heartless bastard. He just didn't let himself feel much. And since he didn't feel much himself, he had a hard time taking the feelings of other people seriously.

Nick had issues stemming from his childhood. (Memo to earthlings: Yes, it all starts in childhood. It's called the human condition and it wasn't *my* idea.) His parents hadn't meant to be cold and judgmental; they just hadn't known any better.

Nick seldom saw his parents or gave them a second's thought, and in his mind that showed how little his childhood had affected him. He believed people who complained about their childhood were pathetic crybabies.

Nick honestly didn't understand what the not-particularly-promising girl was feeling. And most of what she was feeling had nothing to do with him but everything to do with things that had happened to her long before the two of them had met.

Since his relationship with Lauren (and his feelings about her, which he's kept so deeply buried he can't remember them at all), Nick never suffered another painful loss. He conveniently arranged his life to make sure he didn't.

Women had ended it with Nick, but that had always been due to his inability to connect beyond a superficial level. And the women he'd dated had realized that about him right around the time he'd be feeling trapped and wanting out anyway. So the breakup had always come as a relief and saved him the trouble.

Nick knew he'd said things to the not-particularly-promising girl that night that he hadn't meant. But the things he'd said had been said in the throes of passion, and in Nick's mind he couldn't believe that she'd actually taken him seriously. In his mind—and he honestly believed this—most of the scenes women made, all that "drama and hysterics," as he put it, weren't genuine but rather a kind of playacting. A staged overreaction designed to get a certain reaction out of him or make him feel bad.

How will Nick be held accountable for the people he's hurt? What price will he have to pay? Beats me; I'm just a cog in the universal machine. It's out of my hands. All I do know is that one day he'll be *shown* everything he ever did and who it hurt and how it felt to *them,* and it won't be much fun.

Only now, through no real fault of his own, all of Nick's convenient arrangements had been blown to pieces. He'd suffered a major loss, one that cut him to the core: He'd lost his job. Not just lost it, he'd been fired. Nick doesn't know that before it's all over, he's going to have a lot of jobs. And as far as the front office is concerned, your job title is the least interesting thing about you. So far he's been a gladiator, a serf, a beggar, a sheriff, a farmer, a peddler, and a duke. Last time around he was a cowhand.

But Nick's entire identity and sense of self-esteem were centered around his career. Driving home that afternoon, Nick was in a state of complete shock. He couldn't take in the fact that he'd just been fired from his job.

The worst part had been going back to his desk to clean out his stuff. Someone had put a few boxes on top of his desk. God. They'd actually had someone put some boxes on his desk while he'd been sitting in the boss's office getting fired? Probably that bitchy assistant who kept acting like she *wasn't* staring at him.

There hadn't been anyone around when he'd gone to his desk. All of his coworkers had gone home for the day. He'd heard that's how they did it now. Let someone go late in the day on Friday. Make it as painless and as anonymous as possible. Have them gone and their desk cleared out before anyone knows what happened. Nick had thought that was probably the best way to handle it. Until it had happened to him.

Not that he would have wanted anyone to witness his humiliation. On the other hand, having not one single person to say good-bye to made him feel as if he'd never worked there at all. As if the previous three years had been some kind of dream. It made him feel *erased,* as if he didn't exist.

He'd started to clean out his desk when a security guard appeared. At first Nick didn't pay attention, assumed the guy was making rounds or something. But then the guy stopped next to his cubicle, crossed his arms, and stood there. Watching.

"Can I help you with something?" Nick asked.

"I'm here to escort you out, Mr. Wells."

"I don't need an escort, thanks."

The security guard didn't move.

"What?" Nick asked angrily. "Are you afraid I'm going to steal some paper clips? Or take home an extra pen?"

"It's nothing personal, Mr. Wells. Just standard procedure."

It felt personal to Nick. It felt very personal.

Nick threw the stuff he wanted from his desk as quickly as he could into the boxes and hurriedly took down the few pictures he'd hung on his cubicle walls. He could feel the security guard standing there, watching him, but he wasn't going to give the guy the satisfaction of even acknowledging him. In less than five minutes Nick was done.

He put two of the boxes on top of each other and picked

them up. He could come back for the third one. He took a
few steps out of his cubicle, walking past the security guard
without a glance, when he heard the guy picking up his third
box.

"I can get that," Nick said, turning around.

"No problem, Mr. Wells. I've got it."

"Look, I don't want your help. I'll come back and get it."

"It's not a problem."

"It's a problem for me. I don't want you carrying the box,
okay? Just put it down and I'll come back for it."

"They really don't want you coming back inside the building. It's standard procedure, Mr. Wells, nothing personal. I'm
just trying to do my job."

"I don't give a damn about your standard procedure. This is
my stuff and I'll take care of it. Now put the damn box down!"

"I know this is difficult for you, Mr. Wells, but try not to
make a scene. I don't want to have to call someone else."

A scene? Nick thought to himself angrily. He wasn't making
a scene. But he wasn't going to be treated like a criminal. He
hadn't done anything wrong. Who was this jerk to be ordering
him around?

"You think just because you wear a stupid uniform that
you're some kind of big deal?" Nick shouted. "That you have
some kind of authority over me? Forget it. That's my stuff and
my box and I want you to put it down!"

The security guard set the box down on the ground and
took the walkie-talkie off his belt.

"Yeah, this is Beller up on floor six," he said into his walkie-talkie. "I have a situation. Mr. Wells refuses to let me escort him out, and he's becoming very hostile. Could you send Ivans and Cutter up to give me a hand? Thanks."

Beller put his walkie-talkie back onto his belt, crossed his arms, and stood there looking at Nick with a calm expression. Nick stared at him in disbelief.

"You think I'm that dangerous it's going to take three of you to handle me? Just what is it you think I'm going to do?"

"Is there a problem here?"

Nick looked over and saw his boss—his former boss—standing there watching him with a look of distaste. His boss, with whom he'd gone out after work for a couple of drinks and spent half an hour listening to about his kids, was now looking at him, Nick, like he was a virtual stranger.

To hell with it, Nick said to himself, there wasn't anything in that box he couldn't live without. He was out of here.

"No," Nick said, "there's no problem. You can *keep* the damn box."

And with that, feeling as if he'd managed to maintain at least a shred of dignity, Nick stormed off toward the elevator carrying his two boxes. Nick's boss and Beller the security guard gave each other a knowing look, then went back to their respective places of work.

Anna and Nick didn't realize it, but they passed each other on separate elevators. Anna had some things she needed to check on her computer after her meeting, so she was going up to her desk at the same moment Nick was coming down to put his boxes into his rental car. He arrived at the parking garage about the same time Anna walked off her elevator toward her desk.

I watched them pass each other, both of them alone and both of them nursing grudges against the other. Hmmmm, I thought to myself, this might turn out better than I thought. All my previous dealings with Planet Thirty-Seven made this outcome highly unlikely, but it was worth a shot.

The office seemed empty when Anna got off the elevator. People put in long hours but usually tried to clear out by five or six on Friday. Anna didn't expect to run into anyone. She was feeling a little tired and sluggish and decided to see if there was some coffee left in the break room before heading to her desk. There wasn't any, so she got a soda out of the vending machine, hoping the caffeine might perk her up.

It shouldn't take her long to finish what she had to do, but Anna thought she should take a minute and check in with Nick. He'd want to know how it had gone with the detective. He'd probably left her a message on her voice mail. She walked over to her desk and sat down to play her messages. Nick had left one in the morning, asking if she'd talked to Detective Larson yet. Anna cringed a little hearing the detective's name.

Nick had left a second message around one-thirty, asking her to call him when she got in, and asking again how it had gone with Detective Larson.

Anna played her other messages and copied down a couple of numbers, clients she'd need to get back with on Monday morning. She took off her jacket and opened the file she'd brought back from her meeting.

She really should call Nick first and see how he was doing, but along with the apprehensions she'd felt that afternoon, now she was a little angry. He'd told her that morning after breakfast that he wanted to take her somewhere really nice for dinner on Saturday to thank her for being so supportive. But he hadn't mentioned anything about it in either one of his messages. And he hadn't thanked her, either. Not that she was looking for gratitude or had done it for that reason.

But she'd gone out on a limb for him, made a point of letting everyone in the office know they were together and that she stood by him. Hadn't given a thought to how it might affect her reputation at work or her future career, that management might think it showed a lack of judgment on her part. And sometimes, when it came down to making a final decision as to which qualified candidate would get the next promotion, a little thing like that could be the deciding factor.

And all he'd asked about when he'd called—both times— was how it had gone with Detective Larson. Not how it had gone for *her*. He hadn't asked anything about how she'd felt about being questioned. Hadn't thanked her for walking into the office with him or the support she'd shown him. Hadn't even said where, or even if, he'd made their dinner reservations.

Watching all of this play out, I kept my fingers crossed that Anna wouldn't find out until Monday that he'd been fired. Since Nick felt she'd let him down, and she felt he'd let her down, the odds were excellent that neither would call the other. On any given evening, you'd be surprised at the number of people determined, no matter what, not to call the very person they most want to talk to. Human nature is a hoot.

And then, if things went the way I hoped, after a long weekend of stewing about the fact that Nick hadn't called after *all she'd done for him,* after two whole days of nursing her grudge and increasing her doubts and fears, Anna would feel bad for Nick when she heard the news on Monday that he'd been fired. But she would realize she had her career to think about, Nick really didn't have the qualities she was looking for in a man, and it was best that they stop seeing each other.

But unbeknownst to me, a woman named Bethany (recently married and back from her honeymoon, more in love than ever, so she wasn't currently any of my concern) had been forced to stay late that Friday because she had a huge presentation due on Monday, and her boss had made some last-minute changes that afternoon. Bethany had been writing some notes to herself so quietly that no one had realized she was there, and she'd overheard the whole exchange between Nick and the security guard.

When Anna turned on her computer, Bethany got up to see who it was. She needed a break, and she was dying to tell someone what she'd overheard. She wandered over and saw Anna working at her desk. Seeing it was Anna, Bethany wasn't sure whether to say anything or not. She'd heard through the grapevine about Nick and Anna's entrance that morning.

Maybe Anna already knew. No. It had just happened. And surely she wouldn't be sitting there at her desk that calmly if she knew. She'd want to be with Nick. Bethany wasn't sure it was her place to be the one to tell her. But then again, Anna would probably want to know so she could at least call Nick and make sure he was all right. He'd been pretty upset when he'd left. Telling Anna Nick had been fired wouldn't be like gossiping. More like doing her a favor.

"Anna?"

Anna looked up. Bethany stood outside her cubicle with a funny expression on her face.

"Hey, Bethany. I thought I was the only one here."

"Nope. I got stuck, too. Did you just get back, by any chance? I mean, you weren't here earlier, were you?"

"No. I've been gone most of the day at a meeting. I just walked in the door about two minutes ago. Why?"

"I'm not sure it's my place to tell you this," Bethany said uncomfortably, "but I figured you'd want to know."

Anna looked at Bethany curiously.

"Tell me what?"

"I was here working late, and I kind of overheard something I think you should know about." Bethany hesitated for a second, then just blurted it out. "Nick got fired."

"Fired? Nick? You mean they fired him because of that stupid car thing?"

"I don't know. All I know is that he was cleaning out his desk and there was a security guard here to escort him out to his car. And, um, Nick didn't take it very well. He got kind of upset with the security guard. I guess I don't blame him. The guard told him they didn't want him coming back inside the building.

"Nick started shouting and then ended up storming out. Nick's boss was here, too, which I guess didn't help. I hope you don't think I'm being nosy. I thought you'd want to know. Since you guys are seeing each other or whatever."

"This is so unfair. It's such total bullshit. I can't believe they fired him."

"I know," Bethany said, although she wasn't sure it was all that unfair. There had been some rumors going around that morning, rumors that something was wrong with the Shop Smart account.

"Thanks for telling me, Bethany," Anna said, standing up. "I have to go."

Anna didn't turn off her computer or put her file away, or remember to grab her jacket—her favorite jacket—hanging on the back of the chair. She almost forgot to grab her purse as she brushed past Bethany and practically ran to the elevator.

And I knew I'd lost another round.

After spilling the beans and ruining my plans like that, it was a good thing Bethany was happily married. She wouldn't have met another eligible man for years.

sixteen

Nick was sitting inside his condo nursing his third beer when Anna called from her car.

"Nick," she said, "this is Anna. Are you there? Can you pick up?"

She waited a moment, but Nick didn't pick up the phone.

"I just heard what happened. I am so, so sorry. I wish I could have been there for you. That stupid meeting went on forever. I'm on my way over. It's about six-thirty. I left as soon as I heard. I didn't even finish my meeting notes. Not that that matters. I just wanted you to know that I left as soon as I heard. I guess I said that already, didn't I?

"Look, I hope you're just in the shower or something and you get this message. I should be there in about twenty minutes. If you're out and I'm not there when you get back, I'll be at home. All night. If I don't answer it means I'm on my way home, and you can call me on my cell. Whenever you get back call me. Even if it's two in the morning. I can come over, or you can come over to my place, or whatever you want. We can go out or stay in. Whatever you need.

"I'm so angry right now, Nick, I can't tell you. I just cannot believe they fired you. Maybe you can sue. I don't know. We'll figure something out. But please, please, at least call me when you get this message and let me know you're okay. Hopefully I'll see you when I get there, but if not, call me, okay?"

At one point during her message Nick almost reached over and picked up the phone. Almost. She sounded so upset and angry on his behalf, really genuine. But getting fired, even if it was total bullshit, had been humiliating, and he wasn't sure he wanted to see her so soon after it happened.

He just needed a little time to regroup. Hell, it wasn't like it was going to take him long to find another position. He'd always believed that when shit happens you don't sit around feeling sorry for yourself. You get out there and make things happen.

He'd allow himself one night to feel like crap, maybe get a little shit-faced, and then, starting tomorrow, he'd get the ball rolling. If they thought this was going to defeat him, they had another think coming. He had contacts, connections. Maybe he'd start his own consulting business. He wouldn't be down for long.

He had a little money saved, enough to get him through a month or two until he got back on his feet again. And Anna's idea wasn't bad. Maybe he *should* sue the bastards. They might decide to settle to avoid the bad publicity. Give him a nice chunk of change he could use to start his own business. Or buy a house. It would serve the bastards right if they ended up buying a house for him. It was kind of funny when you thought about it.

Nick felt better already. But he still didn't want to see Anna that night. He'd be okay tomorrow. They'd go somewhere really nice, and he'd tell her what he'd managed to line up for himself. He wouldn't be a guy that just got fired, someone she had to feel sorry for. He'd be a guy in charge of his own life, a guy who took the crap life could dish out and came back fighting. Nick stood up and went looking for his wallet to find her cell phone number.

Anna was just pulling into his parking lot when her cell phone rang. She'd spent most of the drive alternating between worrying about Nick and beating herself up for being so self-absorbed, all her doubts and fears and questions now completely forgotten. Hadn't he told her that morning how lucky he felt to have her in his life? And of course he was going to be worried about how it went with the detective. This was his life that was getting screwed with, not hers.

What did she think? That she deserved some kind of medal because she'd been supportive? That's what you're supposed to do for the person you love.

The person I love. She'd never put it that way to herself. She'd said she was in love with him, said she was crazy about him. But calling Nick *the man I love* felt different and more meaningful somehow.

The power of that one little word never ceases to amaze me, and I've seen it all. Wars have been fought, kingdoms destroyed, families torn apart, murders committed, lives lost, noble sacrifices made, all in the name of love or what people thought was love. I'm always there to witness the exact moment when one of you first decides that you love someone else. It's a thrilling moment for *you*, but for me it's just one more headache to add to my collection.

Anna wanted, more than anything, to put her arms around him and let him know it was going to be all right. She'd help him any way she could. And he'd get through this. She had complete faith in him.

And then her phone rang. She picked it up and saw Nick's name on the caller ID panel.

"Nick. I'm so glad you called. Are you all right?"

"A little bruised, but I'll survive. How'd you find out so soon?"

"Bethany Parks happened to be there and overheard what happened. I had to come back after the meeting to put a few notes in my account file, and she came over and told me. I don't think anyone else knows."

"They will by Monday," Nick said, trying not to sound bitter.

"I'm just pulling into your parking lot. Do you want me to order us some takeout or something?"

"Anna, I think I need some time alone. I appreciate you coming over, but I think I need to take tonight and regroup."

"Oh," Anna said, trying not to sound disappointed. But

she was disappointed. She'd had it all pictured. She'd listen to him, let him get it all out of his system, talk all night if he wanted to. Let him be angry or depressed or whatever he needed to be. Hold him if he wanted to be held, keep her distance if he needed her to keep her distance. And she hated the idea of him being alone at a time like this.

But Nick didn't like having people around on those rare occasions when he was feeling down or less than himself. He got uncomfortable when women tried to comfort him. He never knew what to say.

"I still can't believe they fired you over that stupid car thing," Anna said after an awkward silence.

"I wasn't fired because of the car. That was part of it, but there's more, and I don't really want to go into it tonight. Why don't we have dinner tomorrow night? I'll make reservations somewhere nice and pick you up around six."

"Okay, Nick. I mainly just needed to know you were all right."

"I'm going to be just fine. Count on it. So I'll see you tomorrow night."

"All right."

And Nick did get up the next morning and make some calls. It was Saturday—he could have put things off until Monday—but he'd promised himself he wasn't going to sit around moping all weekend. He had a mild hangover, but some juice and coffee and aspirin took the edge off.

Nick apologized to the people he called for bothering them at home on the weekend, but they understood. Would have done the same thing in his place. Nick was very good at networking. He could put a lot of charm and energy into superficial relationships when they were mutually beneficial. He told everyone he called that he'd resigned because his position had no longer been a good fit.

Then he left a voice mail for his former boss threatening that unless he was able to prove his accusations, which Nick knew were groundless, he could count on a lawsuit if he badmouthed Nick to anyone who called for a reference. By the end of the morning he had three interviews set up.

Nick went to the gym that afternoon, had a good workout, saw a few women checking him out on the treadmill, and felt even better. Picked up his dry cleaning and got a few groceries, including a very nice bottle of wine to share with Anna when they got back to his place after dinner. He didn't even think about the cost. He knew he'd have a new position within a week or two. A month at the most.

Anna went into work and finished what she'd left the day before. She saw Mark and Nick's former boss working together in Mark's office, but she made a point of keeping out of their way and didn't even get a cup of coffee out of the break room for fear of running into one of them. Fortunately, no one else was in. Anna had no idea how she was going to act on Monday when she had to deal with everyone knowing about Nick. She got mad just thinking about all of them standing around in little groups, gossiping about Nick getting fired.

Anna spent the rest of the day catching up on errands and housework, and then she worked out to a video and took a long, hot bath in anticipation of her date with Nick. She wondered what kind of mood he'd be in that night. She thought about calling him and then decided not to. He'd asked for some time alone, and she'd give it to him.

Nick arrived right at six, and when Anna opened the door, he gave her a big smile and handed her a bouquet of flowers.

"Nick, they're beautiful. Thank you."

"You're welcome. You look great."

"Thanks. Come on in. I'll put these in water. Do you want something to drink before we go?"

"No. We better head out. Our reservations are for seven, and they've got one of the freeway lanes shut down."

Anna went into the kitchen to get a vase. Nick seemed fine, better than fine. Which was good, although she still felt a small pang of regret that he hadn't wanted her with him the night before. Geez, Anna, she told herself. Quit being so self-absorbed. Men handle a crisis differently. Women call their girlfriends and talk on the phone all night. Men mope for a couple of hours and then get on with their lives.

And Nick felt fine, better than fine. He'd always wondered how he'd face adversity, and now he'd proven to himself that he could deal with whatever life threw at him. This might turn out to be the best thing that could have happened. He liked the idea of a new challenge. Things had been getting a little stale lately.

And Anna. She was turning out to be pretty okay, too. God, she looked hot tonight. He was tempted to skip dinner and lead her right into the bedroom, but he'd been looking forward all day to the shrimp scampi he planned to order. He'd wait. Sometimes the anticipation made it even better.

Anna walked out of the kitchen and put the flowers down on her coffee table. Nick watched her smile as she set them down. He walked over and put his arms around her.

"You like?" he asked.

"Very much," Anna said, smiling.

"Hey, thanks for being there for me yesterday. It helped."

"You're welcome. I'm just sorry things turned out the way they did."

"Don't be. I've got some things lined up already, and it was probably time for me to move on anyway. The job was starting to get pretty routine."

Nick kissed Anna. She sighed with contentment and thought about asking him if he wanted to skip dinner.

"We should get going," he said before she could ask.

Over dinner, Nick explained why he'd been fired. It took him a little time to get up his nerve. He wouldn't have told her about the money part of it, but he knew she'd find out from someone else. These things always get out. Not that he thought for a minute that she'd believe he took the ten thousand dollars. But it was humiliating even to be accused.

And Anna didn't believe it, not for a single second. She was outraged, and it made Nick feel good to see her outrage.

"They wouldn't even give you the chance to prove them wrong? That's outrageous. And Mark! I thought you two were friends. Even if he thought you took the money, he could have come to you. He could have given you a chance to explain. To see if you were in some kind of trouble. But to go behind your back like that. Have you heard from him since you were fired?"

"Anna, I really don't want to talk about Mark."

Because Nick had been thinking the same thing. But he didn't want to think about it, and he didn't want to talk about it.

Anna let it drop, and Nick told her about the calls he'd made and the interviews he'd set up.

"Wow. You really didn't waste any time, did you? God, if it was me, I'd probably spend a week in bed before I even thought about looking for a new job. I'm impressed, Nick. I really am."

Anna couldn't have said anything better. Nick was sweet and attentive and asked her questions about her family and her past while they ate dinner.

And when they went back to his place, he took his time and treated Anna as if she was the most special woman in the world. It was the least he could do. She'd made him feel really good about himself.

The not-particularly-promising girl sat at home eating ice cream, watching television, and crying off and on throughout the night. But they were sad tears, not angry ones, and that weekend she managed to take a shower and clean her apartment. Every once in a while she'd pick up Dr. Grimes's card and just look at it. Like a lifeline.

Nick and Anna, on the other hand, had a wonderful weekend. She spent Saturday night at his place, and on Sunday they went out for brunch, saw a movie, stopped at a farmer's market on the way back to Nick's condo, and cooked dinner together that night.

As I watched the two of them head into the bedroom on Sunday night after dinner—Again! How do you people ever find the time to do your laundry?—I knew the time had come. I'd put it off as long as I could. What I was about to do was risky—it could end up making things worse—but I didn't see any other options.

I'd have to go see Herb and ask for his help.

seventeen

While Nick and Anna were enjoying their mutual ecstasy, I left to get in touch with Herb. (Note from Cupid: Just in case you were worried about it, no, I don't watch when you're doing *that*.) Herb isn't his real name. Like mine, you couldn't pronounce it, and if you actually heard it, well, ashes to ashes and dust to dust, as they say.

To put it in terms you'd understand, Herb is in charge of having crappy things happen to people. Sometimes they've brought it on themselves, and other times it seems as if they've done absolutely nothing to deserve it. However, most people—no matter who they are or how they've lived their lives—sincerely believe they deserve nothing but complete happiness at all times. So Herb gets even more bellyaching and complaining than I do. If he existed on the human plane, he'd look like the oldest and weariest and grumpiest old man you can imagine. I'm a bundle of joy compared to him.

When I say "crappy things," I don't mean wars or plagues or hideous diseases or natural disasters. That's another department altogether. And the moral and ethical dilemmas they have to deal with—to say nothing of the paperwork involved—are far too complicated for me to even begin to understand.

(Memo to earthlings: I know it probably won't help much, but there is a reason for human suffering. I don't always understand it, either, but the universe isn't just screwing with you for the heck of it.)

What Herb mostly deals with is your ordinary, run-of-the-mill kind of crap. Flat tires, cold sores, the toilet overflowing, noisy neighbors, your favorite TV show getting canceled before the story lines get finished—things like that.

Herb was in a bad mood when I found him because Herb is always in a bad mood.

"Hey, Herb, long time no see. How's it going?" I asked him.

Of course, this isn't how we really communicate with each other, but I've translated our interaction into a format you can easily comprehend.

"How do you think it's going?" he snarled. "All day long it's the same thing. *Why me? What did I ever do to deserve this? This couldn't have happened at a worse time.* Why do humans persist in thinking that there's a good time for crap to happen? *Like, okay, if my carburetor had gone out next week, I'd have been fine with it. But why now? At the exact worse time?*"

I had to laugh. No one can imitate a typical whiny human being the way Herb can.

"Aren't they supposed to be rational, intelligent creatures?" Herb continued. "Weren't they given a learning curve? That's what I was told when I got the job. Or was I misinformed? Life is full of crap, that's its design. And yet they all act so shocked every time something crappy happens. Like it's the first they've ever heard of it.

"And if each one of them is a unique individual, why do I hear the same old crap all day long, day in and day out? Can you answer me that?"

"Wish I could, Herb. But they drive me nuts, too."

"What a life, huh?"

"Yeah. What a life."

We both pondered that for a minute.

"Listen, Herb, I've got a favor to ask you. I've gotten myself into a bit of a jam, and I need your help."

Herb looked at me and sighed.

"I don't think I like the sound of this."

"I didn't think you would. The thing is, I let the frustration of dealing with the humans get to me, and I made a mistake."

"What kind of mistake?" he asked unenthusiastically.

"I get fed up, too. All day long I have to hear them whining about wanting true love. And most of the time they don't want to do any of the things that it takes to have true love, or make it last. They want to have it just drop in their laps and last a lifetime. And when it doesn't, what do they do? They whine."

"So typical of them," Herb muttered. "You know what I

think it is? They all remember the garden, back when they had the good life. They forget they couldn't handle the garden, and that they found a way to screw up paradise. They still think that's what they deserve. Bunch of idiots, if you ask me. I don't know why the universe goes to so much time and trouble with them. Now Planet Nineteen, that's a planet worth something. Have you seen what they've been able to do for themselves?" Herb sighed again (Herb sighs a lot). "I keep putting in for a transfer, but they keep telling me I'm where I'm supposed to be."

I nodded my head.

"I tried that a couple times. Me, I'd love to work out at Planet Forty-Three. But I guess that isn't up to us. Anyway, one night last week I was watching this woman named Anna on a date with this guy named Nick. And I don't know. It was like all my frustration came to a head and I did something stupid. Real stupid."

"What did you do?" Herb asked, looking at me with a sly grin.

"I sent her an arrow of true love."

"Whoa," Herb said, then let out a low whistle. "That's some major cosmic shit. You gotta get approval for one of those things."

"I know, I know. It was stupid. I shouldn't have let her get to me. But day after day, year after year, watching them do the same stupid things over and over, I guess I just reached my limit."

"If you ask me, you've been pretty patient considering what you have to put up with. But I don't think *they*"—Herb pointed upwards—"are going to see it that way."

"I know they aren't."

I told Herb the basic story of what had happened so far between Nick and Anna. "Maybe I made the arrow too strong. I don't know. All it does is get the ball rolling, and then it's up to *them*. It should have worn off by now. But this Anna keeps surprising me. My annual report is due in three months, and I think she's still going to be feeling true love, and I'm going to have a lot of explaining to do. I'm surprised I've gotten away with it for this long."

"Hmmm," Herb said without conviction.

"I need some help here, Herb, or my ass is grass. I need you to throw some crap Nick's way. He isn't very good about crap happening to him, and he's already having to deal with being fired. Some of your really good stuff so he'll get stressed out and drop the nice-guy act and Anna can see what a jerk he really is."

I sat quietly, waiting for Herb to say something. I knew begging wouldn't help. Herb hates begging; he hears it all day long. *Please let that pain in my tooth go away. Please let that noise in my car just be a loose hose. Please let somebody be pulling out so I can get a parking space right up front.* How many times had I heard him imitate people begging the universe or God or whoever they thought was in charge of things to please make this crap go away?

Herb was either going to help me or he wasn't. I just hoped he remembered all the times I'd sat with him over the course of human history, listening to him let off steam.

"Would this Nick guy you're talking about be Nick Wells,

by any chance?" Herb finally asked, surprising the hell out of me.

"Yeah. How did you know?"

"You can rest easy, old pal. I got the orders a few days ago. Nick didn't get fired through no real fault of his own for no reason. And he's in for some major crap over the next few weeks."

"He is?"

"It's going to be some good stuff, too," Herb said with a chuckle.

"Did they say why?"

Herb gave me a withering look.

"Why? So he can learn what he needs to learn. You should know the drill by now."

"I mean did they say why now? Was it anything in particular?"

"You think I got some special pipeline to the Creator or something? I know about as much as you know. Just enough to do the job, but not enough to keep the job from driving me crazy most of the time."

"They were just regular orders, though, right? Nothing out of the ordinary?"

"Just regular orders," Herb replied. "You've got to chill out, buddy. Everything will work out for the best in the end."

"Says who?" I asked sarcastically.

"The front office. The archangels. All the other gods and spirits. The Creator. If I remember correctly, it's the basic foundation of creation."

"Since when did you become such a cheerleader?" I asked. It was a pretty sad state of affairs when I found myself getting a pep talk from Herb, of all spirits.

"I may be old and worn out, buddy, but I haven't lost the faith. And I think you're letting yourself get all worked up over nothing. You've done a good job for them over the centuries. Why not just tell them what happened? Maybe they'll go easy on you. They've mellowed out a little since the old days."

"Fat chance," I muttered. "Thanks for the info, Herb."

"Hope it helped."

It hadn't. Not much. I thought I'd feel better after talking to Herb, but I still felt as if things were veering completely out of control in my little domain.

And despite Herb's reassurances, I knew that when the front office caught up with me, which could be any time now, there wasn't a chance in hell that they'd go easy on me.

eighteen

On Monday morning, Nick felt back to his old self. He and Anna had spent a great weekend together—she'd just left that morning—and he had his first interview at ten. He'd just finished getting dressed when the phone rang.

"Nick? It's Rick Miller."

"Hey, Rick, I was just getting ready to head out the door in a few minutes. I'm really pumped about the interview."

"Yeah, about that. I hate to have to tell you this, but it turns out we have a hiring freeze on. I guess our profits for last quarter fell short. I just found out this morning. I feel like a louse getting your hopes up for nothing."

"Don't worry about it," Nick said, swallowing his disappointment and forcing himself to sound nonchalant. "I've got some other leads."

"Good. I'm glad to hear it. And I'll definitely keep my eyes and ears open. If I hear of anything, you'll be the first to know."

"I appreciate it. And hey, maybe we can get together one of these weekends and play some golf."

"Sounds good, buddy."

Nick was a little disappointed when he hung up the phone but not too worried. Hell, he had another interview that afternoon for a better position anyway. Since he didn't have to be there until two, he decided he'd go to the gym and have a good workout. That always energized him.

Anna wasn't having a good day at work. Everyone was acting so weird. She'd known it was going to be awkward having to face everyone, but she hadn't anticipated just how awkward it would be.

Nick was the hot topic around the office. Wild rumors were flying, and it was all anyone wanted to talk about. But they couldn't talk about it with Anna around. Everyone was dying to know how she was taking the situation, but they couldn't come right out and ask her. So they avoided her.

If she'd walk past a group of people, they'd grow suddenly silent, and she'd feel them staring at her as she walked past. The people she had to actually deal with that day acted nervous and ill at ease, making her feel more and more uncomfortable as the morning wore on. Even a simple question like "How's it going?" felt forced.

She thought about calling Nick, but she was afraid people might overhear. She hated herself for it, but it was how she felt. And anyway, he'd be tied up with interviews all day. She'd call Joan, that's what she'd do. See if she was free for lunch. Being with Joan always made her feel better.

Nick returned home around noon and had two phone messages waiting for him. The first one was from his former boss.

"I got your message, Nick," his former boss said, "and I have to wonder where you get the balls to threaten me or this company with a lawsuit. We might not have enough evidence to convict you in a court of law, but a civil suit? That's not reasonable doubt, Nick. That's a preponderance of evidence. And we have that in spades. So here's what I'm going to do. If someone calls here for a reference, I'll make sure my assistant doesn't put the call through. And I won't call them back. In other words, I won't 'bad-mouth' you, as you so eloquently put it. But I'm damn well not going to put in a good word for you, either.

"And if you are really stupid enough to be thinking about suing us for wrongful termination, you'd better think twice about that. Like I said, we have evidence. And we also have a team of lawyers that would crush anyone dumb enough to take your case. Please don't call here again."

Nick shook his head in disgust. What kind of evidence could they have when he hadn't done it? Maybe the bastards had rigged the numbers to make sure he'd look guilty in case he tried to sue. He should have known they'd find some way to cover their asses. Hell, maybe his boss had taken the money and used Nick as his fall guy.

But Nick's former boss hadn't taken the money and thought

he did have enough convincing evidence to make it appear that Nick was the guilty party. Mark had seen to that. Mark knew Nick's access code, and he'd needed money. Badly. Badly enough to screw over a friend. He'd developed a gambling habit, and it wouldn't be long before it all came crashing down around him. And when it's discovered that Mark took the money, Nick's former boss won't have the grace to call Nick and apologize. But Nick's boss is a different story, and Mark is a different story, and currently not my problem. We have more than enough problems with this story as it is. And Herb will have all kinds of really nasty crap waiting down the road for Mark.

The second message waiting for Nick was from Steve Woods.

"Nick, it's Steve Woods. I hate like hell to let you down, but that position I was telling you about on Saturday? They just filled it. I can't believe it. It's been open for weeks. And then this morning some hotshot interviewed for it and they offered him the job right on the spot. Sorry about that, buddy.

"You're still welcome to come in and talk to personnel, but I can't think of anything else here that's open right now that would be right for you. But I'll be on the lookout. If I hear of anything, you'll be the first to know. Hang in there. Something will turn up. And maybe we can get a poker game together one of these nights or do lunch. Give me a call."

Now Nick was starting to panic a little. When he'd had three interviews, he hadn't had a doubt in the world that he'd land a position out of one of them. But a single interview was a crapshoot. He wasn't feeling like his old self anymore.

He'd call Anna. That's what he'd do. See if she was free for lunch. Talking to Anna always made him feel better.

Anna was just getting ready to leave for lunch with Joan when the phone rang.

"Hi," she said when she heard his voice. But she didn't say "Hi, Nick," the way she usually did. The way she usually loved saying his name. "I thought you'd be gone by now."

"My interview got canceled," Nick said cheerfully, "so I've got some free time, and I was wondering if I could take you to lunch."

"That would have been great, but I was just getting ready to go meet Joan for lunch."

"Oh."

"I'm free for dinner, though," Anna offered.

"Whatever," Nick said brusquely. "Give me a call when you get off."

When Nick hung up, Anna stood there for a second, wondering if she should call him back and offer to cancel her lunch with Joan. She didn't normally do that, cancel plans with a friend to be with a guy. But this was a special situation. It was his first day of being unemployed and one of his interviews had been canceled. The way he'd hung up on her indicated that he was obviously hurt, and obviously a lot more rattled by getting fired than he'd let on. She should have realized that.

Joan would understand. Anna picked up the phone again and dialed Nick's number, trying really *hard* not to feel worried about people overhearing, but he didn't answer.

She knew he was probably still there, knew he was probably

hoping it was her calling him back. All she had to do was say his name, and he'd pick up the phone. But she couldn't bring herself to do it. There were too many people around. So she slowly hung up the phone, feeling like a total piece of crap.

But Anna was wrong. Nick wouldn't have picked it up if he'd heard her voice. He was too angry. She made such a big deal about wanting to be supportive, but then the first time he needs her, the first time he asks her for something, she turns him down. Nick had thought about making some more calls, but now he wasn't in the mood.

"So how's the last nice single man living in America doing these days?" Joan asked Anna as she sat down across from her at the table in the Chinese restaurant.

Anna frowned.

"He got fired on Friday."

"What?"

"Yeah. I don't want to go into details. But it was completely unfair and unjustified and there's nothing he can do about it."

"Wow. I'm sorry, Anna. How's he taking it?"

"Better than I would," Anna said. "He got up Saturday morning and set up some interviews with some of his contacts and buddies. I'm sure he won't have any trouble finding a new position."

"That's good."

"Yeah. The only problem is, I found out today that I'm a total chicken shit."

Joan laughed.

"A *total* chicken shit?"

Anna nodded her head. "Total."

Their server arrived just then, but Anna and Joan didn't need to look at their menus. They always ordered the same thing when they came there. A number twelve for Anna and a number seven for Joan.

"So why are you a total chicken shit?" Joan asked after they'd ordered.

"Today at work, Nick was the hot topic of conversation. It was all anyone wanted to talk about. But since they know I'm seeing him, they felt awkward around me, and it just got weirder and weirder as the day wore on. It got to the point where I was afraid to leave my desk even to get a cup of coffee."

"That doesn't make you a total chicken shit, Anna. It makes you human."

"It gets worse. Nick called me a little while ago, and I made a point of not saying his name, in case anyone heard me and knew who I was talking to. And then I tried to call him back. And I couldn't do it. Because it would mean saying his name out loud and wondering if people were trying to eavesdrop."

Joan smiled at Anna.

"That's not so bad. Well, it's kind of bad, but not horrible. This is your *work* you're talking about. I wouldn't want to be in your position. I've seen careers killed by gossip. You're trying to figure out how to handle the whole thing, and it's going to be tricky. Now stop beating yourself up. Here comes our soup."

Their server set down their wonton soup, a pot of tea, and

two cups. Joan picked up the teapot and poured a cup for herself and one for Anna.

"Joan, I always thought if I really loved someone, I'd be willing to walk through fire for him. This is the man I want to spend the rest of my life with, and I couldn't even stand up to a little gossip. What does that say about me? I mean, if I can't—"

"Whoa," Joan said, interrupting. "Back up a minute. The man you want to spend the rest of your life with? I thought you two just started seeing each other."

"I know. It sounds crazy. But I'm completely serious. Don't give me that look."

"I'm sorry, but you've got me a little worried. This isn't like you. Are you sure it's love and not just the infamous ticking of your biological clock?"

"I'm sure."

"Okay. I'm going to suspend judgment here and let you tell me how you know this is the man you should spend the rest of your life with. This unemployed man, I might add."

"Ha-ha."

"Sorry. Go ahead."

"I can't."

"You can't what?"

"I can't explain it. I could try. But anything I said would sound corny because it's not something you can put into words."

"Uh-huh."

"Really. Remember that documentary we went to see about the Buddhist monks? And how they would talk about finding enlightenment, and their faces would light up, and you'd look at their faces and know whatever they'd been experiencing had been so completely incredible? But then they'd try and put it into words and they couldn't? Or they would try and it would just sound kind of lame?"

"You're saying Nick is like a religious experience?" Joan asked. "That must be some sex you're having."

"Yes, as a matter of fact we are, but that's not the point."

"Uh-huh."

"But it doesn't hurt."

The two of them laughed.

"What I'm saying," Anna went on, "is that I could sit here for hours trying to explain it to you, and in the end, you probably still wouldn't believe me. But I know what I feel and I'm choosing to trust that feeling."

"And how is it going to feel if you're wrong?"

"You mean if Nick and I don't make it?"

Joan nodded her head.

Anna thought about it for a minute.

"I would be very sad. But the feeling itself? That could never turn out to be wrong."

Joan gave Anna a long, appraising stare.

"What are you thinking?" Anna asked.

"I guess what I'm thinking is that if this thing with Nick is as real as you think it is, or know it is, then you have to ask yourself what's important to you. And do you have the courage to act on your convictions if it comes down to making a choice."

Anna stared back at Joan.

"Sorry," Joan said. "That was incredibly self-righteous of me, wasn't it?"

"No," Anna said quietly, "it wasn't."

Anna steered the conversation onto other topics while she and Joan ate lunch, but she only paid scant attention to what they talked about. She thought about what Joan had said. And she thought about how small she had felt all morning when she'd acted so cowardly. And then an idea came to her, something she could do to feel better, but she didn't know if she had the strength to go through with it. So she thought about it and agonized. She imagined herself doing the right thing over and over, thinking that if she could imagine herself doing it, then it would make it easier to actually do it in real life.

After Anna said good-bye to Joan in the parking lot, she got inside her car and took her cell phone out of her purse. She talked to the party on the other end for about twenty minutes, and when she hung up, the deal was done. She just had one last thing to do to make the transaction complete.

Half an hour later Anna sat in front of her computer typing. When she thought she had it down right, she printed out the piece of paper and read it over. It sounded fine. She stood up, holding the piece of paper, and walked out of her cubicle. Everyone watched her as she walked past, the way they had all day long. They couldn't help themselves.

Anna knocked on her boss's door, walked inside, sat down, and turned in her resignation.

nineteen

Anna returned to her desk after turning in her resignation and picked up the phone to call Nick. He answered on the second ring, but only because he thought it might be Matt Robbins returning his call.

"Nick," Anna said, loudly enough that anyone nearby could hear, "it's me. How's it going?"

"Okay," Nick said curtly. His third interview had just been canceled, it had been two hours since he'd put in the call to Matt, and he was still put out that Anna had ruined his afternoon.

"Listen, I'm going to take off early this afternoon. I've got some news for you, and I was wondering if I could swing by."

"I don't know, Anna. I've got things I need to be doing, and I don't know if I'm up for company at the moment."

"You'll want to hear this. I promise. And I don't have to stay long. But I want to tell you this in person."

"Okay. Could you do me a favor and pick up some beer on your way over?"

"Sure. I'll be there in about an hour."

Anna didn't notice the contradiction between Nick's supposedly having so much to do and his wanting her to get him some beer.

When Anna arrived at Nick's condo, he didn't open the door for her. He just yelled out, "It's open," when she knocked on the door.

"Did you get the beer for me?" Nick asked when Anna came inside, his eyes glued to the television, where a discussion of tonight's football game was in progress.

"Yeah, it's right here. How'd your interview go?"

"I told you. It got canceled."

"I meant the other one."

"They *both* got canceled."

"Oh, Nick. I'm sorry."

"And as of half an hour ago, my third one got canceled, too. All in all, it's been a great day."

"If I'd known—"

"Whatever. Can I have one of those?" he asked, looking at the bag she was holding.

"Sure. Do you want a glass?"

"Nope."

Anna pulled the six-pack out of the bag and handed him a bottle of beer. He took it from her, then looked back at the television. Anna hesitated a moment, then walked into the kitchen and put the rest of the beer inside the refrigerator. She closed the refrigerator door and stood there, watching Nick.

I watched the unfolding scene with anticipation. Herb had been right. Crap was definitely happening to Nick. And just as I'd predicted, the nice-guy act was gone and Nick was turning into a jerk right before my very eyes.

Come on, Anna, I thought. Get out while the going's good. I'll find you someone else. In fact, you've been such a trooper I'll go through regular channels and submit your name for true love. With the right guy, one the front office approves of. Not this jerk that you weren't ever meant to be with in the first place.

But just my luck, Anna saw Nick in a light entirely different from mine. She saw a guy who was hurting and didn't know what to do about it. He'd put on a good show over the weekend, but now the reality had set in. She knew losing a job did a real number to a guy's self-esteem. He probably thought *she* thought less of him, which wasn't true. Nothing could be further from the truth.

And her heart ached for him. He looked like a little boy, sitting there pretending that nothing was wrong. She wanted more than anything to put her arms around him, but she knew instinctively that she shouldn't, that right now it would be the worst thing she could do.

(Memo to earthling guys: No matter how much you hate analyzing your relationship, and even worse, yourself, women do it all the time, regardless of whether or not you participate in the process.)

But Nick didn't realize what she was thinking. He thought he was *showing* her. *Nothing wrong here. Just a guy drinking a beer and watching a sports show. Maybe a little pissed off that you couldn't take an hour out of your busy day and have lunch. Hell, I did just get fired, and it might have been nice to show me a little support. But it's not like I'm lying in bed with the covers pulled over my head. Just enjoying a little leisure time before I find another job.*

Anna walked back into the living room and sat down on the couch.

"Nick?" she asked hesitantly.

"I'm trying to watch this."

"I need to tell you something. But it's a good something."

"Can it wait until the commercial?"

"Sure."

Anna waited patiently while Nick watched three men discuss the offensive and defensive options available to the two NFL teams playing against each other that evening. She pretended to watch attentively, although she had no idea what the three men were talking about. Nick, however, appeared completely absorbed.

After resolving that both teams were going to have to rely on their defense—neither had a good offense—the show went to a commercial. But Nick continued to keep his eyes glued to the television set.

"Nick?" Anna said again.

"Yeah?"

"Can you turn the sound off a minute? There's something I need to tell you."

Nick pressed the mute button on the remote but continued staring ahead.

"So—" Anna started.

"Can you hold on a second?" Nick asked. "I want another beer."

Nick stood up before Anna could reply, then he walked into the kitchen.

"You want anything?" he called out, more to put off the conversation than out of courtesy. Nick had a horrible feeling that Anna didn't have any real information to tell him. He was afraid that what she had to tell him was going to be more along the lines of a pep talk. And the *last* thing he needed right about now was a pep talk.

She'd tell him this great quote she remembered out of some self-help book she'd read, or something she'd heard on *Oprah*. Something she thought would cheer him right up, or show him exactly what he needed to do to handle the situation.

God, if he had a dollar for every time some woman had quoted him something she'd heard on *Oprah*. As if by hearing it he'd suddenly see the light, become a completely different person, and she'd have the kind of relationship she—not he—had always dreamed of.

The last thing Nick wanted was a pep talk, or to hear her brilliant idea on how to find the job of his dreams. Or listen to her drone on about how everything happens for a reason.

Everyone he thought he could count on had dropped the ball. It was one thing to go in for an interview prearranged by one of his connections, when all the gears had been oiled and the way had been paved. Now, unless Matt ever called him back, Nick would have to be one of those schmucks calling headhunters, looking through the classifieds, and sending his résumé out to employment agencies.

Nick walked back into the living room, carrying his beer and dreading the conversation they were about to have. Maybe they needed to take a break until he got back on his feet. It was hard enough dealing with not having a job; he didn't have the energy to deal with Anna watching his every move, checking in to see how he was doing, looking worried just because he'd decided to take an hour or two for himself and have a couple beers, watch a little TV.

She wasn't fooling him with that casual attitude of hers, pretending to watch TV when he could feel her glancing at him out of the corner of her eyes when she thought he wasn't looking.

Nick sat down on the couch, put his feet up on the coffee table, and took a sip of beer.

"So—" Anna started again.

"This isn't going to be a pep talk, is it?" Nick asked, interrupting. "Because I really don't think I could handle that right now."

"No," Anna said, starting to feel a little impatient.

"Just because I want to have a couple beers and watch a little TV doesn't mean I'm not trying. It's only the first day, you know. And it's not like I'm going to be out on the street next week asking to work for food."

"I know that. I told you I think you're handling it much

better than I would," Anna said, wondering why men didn't ever *listen*. "You deserve a little break after what you've been through."

"It's not like I need a break," Nick said dismissively. "I lost my job. Okay, it sucks, but it happens all the time. We don't need to go on and on about it and run it into the ground. It really doesn't help anything to talk about it to death."

The last thing he wanted was for her to go all overboard with sympathy, like he was some object of pity. Why did she have to make such a big deal about everything? It wasn't as if he couldn't handle it.

Anna looked at him with a hurt expression. She didn't mean to, the last thing she meant to do was make him deal with *her* stuff at a time like this. Nick doesn't know what you've done for him yet, she reminded herself. He's hurt and angry and lashing out at you, because that's what people do at times like this. They lash out at the people they love.

And Nick, feeling pissed as hell when he saw her hurt expression—*Great! Like I don't have enough on my plate*—watched in disbelief as she suddenly went from looking hurt to getting this weird, goofy smile on her face.

Do you see what I have to deal with? Anna and Nick are so far apart from understanding what the other is thinking and feeling that they might as well be on different planets. And shouldn't it be obvious as the nose on her face that if Nick gets mad when she doesn't show enough sympathy—and then gets mad when she does show sympathy—this is kind of a no-win situation for Anna? Why do you people insist on staying in no-win situations? Do you not understand the meaning of the words *no win?* As in, you cannot win, no matter what you do?

And then I have to hear all the whining and moaning when it's twenty years later and you're sitting in your living room crying because you just got served the divorce papers. "But I tried," you'll say, "I tried so hard." You stayed in a no-win situation for twenty years, trying as hard as you could, and in the end, what do you know. You didn't win! How you people ever got a man on the moon, I'll never know.

Okay, Anna told herself, let's not go overboard. He doesn't necessarily love you. But he's not putting on a show. He's letting you see how miserable he's feeling. He feels comfortable with you. He's *letting you in.* And that's huge.

And made her feel comfortable as well.

"Nick, sweetie," Anna said happily, "could you please shut the hell up and let me tell you my news?"

What in the hell? Nick thought to himself. One minute she's looking hurt, the next minute she's smiling, and now she's making jokes. Did women have any idea how impossible it was to keep up with their moods?

"Go ahead," he mumbled.

"I quit," she announced.

Nick stared at her, looking puzzled.

"Quit what?" he asked.

"My job, silly."

"You did what?"

"I quit my job," Anna repeated, looking very proud of herself.

Nick simply stared at her.

"Why?" he finally asked.

"Because of you."

"Me?"

"Um-hmmm," Anna said, nodding her head. "Because of the way they treated you. I told them I couldn't stay with a company that treated one of its best employees in such a shabby way, accusing them of something they hadn't done without even giving them a chance to defend themselves."

"I don't know what to say," Nick said, as she continued looking at him. What in the hell did she expect him to say? "Are you sure that was wise?"

He still couldn't take it in. She'd quit her job because of him? No one had ever done anything like that for him before. But he hadn't asked her to. Why would she do a crazy thing like that? And what was she going to expect in return? He felt like he was somehow responsible for her decision, and he resented feeling that way. He had enough problems of his own at the moment.

And now they were both going to be looking for a job? What the hell had she been thinking? That he'd be so grateful she'd have him right where she wanted him?

"I don't know if it was wise," Anna snapped.

I perked up. I'd heard the tone in Anna's voice. Dripping with anger and resentment. Maybe, finally (and it was about damn time), Anna had reached her breaking point. She wasn't a saint who could just keep on giving and giving without getting something in return. Even true love has its limits.

Anna had never snapped at Nick before. He flinched. She looked really pissed. It was one thing for him to decide they needed a break, that things were moving too fast and he had enough to deal with as it was. But seeing Anna angry at him, Nick felt a sense of panic.

He had no job, no immediate prospects, his life was getting away from him. The thought of not having Anna, either, of her getting fed up and walking out the door and never coming back, suddenly made him feel terrified.

"I'm sorry, Anna," he said as his panic grew. "You just took me by surprise. Maybe I'm not handling this as well as I thought I was. I guess I freaked out a little at the thought of both of us being unemployed."

"You don't have to worry about that, Nick," Anna said, feeling bad now about snapping at him, her anger gone, and yes, oh yes, she'd definitely noticed the way he'd used the word "us." "I have another job."

"You have another job?"

"Yeah. I had an offer a few weeks ago, but I turned it down. I wasn't ready to make a change. I called them today to see if the position was still open. They told me it was, so I gave Brown my resignation. I finish out the week, and that's it."

"Oh. That's great," Nick said, feeling relieved and resentful at the same time. She had another job *already*, and he couldn't even get a damn interview. "I'm glad you don't have to go through what I'm going through."

"You'll find something. I know you will."

"Yeah, I know," Nick said with a forced smile.

Nick never really thanked her that night for what she'd done. Not in so many words. He spent the rest of the evening consumed by conflicting emotions. One part of him was grateful that Anna had felt strongly enough to quit her job. Another part of him felt a great deal of discomfort at the thought of what she'd done. It felt good to have someone on his side, especially since all his buddies had let him down. He understood, kind of, about the jobs falling through. But had any of them called to take him out for a beer or ask him over to watch the game?

What Anna had done on his account was incredible. And he didn't know what he was supposed to do about it, how he was supposed to act. He resented feeling that way. One minute he'd think what a great thing it was she'd done for him. And then, feeling that sense of gratitude come over him, he'd remind himself that she hadn't *really* quit her job for him. She'd *changed* jobs for him. There was a difference.

He needed her, and he resented needing her. He wanted to be left alone, and then he felt terrified at the thought of being alone.

He was torn between a desire to simply quit pretending and talk about how lousy he was feeling and an equally strong desire to *never* let her know how lousy he was feeling.

Anna made dinner for him and watched four different sets of guys talk about the game scheduled for that night (some of whom felt the game would depend on the offense strategies, not the defense). She sat through the game with him, and although she found it extremely dull (she couldn't believe how long it took those teams to move that damn ball down the field), she tried not to bother him or talk too much.

Later that night, after they'd made love (that was how Nick expressed his gratitude, and he hoped she appreciated it after the day he'd had; he was worn out), and Anna was just starting to drift off to sleep, he asked her something that had been bothering him all night. Something he hoped would help him gauge just how grateful he was supposed to feel.

"Anna," Nick said, "can I ask you something?"

"Ummmm," Anna said sleepily.

"If you hadn't had another job lined up, would you have still quit?"

"I'd like to think so," Anna answered honestly.

Which was no help to Nick whatsoever.

I left the two of them and went to see Herb again. I knew I was grasping at straws, but I was all out of ideas, and I had nowhere else to turn.

"Don't worry," Herb told me. "This is just the beginning. There's all kinds of crap coming Nick's way."

"Good crap?" I asked hopefully.

"Some of the best. Stuff that's almost guaranteed to ruin a romance."

"Like what?"

"You know I can't tell you that. But let's just say this would have to be one of the greatest loves of all time for her to want to stick around."

Unfortunately, that's just what I was afraid of.

twenty

Two weeks went by, and Nick didn't get so much as a nibble. He woke up each morning determined not to let it get to him, but by early afternoon depression and hopelessness would set in.

He couldn't believe the bad luck he kept running into. It felt as if someone had placed a hex on him. Interviews would be set up, then canceled. He'd make appointments with an agency, and some emergency would come up and the person he was scheduled to see wouldn't be in.

He called some of his so-called buddies to see if they had any new leads. None of them did. It took every ounce of strength he had not to sound desperate—never, ever let them hear you sound desperate; it's the kiss of death—but they must have heard something. They all made excuses to get off the phone as soon as possible. And nobody was setting up poker games or golf matches with him.

Anna came over almost every night to be with him. She loved her new job, but she kept her comments about it to a minimum. Nick could tell. She was glowing and bursting with energy, and he resented it. To his credit, he tried not to resent it, but he couldn't help himself. Why were things so easy for her and so hard for him?

Anna didn't have a good time at Nick's. He didn't talk much, snapped at her over little things, and they spent most of their time watching TV. Watching what he wanted to watch. He never even asked for her input.

But she was determined to see him through this. She never lost faith in him or doubted that he'd find something one of these days. We'll look back on this one day and laugh, she told herself. And on those nights when she felt as if she might scream if she had to watch one more rerun of *Miami Vice* or one more group of guys talking about the upcoming game, or the game that had just finished, she reminded herself that this was her choice. She was in it for the long haul. You didn't bail on the person you loved because they were going through a hard time. And she probably would have been acting just as bad if she were the one out of a job and having no luck finding a new one.

She didn't ask herself if Nick would have come over every night and sat with her watching tearjerkers on Lifetime or reruns of *Will and Grace* if the situation had been reversed. What Nick would do for her wasn't the point. She was choosing to do this for him because she wanted to.

But one morning, as Nick forced himself to take a shower and get dressed and blow-dry his hair—something was going to break for him today, he could just feel it—he noticed some hairs in the sink. He looked at his comb. He didn't ever remember seeing that much hair in his comb before. He peered closely at himself in the mirror, bent his head down, and gasped with horror. His hairline was receding. And there, on the left near his part, his hair was *thinning*.

No. He was only thirty-one years old. This couldn't be happening to him. His dad was twenty-five years older than Nick and still had practically a full head of hair. So did his mom. It was one of the things Nick had always felt a little smug about, the knowledge that he wouldn't ever go bald. He used to snicker at hair loss commercials, secure in the belief that he'd never have that problem.

But now, at only thirty-one, all the signs were there. This couldn't be happening. Baldness was supposed to be hereditary. That's what they said. It was hereditary, dammit. And now he was going to be one of those guys buying Rogaine and worrying about how his stylist parted his hair.

Nick didn't make a single call that day. He was too depressed. He didn't go to the gym or check out the classifieds. He kept his curtains closed and lay down on the couch and switched back and forth between ESPN and the Spike Channel for Men. At one point he noticed that his jeans felt a little snug, which didn't help matters. But it didn't stop him from drinking a few beers and opening a bag of potato chips.

When Anna arrived that night, Nick was in a horrible

mood. God, did she always have to be so cheerful? Look at her. Miss Professional with every hair in place. She'd probably gone to the gym at lunch and had a healthy low-carb lunch afterward. Couldn't afford to let herself go, not when she had such a great career going for her.

Anna had had a long, hard day at work. When she walked in and saw Nick lying there, beer bottles and a potato chip bag on the coffee table, she felt a moment of complete exhaustion. She really wanted to go home, take a long, hot bath, and crawl into bed with a good book.

"I brought Chinese," Anna told him, hoping he didn't hear the exhaustion and frustration in her voice. "I hope that's okay. I didn't feel like cooking tonight."

Of course not, Nick thought. It's hard to come home and cook when you've been working all day.

"I don't really feel like Chinese," Nick said, keeping his eyes on the TV. Actually, it smelled great, but he was sick of her bringing him food like he was some kind of invalid. If he wanted dinner he'd make himself some dinner. He just didn't happen to want any dinner.

"Okay," Anna said. "Do you want me to make you something?"

"No, I don't want you to make me something. I don't want a home-cooked meal. Or a pizza. Or some tacos. If and when I do want to eat something, I'll get up and make myself something. Is that all right with you, Anna? Or should I get your permission first?"

Anna looked at him for a moment.

I didn't get hopeful or excited this time. I was beyond that now. Anna might feel momentary anger, or some resentment, but she'd rise above it and simply choose to keep loving him. At this point I knew the routine by heart, pardon the pun.

Anna walked into the living room, sat down on the couch, picked up the remote, and turned off the TV.

"I was watching that," Nick snapped.

"Nick," Anna said, "I think we need to talk."

Oh boy, Nick thought to himself, here it comes. The "I've tried to be patient" talk. Or the "I've had it up to here" talk. Or the "It doesn't do any good to wallow in self-pity" talk. Or the "I'm tired of you taking everything out on me when I'm just trying to help" talk. As if I need this right now. Like she has any idea what I'm going through.

And me? Cupid? The guy with the *worst* job in the universe? I'm paying close attention again. "Nick, I think we need to talk." That's what she'd said. What's the sound of no hands clapping? That's the sound I was making. Because when a woman says the words "I think we need to talk," she's not about to say something a guy wants to hear.

Nick closed his eyes, groaned, and braced himself.

"Go ahead," he muttered, "get it over with."

"I think," Anna said, "that you should move into my place."

"Huh?" Nick asked, opening his eyes.

Leave it to Anna to be the only woman on the planet who had something good to say when she said, "We need to talk." She was driving me right around the bend.

"I've given this a lot of thought, and I think it would take some of the pressure off of you. You could rent out your condo so you'd have some money coming in. You wouldn't have to pay me rent, just help out with the groceries. And that way you'd have less stress weighing you down and it would make it a lot easier to look for a job. And you could take your time instead of having to take the first thing that came along."

To say Nick was flabbergasted would be to put it mildly.

He'd never thought about the two of them living together, but when he thought about not having to try and maintain his condo without a regular paycheck coming in, thought about the financial cushion it would give him, and the extra time to find just the right job, he felt an overwhelming sense of relief.

"What do you think?" Anna asked.

"I think I feel like a real shit for the way I've been treating you," Nick said, sitting up. He wrapped his arms around her. "Thank you," he said simply, and meant it.

"Does that mean yes?" Anna asked.

"It means yes, and it means thanks for putting up with me."

Anna felt wonderful. This one moment made all the nights of frustration and exhaustion, and yes, even boredom sometimes (which she hadn't expected—how can you be bored when you're with the person you love?) worth every single minute.

Walking in that night, seeing him lying there on the couch, she'd had second thoughts about offering to let him move in with her. And when he'd gotten rude and sarcastic, she'd come very close to telling him to go to hell and walking out the door. But when she'd pictured giving up on him and walking out the door, it had felt so ordinary. Small and ordinary and run-of-the-mill. Loving Nick was the only extraordinary thing she'd ever experienced. She didn't want to go back to being small. So she'd taken a deep breath, fought back her doubts and fears, and chosen to keep loving him in spite of how he was acting.

Nick felt like a new man. He'd go to the gym tomorrow, and make some calls. And that thing with his hair? No way he was going bald. It was just stress. Now that he had a second chance, thanks to Anna, his hair would stop falling out. And a few trips to the gym would get rid of the little beer belly he'd developed. The relief and gratitude he felt for Anna at that moment was the closest Nick Wells had ever come to feeling genuine love as an adult for another human being since he'd been with Lauren.

I can't tell you how thrilled I was.

twenty-one

anna took care of everything. She put the ad in the paper, found a storage unit, called the movers, got the boxes, helped Nick start getting his stuff packed, and found a cleaning agency to come and get the place ready for prospective renters. She did most of it on her lunch hour so Nick could keep his phone line free in case someone was trying to get through about an interview.

Nick felt kind of bad that he wasn't really doing much in the way of job hunting. He did keep his pledge to go to the gym every day, and he started eating a healthy diet again. But he didn't see the point of trying to set up interviews when he was busy packing and getting ready to move. It made a lot more sense to wait until he'd moved in with Anna and he could give job hunting his full concentration.

The second couple who came to see the place decided to take it, so by the following Sunday Nick was moved into Anna's, and they celebrated by going out to dinner. Nick insisted on picking up the check over Anna's objections. But she didn't object too much. It did her good to see him feeling confident again.

Nick had big plans for Monday. Now that he had a little breathing room, his energy had returned. There were plenty of people he hadn't called. Not actual buddies, but people who'd worked with him over the years and knew what he was capable of. He couldn't believe he'd let himself get so down and feel so defeated. Thank God he had Anna in his life. He wasn't sure what it was he felt for her, but she'd definitely been a lifesaver.

Though it was a little annoying, the way she had a place for everything and acted as if it were obvious where everything should go. Like the paper towels. What did it matter if he left them out on the counter? Where was it written that they had to go back underneath the sink when he was done using them? She hadn't gotten mad or anything, had said it kind of jokingly, but he could tell she fully expected him to remember it in the future.

And the bathroom. Why was it that women had to have three different kinds of shampoo and two different kinds of conditioner? Either a shampoo worked or it didn't. You keep the one that works and throw the rest away. It was only logical. He barely had room in the shower to keep his own bar of soap. Things would have been a lot simpler if she'd had another bathroom.

Not that he was complaining. He'd be a real shit to be complaining at this point. Hell, what other woman would have put up with the crap he'd given her the last couple of weeks? And then asked him to move in to make things easier for him? None that he could think of. He owed Anna a lot.

Of course, he'd pay her back someday, when things got back to normal. Nick Wells wasn't a charity case.

And it wasn't like she wasn't getting something out of it. How many orgasms had she had last night? Three? Four? He was surprised the neighbors hadn't complained.

Nick fully planned to help out around the place as long as he was living there. Do some of the cleaning, have dinner ready for her when she came home. If he had time, that is. She'd have to understand that looking for a job was a full-time job in itself, and some days he might not get home until late. And might be even more beat than she was.

On Monday morning, Nick got up and made Anna breakfast while she showered. He'd pretended to roll back over and go to sleep when she'd first gotten up so breakfast would be a surprise.

"Nick!" she said, walking into the kitchen, wearing a robe and drying her hair with a towel. She'd smelled the bacon frying. "You didn't have to do this."

"It's the least I could do. Have a seat. We have juice and bacon and coffee, and your waffle is just about done."

Anna sat down and wrapped the towel around her hair. She didn't really have time for breakfast, but there was no way she'd hurt Nick's feelings. Not after he'd gone to all this trouble for her.

"So what are you going to do today?" Anna asked innocently while Nick poured her a cup of coffee.

Nick bristled. Was this how it was going to be? Was he

going to have to start justifying himself and accounting for his whereabouts? He should have known. Maybe he'd made a huge mistake. Only now he already had his stuff here, his place was rented, and he was stuck.

"This and that," he said evasively. "Make some calls. See where they lead."

"Sounds good," Anna replied. "That waffle smells delicious. I can't remember the last time I had a waffle for breakfast. And such a cute chef, too," she added, smiling up at him happily.

Nick relaxed a little. He needed to chill out. She hadn't been grilling him, just asking about his day. Hell, if you live with a woman you've got to expect to talk about your day. It would be the first thing she'd ask him when she got home that night. *How was your day?* went with the territory.

After Anna left, Nick sat down to have another cup of coffee and read the paper. He planned on turning right to the classifieds, but a story on the front page caught his eye. He ended up reading the entire first three sections and having two more cups of coffee.

Come on, guy, he told himself, it's time to get a move on. Grab a cup of coffee and start reading the classifieds. Nick stood up to get some more coffee and looked out the window. It was a beautiful day. He noticed the pool in the courtyard. He hardly ever got a chance to go swimming, except at the gym. Maybe he'd go down and take a dip in the pool instead of going to the gym later. Get himself energized, and then come back up and read the classifieds.

Nick put on his swimming trunks and went down to the pool. He swam for about half an hour to get his heart rate up, and then got out of the pool. Nick was just drying off when he saw a tall, blonde woman with a great rack walking toward the chaise longues set around the deck. She had on a black thong bikini that showed off everything she had to its best advantage. *Wow,* Nick thought, watching her, *she's hot.* He wouldn't mind going a few laps around the pool with her.

"Hi," he said as the woman sat down on one of the chaise longues.

"Hi," she answered, taking a tube of suntan lotion out of her tote bag.

"I'm Nick," he said, wrapping the towel around his belly. Not that he had anything to hide or conceal. Those last trips to the gym had gotten him just about back to peak condition.

"I'm Tina," she said.

"Hi, Tina," Nick said with a grin. He walked over and sat down on the chaise longue next to hers. He wouldn't mind getting a little sun for a few minutes. Give his face a little color, make him look fit and healthy for interviews. Might as well enjoy the scenery and take advantage of having some downtime while he still had the chance.

"You live here?" Nick asked.

"Uh-huh."

"Great day, isn't it?"

"I guess."

"I don't usually get a chance to lay around the pool like this. It's kind of nice."

Tina applied some lotion to her calves and thighs. Nick tried not to stare, but it wasn't easy. What a body. Didn't seem to have much of a personality, but with a body like that, she didn't need one.

"I guess that's one nice thing about being between jobs," Nick joked. "You finally get a chance to get outside."

"I guess," Tina said. "I'm not out of a job, though. I work nights."

"What do you do?"

"I'm a nurse."

"That must be interesting."

"Not really. Not unless you like sick people and paper-work."

"I bet you see a lot."

"Yeah. I get to see a lot of rude doctors." Tina hated doctors. She'd gone into nursing hoping to marry one, but after three years and numerous attempts, she'd had lots of mediocre sex and not one single marriage proposal.

"But it must be rewarding. You help people."

Tina snorted. "Well, it's not like they appreciate it."

Tina was cynical, bitter, depressing, and virtually humorless, with very limited social skills. But she had extremely large breasts, and Nick would have been content to spend the rest of the day talking to her. Unfortunately, her current boyfriend— the best she could do at the moment—chose that moment to come strolling up to the pool. He was a lab technician at the hospital where Tina was employed, and he also worked the evening shift.

"Hi, babe," Tina's boyfriend said, eyeing Nick suspiciously.

"Hello," Tina answered lethargically.

"Hey," Nick said, nodding at Tina's boyfriend. "How's it going?"

"Okay."

Tina's boyfriend sat down on the chaise longue on Tina's other side and leaned over to kiss her. Make sure this guy knew what was what. It was great having a girlfriend with big tits, but man, he got so tired of every guy she ran into hitting on her all the time.

"Well," Nick said, standing up, "I should get going. Gotta hit those want ads. It was nice meeting you."

Tina and her boyfriend continued kissing and didn't bother to reply.

Damn, Nick thought as he walked upstairs. Just when we were hitting it off. Not that he'd planned on doing anything. He wasn't that big a shit. He wouldn't do that to Anna, not after all she'd done for him. It wouldn't have gone any further than a little innocent flirtation. Maybe take a swim together and get a chance to see how Tina looked getting out of the pool in her wet bathing suit. A little harmless fun, that would have been. But it would have been a nice way to spend the morning.

Nick decided he'd take a shower and get dressed before looking at the classifieds. He hated the feel of clammy swim trunks, and he could smell the chlorine in his hair.

When Nick got out of the shower, he threw on some jeans and a T-shirt and went into the bathroom to comb his hair. They were there again. No. This wasn't possible. This wasn't happening. There were even more than last time. It looked as if there were hundreds of them. Hundreds of hairs that should have been on his head but were sitting there in his comb.

Nick stared in disbelief. This WAS NOT HAPPENING TO HIM. It couldn't be. He peered at his reflection in the mirror, and he could have sworn there was a patch of scalp showing through on the left side of his head. He moved his hair around a little, and it helped, but he still knew. Knew that he, Nick Wells, who was only thirty-one years old, had a spot on top of his head that was balding.

If he still had a job, he could have made an appointment with someone. Whoever it was that you went and saw about something like this. A regular doctor? A dermatologist? Nick wasn't sure, but he would have found out. It probably wouldn't have been covered by his insurance, but he would have had the surplus income to pay for it. But he didn't have a job, and money was tight.

He'd go out and buy some Rogaine. He was pretty sure you didn't need a prescription anymore, thought he'd noticed some boxes of it sitting on the shelf in the store one day when he'd been out buying shampoo. Back in the good old days when he could see a box of Rogaine and snicker at the poor slobs who were forced to use it.

Nick got dressed and drove to the store. He bought some Rogaine, skipping the register with the hot young checker that he normally preferred. But not today. When he got back to Anna's place, he'd get on her computer and see if he could order some Rogaine over the Internet and avoid this kind of embarrassment. And before he ordered it, make sure they mailed it in a plain brown wrapper.

He read the directions and put on his first application, then found a place to hide the box in the back of one of the dresser drawers that Anna had cleaned out for him.

By the time he got all that done, it was going on two o'clock and Nick didn't feel like looking at the classifieds or making any calls. Hell, it wasn't going to hurt to wait until to-morrow to get going. It wasn't unreasonable for him to take a day or two and get used to living in a new place. Moving was stressful.

Hey, Nick thought to himself, maybe that's it. Some of the stress may be off now that I don't have so many financial wor-ries. But I lost my job, I got fired through no fault of my own, I gave up my condo, I had to move. No wonder I'm losing my hair. I'm not going bald, I'm just under a lot of stress. I'll keep using the Rogaine for a few weeks, just to make sure I don't lose any more while I've got all this stress in my life.

Nick felt good enough now to sit down and enjoy a hockey game on TV. When it was over, he looked at the clock and saw it was almost five. He debated cooking something for him and Anna for dinner, but he didn't see anything in the refrigerator that appealed to him. And he was tired. It had been a long, frustrating day.

Anna left the office as soon as she possibly could. She could hardly wait to get home and see Nick, find out what he'd been up to all day, see if he'd gotten any leads.

When she walked in the door, Nick was watching the news.

He'd actually had a sports show on, but he'd changed channels when he'd heard her footsteps approaching. Not that he had anything to hide. He just didn't want Anna to get the wrong idea and think he'd spent all day watching sports.

They said hello to each other. Anna had kind of hoped that Nick had made dinner. She hadn't actually asked him to. She didn't want him to think she expected him to be her cook and housekeeper just because he was staying with her and had no job. She didn't want him to feel like he had to earn his keep.

It just would have been nice to come home after a hard day and have dinner waiting. But maybe he'd been busy all day with phone calls and interviews. For all she knew, he might have arrived home a few minutes before she had and just turned on the news while he waited for her.

"I thought we'd go out for dinner," Nick said as she put her purse down. "I was going to cook, but I couldn't find anything."

"I had some chicken in there."

"Hmmm. I guess I didn't see it."

"I don't really feel like going out. How about if I get out of these clothes and make us some omelets?"

"Sounds good," Nick told her, thinking maybe he should get up and offer to make the omelets. But he was bushed. And he'd offered to take her out.

Anna changed her clothes and went into the bathroom to splash some water on her face and tie her hair back in a ponytail. She turned on the faucet at the sink, and as she put her hands under the faucet, she saw something in the mirror: the reflection of Nick's royal blue swimming trunks hanging in the shower.

He went swimming? she thought to herself. I'm out working all day, and I come home to find him sitting on the couch watching TV? He couldn't be bothered to even make a salad or open a can of soup, and conveniently doesn't see the chicken sitting right there on the top shelf of the refrigerator? But he had time to go swimming? Anna turned off the faucet and dried her face and hands, weeks of buried frustration coming to the surface.

"Did you have a nice swim?" Anna asked, walking into the living room.

"What? Oh yeah. I thought it would save some time to take a swim instead of going to the gym. That way I'm right here instead of wasting all that time driving back and forth, and I can get right on the phone."

"And is that what you did? Got right on the phone?"

Nick looked up from the television.

"What is this? The third degree? You think I just sat around all day?"

"I don't know, Nick. You tell me. I come home to find you watching TV, you've got stuff thrown all over the place."

"What stuff?"

"Newspapers. And you left your towel on the bathroom floor. And it might have been nice to at least get something started for dinner. Like that chicken that was sitting right there where anyone could see it."

"If you wanted me to cook the chicken, then you should have told me to cook the chicken. I'm not a mind reader."

"I didn't think I'd have to tell you. I thought that since you were living here now it was understood that you'd help out. And could you please turn off that television."

Nick picked up the remote, turned off the TV, and threw the remote down on the coffee table with a thud. He stood up, grabbed his wallet and keys off the coffee table, and walked toward the front door.

"Where are you going?" Anna asked.

"Out. Maybe while I'm gone you can type me up a set of rules and regulations so I know what's expected of me as your boarder."

Nick opened the door.

"Nick!"

Nick walked out the door, slamming it behind him.

Now this is more like it, I thought, watching Anna storm around the apartment after Nick left. For the first time since she'd met him, Anna's heart was seething with anger and frustration. Nick's heart seethed with anger, too, mixed in with some shock and a dash of guilt. And I knew how much Nick hated all those feelings, the lengths he would go to in order to avoid those feelings. Especially guilt. There wasn't anything Nick hated more than feeling guilty.

And this was just day two of sharing the same living space. Excellent. I'd become so pessimistic when Anna had asked Nick to move in that my near constant state of terror and despair had made me forget one of the eternal truths about romantic love: Two people can start out madly in love with each other and still find it absolutely impossible to share a bathroom.

twenty-two

When Nick walked out the door, he had every intention of going to a bar. But then he realized that would make him one of those pathetic losers—a guy with no job who's just had a fight with his girlfriend, sitting at a bar telling the bartender his problems. Nick was not that guy. He wasn't going bald, just losing a little hair because of the stress he was under, and he was not that guy. Was never going to be that guy, no matter how long it took him to find another job.

So he went to a drive-through, ordered a cheeseburger and onion rings, and drove around for a couple hours. Gave Anna time to cool off. He'd apologize when he got back. She'd make his life miserable unless he did.

And he supposed she had a point, after all. He could at least have made something for dinner. He owed her that much. But he didn't like the feeling of owing her something. He needed to get off his ass tomorrow and get moving. Set himself a goal that in one month, two at the most, he'd be back on his feet and ready to move into his condo. He hadn't had the couple sign a lease, just had them pay their rent month to month, so he could give them notice the minute he was able to move back in.

After Nick left, Anna got the chicken out of the refrigerator. How could Nick *not* have seen the chicken? Any closer and it would have bitten him. She threw it into a pan to sauté, tossed in some olive oil and lemon juice, and added some mushrooms and herbs. Honestly, how hard was that? It took what, ten minutes? She left the chicken simmering on the stove.

While the chicken was cooking, Anna picked up the newspapers Nick had left laying around and, muttering to herself, threw them in the recycling bin. Then she marched into the bathroom and put his wet towel into the laundry hamper. Still muttering to herself, she turned around, and then she saw her reflection in the mirror.

Anna stared at herself, at the hardness in her eyes and the tightness around her mouth, and she didn't like what she saw. She closed her eyes, her anger evaporating as she rubbed her temples. She'd blown it. Two days of living together and all her good intentions had gone right out the window. She'd sworn to herself that she wasn't going to start expecting things from Nick when he moved in. That if he chose to clean the place up or cook dinner, she'd be pleasantly surprised. That she'd never lose sight of the fact that she'd offered him a gift of her own choosing, not a set of obligations she expected him to fulfill. She didn't want it to be *I did this for you, now you have to do this for me.*

It would have been one thing if she'd told him that until he got a job she expected him to make dinner for her. But she hadn't, she'd deliberately *not* given him a set of chores and duties.

When Nick got back—he had to come back, of course he did, his stuff was here—she'd apologize. Not about the towel and newspapers. She hadn't handled it well, but she didn't feel guilty about expecting him to clean up after himself.

What she felt guilty about was that she'd violated her own intentions, the very reasons she'd asked Nick to move in with her in the first place.

Anna wasn't able to eat more than a few bites of dinner. What if Nick stayed out for hours? Worse yet, what if he stayed out all night? Called up some old girlfriend, one who didn't scream and nag at him, and stayed over at her place? Came back tomorrow morning, got his stuff, and moved out to go live with someone who wouldn't start screaming at him the minute she walked in the door, before he'd even had a chance to explain himself?

Anna caught herself and set down her fork. There it was, that old familiar feeling of smallness. Something became clear in her mind; a firm resolution was formed. No matter what happened from here on in, no matter what Nick decided—even if he left—Anna didn't ever want to feel small again.

During the twentieth century, bad language among the spirits of Planet Thirty-Seven got to be a bit of a problem, and the front office issued strict guidelines as to which words were inappropriate to use when discussing or reacting to the behavior of human beings. So I kept my thoughts regarding Anna's latest emotional breakthrough to myself.

I needed a break from her and her never-ending emotional breakthroughs anyway. I decided I'd go and see how the not-particularly-promising girl was doing.

I found her coming out of Dr. Grimes's office, dabbing her eyes. To the human eye she probably looked like hell. Her eyes were red and puffy, and her face was swollen from all the crying she'd done. But I read her heart, and I knew she was making progress. There was a lot more sadness there, but a lot less rage. So I returned to Anna's apartment to observe whatever nauseating scene I'd have to sit through next.

When Nick walked in the door an hour later, Anna gave him a radiant smile. He shut the door, trying to figure out what her smile meant. He'd been ready for tears and recriminations—*How dare you just walk out on me like that! I've been worried sick!*—and was fully prepared to apologize and take his medicine. The smile thing threw him off completely.

"Hi," she said softly.

"Hi," he answered warily.

"I'm sorry about earlier," she said.

"Yeah, me too."

"There's some chicken in the refrigerator if you're hungry."

"I got a burger while I was out."

"Oh."

"Don't you want to know where I've been?" he asked after a moment, wishing she'd stop smiling at him.

"If you want to tell me."

"I got a burger and drove around."

"Was it a good burger?" Anna asked.

"I guess." *What the hell kind of question was that?* He wished she'd quit smiling. It was making him nervous. "What are you so happy about?"

"I got to spend the last three weeks with Nick Wells."

"Huh?"

"That's what I've been sitting here thinking about. How lucky I am that I got to know you."

Nick really had no idea how to reply to that.

"So if you don't want to live here anymore," Anna said calmly, "if that's what you came back to tell me, you don't have to worry. I'm not going to scream or cry or make a scene. You don't owe me anything."

"What are you talking about?"

Was this her weird way of kicking him out? He just got here. Where in the hell was he going to go if she kicked him out?

"That's where I went wrong earlier tonight. Thinking you owed me something. I asked you to live here. I wanted you to live here."

Nick didn't like the way she kept putting everything in the past tense.

"And I'd like you to stay."

Finally, Nick thought. Why couldn't she have just said that instead of making me stand here like an idiot trying to figure out what she was getting at.

"I wasn't planning on going anywhere."

"Good. I want you to stay as long as you need to. I'm not saying you can do whatever you want. You can't set the place on fire or anything, and you need to pick up after yourself, like the newspapers laying around and the wet towel on the bathroom floor."

"Okay," Nick said, thinking that she really didn't need to add that last part. Just because he'd left some newspapers around one time didn't mean it was going to become a habit. "That sounds fair."

"But you don't have to do anything extra, like you owe me or need to pay me back. That's what I'm trying to say."

Like I told Herb later that night, listening to Anna then, I figured I was doomed no matter what kind of crap Nick had coming his way. The woman was *unshakable*. Where had she learned this stuff? But Herb didn't do much to cheer me up. It's not exactly his strong suit. And he doesn't understand the love game, has no idea what I'm up against. When I look back on it now, I should have noticed Herb was a lot more gloomy than normal, and acting a little strange even for him. But I had a lot on my mind.

Nick stood there, unsure what else to say. He'd always enjoyed it when women told him how great he was, how special he was, how much they enjoyed spending time with him. Hell, what guy wouldn't have? But he'd always known that they expected him to say the same kind of stuff back. Which, depending on how hot she'd been, or what the chances had been of him getting lucky, he usually did.

But Anna seemed perfectly content that he wasn't saying anything back. He didn't get it. And he wasn't sure he liked it. He didn't know why he didn't like it. But something about it bugged the hell out of him.

Anna stood up, and Nick was terrified she was going to come over and hug him. He didn't want her hugging him. He didn't know why he didn't want her hugging him; he just didn't.

But Anna simply gave him a kiss on the cheek.

"I'm bushed," she said. "I'm going to bed."

And then she walked into the bedroom and shut the door. Didn't stay in the living room and watch TV with him the way she usually did. Didn't ask him if he was coming to bed, or when he was coming to bed, seemed perfectly fine going to bed by herself. And Nick, for his part, had absolutely no desire to follow her into the bedroom and have sex that night. Which really threw him for a loop.

This was a perfect opportunity for some great make-up sex, which was some of the best sex he'd ever had, and he was passing it up, wasn't even tempted. Feeling perplexed and vaguely ill at ease, Nick sat down on the couch and turned on the TV. Maybe there was a game on.

Anna slept like a baby that night. Nick tossed and turned when he got into bed a little after midnight, and he got very little sleep at all. And when he woke up the next morning, long after Anna had left, he found a big clump of hair on his pillow.

twenty-three

Nick's hair continued to fall out day after day. He started doing more than one Rogaine application at a time, even though the directions specifically said not to exceed the recommended amount. He went to the health food store and got some vitamin supplements. He massaged his scalp because he'd read somewhere that poor circulation contributed to hair loss. He bought shampoos and conditioners designed to make your hair look thicker, being sure to hide the bottles away in his dresser drawer after he showered. He put volumizing mousse in his hair and stopped using a blow dryer. But nothing helped. It kept coming out into his comb and onto his pillow. Whenever he took a shower, he'd find big strands of his hair sitting in the drain.

Anna never said a word about it, but she had to have noticed. How could she not have noticed?

Seeing all that hair, hair that used to be on top of his head, Nick got so depressed every morning that he'd head down to the pool for a swim, thinking some exercise might help get him motivated. He kept hoping to run into Tina again—not telling himself he hoped to run into her but hoping it all the same—but she hadn't been around lately.

So he'd go down by the pool and sit down on a chaise longue, waiting to see if Tina might make it that day, but not admitting that to himself. And tell himself he needed to get moving but somehow never getting up the energy to jump into the pool. Part of it was being afraid of how his hair might look when he got back out.

He'd sit, getting more depressed, looking down to see if any of his hair had fallen onto the chaise longue. Sometimes he felt as if he left a trail of hair everywhere he went. But even when it was too cold to swim, he'd go down and sit by the pool.

Since he didn't get any real exercise anymore, and ate a lot of crappy food when he watched TV, Nick started getting a paunch and some love handles. He saw them, the paunch and the love handles, when he got out of the shower. And he'd swear that tomorrow morning, first thing, he was going to take a good, long swim. Maybe go to the gym, too. Get a grip on his weight before it got out of control. Because it didn't take long. You could spend years of your life working out, building muscle tone, but it only took a few weeks to get completely out of shape.

Nick knew he was running low on funds, and he couldn't afford to waste much more time. He needed to get off the stick and start looking for a job. And he intended to, each and every single morning.

But then he'd get up and see the hair on his pillow, sit by the pool, notice his paunch and love handles when he took off his robe to take a shower, and lose his energy and motivation. All he managed to get done most days was clean up after himself. Some days it was at the last minute—Shit! It's six already?—and he'd run around the apartment like a maniac getting his mess put away, but Nick always got it done.

Anna would come home at night, make them some dinner, and then go into their bedroom to read or do some work from the office. They hardly ever made love anymore, and they seldom talked. She never asked him if he'd had any luck that day in his search for a job.

Nick alternated between feeling grateful that she left him alone and didn't bother him with a lot of questions and feeling baffled at how she was acting. Trying to figure out what she was getting out of this. This couldn't be any fun for her. They were worse than an old married couple. She had to have an idea he wasn't putting his whole heart and soul into finding a job, but she never bugged him about it. Sometimes he felt guilty and vowed to do better. But then morning would come, the hair would be on his pillow, and the whole routine would start up all over again.

"How do you stand it?" Joan asked Anna one day when they were having lunch. "It sounds like all the guy does is lie around the house." Joan had never met Nick, but she'd decided she didn't like him very much. He sounded like major bad news.

"I don't stand it," Anna answered. "That's not how it is for me."

"How is it for you? Because I have to say I don't understand this at all. What do you get out of it?"

"I'm not looking to get anything out of it. I drove myself crazy for years worrying about what I was getting out of my relationships. I love him. That's it. That's enough."

"But, Anna," Joan persisted, "that's not how it works. Love can't be a one-way street. The other person has to give something."

"Says who?" Anna asked.

"I don't know. Says everyone. Anyone with any self-respect. This isn't like you. You're letting him walk all over you like a doormat."

"No, I'm not," Anna said calmly. "I'm choosing to do this. I don't resent him, I'm not angry with him, I'm not pretending everything is okay when it isn't, I'm not clinging to him out of desperation. I'm letting him be where he is right now. And I know it's not a great place. But I'm choosing to keep on loving him in spite of all that, and having faith that he'll pull himself out of this when he's ready."

"But what if he doesn't?" Joan asked. "You can't go on like this forever."

"I don't know. All I have is today and today is another day I get the opportunity to love Nick. And that makes my day better."

Joan nodded her head as if she understood what Anna was saying, but Joan actually thought Anna had gone off the deep end.

It wasn't until they were getting ready to pay the bill that Joan found the nerve to bring up the subject of Nick again.

"I just want to say one more thing about Nick," she said to Anna, "and then I'll drop it. You say you love him. I assume that means you want what's best for him, right?"

"Of course I do."

"Are you really sure what's best for him is to allow him to not have to do anything? Is it really best for him to get a free ride? If you weren't taking care of him, wouldn't he have to do something about his life? Is lying around on your couch going to make Nick Wells the best Nick Wells he can be?"

That same day, Nick didn't go down to the pool until early afternoon. He was sleeping later and later every day. Partly because he was staying up later and later each night. He'd tell himself he was going to shut the TV off promptly at eleven and get to bed at a decent hour, but then some promo would come on for Letterman or Leno, and he'd decide to watch the first half hour or so before going to bed.

He'd channel surf during the commercials while watching Leno or Letterman and get interested in some movie over on TNT, and the next thing he'd know it was two in the morning and he'd done it again. Stayed up all night.

And it wasn't as if he had some great reason to leap out of bed in the morning these days. The job market sucked, he was losing his hair, he didn't even feel like having sex much anymore, and none of his so-called buddies had lifted a finger to help him. It was a miracle that he got up at all.

Walking to the pool that day, Nick felt like hell. Until he

saw Tina lying on one of the chaise longues. Wearing that great black bikini of hers. She was lying on her stomach, and she had the straps to the top of her bathing suit pulled down. With what she had, he was bound to get a glimpse of something. Nick sucked in his gut and slicked back his hair.

"Tina," he said, walking over to the chaise longue. "Long time no see."

"Yeah," she said, looking up. "I've been on vacation."

"Go anywhere nice?" Nick asked, sitting down.

"My boyfriend took me to Acapulco. I feel like I'm starting to burn. You want to put some lotion on my back? It's in my bag. Right there on top."

"Sure," Nick said. "So how was Acapulco?" he asked, reaching into her bag for the suntan lotion, hoping his gut didn't hang out when he leaned over.

"Boring. We didn't exactly go on the deluxe package. And it's a drag eating Mexican food all the time."

Nick laughed.

"Sombreros, mariachis, and tostadas. After a couple days, they start getting real old."

Nick laughed again, rubbing the lotion on her back.

Guys always laughed at the things Tina said. She knew it was because she had big boobs—usually when they were laughing they were also sneaking peeks at her chest—but she'd just never figured out why big boobs made all the stuff she said seem so funny. Especially when she wasn't making a joke.

"So where's your boyfriend?" he asked.

"Who knows," Tina said. "And who cares?"

"You two split up?" Nick asked casually.

"Yeah. I dropped him when we got back. Let's just say you can really get to know a person when you share a dumpy hotel room with them for ten days. Get to know them a little *too* well, if you know what I mean."

"I'm sorry."

"Don't be. It wasn't anything serious anyway. He was just someone to kill time with. What about you? Are you seeing anyone?"

"Kind of."

"Uh-huh," Tina said knowingly. She knew what *that* meant. But Tina was bored, and at loose ends, and all the cute doctors at the hospital were taken. She might be in for a bit of a dry spell.

"I've got a couple hours to kill until I have to get to work," she said, raising her head and shoulders a little to give Nick a nice eyeful. "What do you say we go back to my place?"

twenty-four

I saw the whole thing. Well, up to a certain point. I ducked out after the first kiss (and from what I saw, it didn't look as if Tina was a very good kisser).

But I'd learned my lesson, and I didn't let myself get hopeful. I couldn't delude myself anymore. Anna just wasn't going to give up on this guy, no matter what. Even if she found out about Tina, she'd probably forgive him, go on loving him and believing in him, tell herself it hadn't meant anything, he'd just done it because he was feeling so down on himself, etc., etc.

I was so sick of Anna at that point, so disgusted by the whole situation—it was really unfair of her to turn into this selfless, loving person without showing any of the usual warning signs—that I gave myself a break and left her alone all afternoon. It wasn't like she needed me.

It was ironic. I usually get a big kick out of irony—watching you people attempt to love each other has given me plenty of chances to see it firsthand—but not this time. Anna had become a sterling example of what human love can be and of the potential for growth and change that people are capable of. Under normal circumstances I'd have highlighted her in my annual report to the front office. They *live* for this kind of stuff.

But now, in an ironic twist of fate (and personally, I've never cared for Fate. I've met him a few times, and he's a humorless, pompous prig), not only wouldn't Anna earn me a single point of credit, but she was actually going to be the cause of my downfall as well.

I probably needed to start tying up some loose ends while I still had time. And say good-bye to those fellow spirits whose company I'd enjoyed over the course of human history. First and foremost was Herb. We'd had some good times watching all of you bumbling around. And Frank over in Déjà Vu. A minor spirit, but a stand-up guy. There's no real reason for déjà vu. The universe just threw it in for fun.

And Stella, of course, from the annoying weather division. Her specialty was unexpected rain showers. The way she could imitate the expression a human being gets, peering up at the sky when they feel a drop of rain as if they'd never seen one before—that still cracked me up every time she did it. Or how she'd mimic the way you'll ask each other, "Is that rain?" Like water coming out of the sky could be anything else.

Yeah, I'd miss them. And meanwhile, until the front office caught up with me and I had to face the music, I'd keep doing my job. So I waited outside Tina's apartment until Nick walked outside to see how his heart was feeling about what he'd done.

Nick returned to their apartment, his and Anna's, feeling like a complete and total piece of shit. Tina hadn't even been that good. A great body, but kind of boring once they got started. Hell, she wasn't even a good kisser. And that voice. How had he missed noticing what an irritating voice she had?

He felt guilty as hell. God, what had he been thinking? He hadn't been thinking. Not with his brain anyway.

Never again. He'd stop going down to the pool, start going to the gym and getting back in shape. He'd go to bed early, get up when Anna got up, and spend every day—all day—looking for a job.

He'd start making changes, big changes, right now. When Anna got home, the place would look spotless. He'd dust and vacuum, dinner would be on the table, and they'd spend the evening doing what she wanted. If she wanted to talk, they'd talk. If she felt like catching a movie, he'd take her out. Or go to the video store and rent something. Something she wanted to see. He was willing to sit through *Fried Green Tomatoes* or *Terms of Endearment* or *Steel Magnolias*. Whatever she wanted.

But first he'd take a shower and get cleaned up. Have a little lunch. Something healthy, not that crap he'd been eating. Maybe he should force himself to go to the gym. No. Not enough time. By the time he showered and ate, got the place cleaned up and started dinner, the rest of the afternoon would be gone. Hell, it was already three. Anna would be on her way home in a few hours.

Nick showered, got dressed, and applied his Rogaine. It looked to him as if there had been less hair left in the drain today. Maybe the stuff was starting to work.

He made himself a turkey sandwich and cut up some carrots to go with it, leaving the potato chips behind for a change. He grabbed the paper and went into the living room. He was so used to eating in there that he didn't think about having lunch at the dining room table.

Nick sat down, took a bite of his sandwich, and opened the paper. Man, he was tired. All the late nights and junk food were catching up with him. He started reading the front page, but it was too hard to concentrate. Nick yawned. Hey! he thought, three-fifteen. Sports talk is on. I'll watch the last half, finish my sandwich, and then start getting the place cleaned up. See if there's something in the freezer I can defrost for dinner.

At three-thirty, Nick turned off the TV, picked up his plate, and headed for the kitchen. He rinsed off his plate, put it in the dishwasher instead of the sink, like he usually did, and felt a real surge of pride at his accomplishment. Then he opened the freezer, checked its contents, and decided to take out the tuna fillets. They were freeze wrapped, so he could put them in a pan of water and they'd be defrosted and ready to cook in a couple of hours.

After taking care of the tuna, he got out some vegetables to make a salad. He could let it keep in a bowl in the refrigerator, then spend the next two hours or so cleaning, and dinner would only take about half an hour to throw together.

When Anna came home that night, she'd see how he hadn't just been lying around on the couch watching TV, see he'd done some cleaning, even made her a nice dinner. He'd set the table, too. Get out her good dishes, the ones they never used because she saved them for special occasions. Light some candles . . . wait a minute. What if it made her happy at first but then she got to thinking about it and wondered why he'd gone to all this trouble? What if it made her suspicious?

Nah. Anna trusted him. She'd never think . . . but women had a way of knowing these things, like they had some kind of special radar. He wasn't afraid of Tina spilling the beans. It wasn't like they were going to run into her. He never saw Tina other than at the pool. He doubted Anna even knew who she was. And Tina had been totally cool when he'd left. Hadn't asked when they were going to see each other again, thank God.

Although, now that he thought about it, she hadn't been very grateful. Despite the fact that her performance had been lackluster—to say the least—he'd made sure he'd put a smile on her face. And it hadn't been easy. It had taken some real effort on his part. A lot of guys would have given up and just taken care of business.

And all Tina had said when he left was to be sure and lock the door on his way out 'cause she needed to hop in the shower if she was going to be on time for work.

But then again, he hadn't been up to his usual level. He'd been good—he was always good—but not at his best. If she ever got a chance to see him at his best, when he wasn't so tired and out of shape, under so much *stress,* that would be a different story. She'd be begging for more. He'd like to have the chance to show her . . . no. Don't even go there, Nick.

But Nick decided he wasn't going to take any chances. There wasn't any point in going overboard and maybe raising some red flags for Anna. He'd cook dinner, that would make her happy, but he'd skip the dusting and vacuuming. Besides, he was beat. What he *should* do was take a nap for an hour or so. Then he wouldn't be so tired when Anna got home. He'd have the energy to pay some attention to her. Not too much attention, but enough to make it seem natural when he went into bed with her. It had been too long. He didn't know how she was able to stand going without it for so long.

Unless . . . Nick felt a minute of absolute agony at the thought of Anna being with someone else. But then he told himself no. No way. No way was Anna getting some on the side. The idea was ridiculous.

He threw a salad together, nothing fancy, and then went into their bedroom. He pulled the curtains, set the alarm for five, and got under the covers. At five o'clock the alarm went off. Nick rolled over sleepily, turned off the alarm—fully intending to get up in a few minutes—and rolled back over to sleep.

When Anna got home that night around seven, the apartment was dark, the TV wasn't on, and Nick was nowhere to be seen.

"Nick?" she called out, turning on the living room light. His car was in the parking lot, so she knew he hadn't gone out. "Nick?" she called again. Nick, however, was sound asleep and didn't hear a thing.

Anna set down her purse and briefcase and walked out of

the living room and down the hallway. She turned on the hall light and glanced in the bathroom. Then she walked to the end of the hall and looked in their bedroom. Nick was in bed, snoring lightly. She looked at him for a minute, smiled, then walked back down the hallway, turning off the light when she reached the living room.

Anna couldn't believe how calm she was, considering what she had to tell Nick that night. The two important things she had to tell him that night. If he woke up. She might have to wait until tomorrow if he slept all night, but that was okay. She didn't feel rushed or anxious about what she had to say.

She'd have something to eat, get a little work done, and read her new *Vanity Fair.* Talk to Nick tonight if he got up; tell him tomorrow night if he didn't.

Anna walked into the kitchen and found the tuna fillets Nick had set out earlier. She didn't know how long they'd been sitting in that pan of water, but it looked like it had been hours. She didn't want to take any chances on their being spoiled, so she dumped out the water, picked up the fillets, and threw them in the wastebasket.

When she opened the refrigerator and found the salad Nick had made, Anna smiled to herself, picturing how it must have gone. Nick had had every intention of making dinner for her that night. He'd made the salad, taken the tuna out of the freezer to defrost. But then he'd decided he was tired. He'd taken a nap. Had probably set the alarm so he'd be sure to get up in time to have dinner ready for her, then rolled over and gone back to sleep after he'd turned it off.

Imagining all that, Anna knew she'd made the right decision and for the right reasons.

When Nick woke up, he looked at the alarm clock and saw that it was seven-thirty. He swore at himself, threw the covers off, and jumped out of bed. He found Anna in the kitchen, tossing the salad.

"Hey, sleepyhead," she said, smiling at him, which made him feel like a bigger shit than ever.

"I was going to make you dinner," he said sheepishly. "Did you find the tuna? Here, let me finish that and cook the tuna. You go sit down."

"That's okay. I've got it."

"Okay. You do the salad and I'll do the tuna."

"The tuna looked a little funny. I think it sat out too long, so I threw it away."

"Oh, man. I'm sorry, Anna."

"It's okay. I boiled some eggs, and there's some cheese. It'll be fine."

"Let me finish that. You go sit down. You've probably had a long day."

"It's fine, Nick," Anna said. "Cooking relaxes me. Why don't you get a beer and watch some TV. Isn't *Sports Buzz* on?" Living with Nick these past few weeks, Anna had the ESPN schedule virtually memorized.

"I really wanted to make you dinner," Nick said, pouting, as if Anna had somehow robbed him of his big surprise.

"It's okay, Nick. It really is. Go watch your show."

Nick took a beer out of the refrigerator and went into the

living room. He turned on *Sports Buzz*. Every few minutes he looked over his shoulder to watch Anna. Her shoulders weren't tense and tight—a dead giveaway he'd learned over the years; they act like they're not upset but their body language screams hostility—and once or twice he heard her humming to herself.

Nick was relieved she hadn't gotten on his case about falling asleep. He wouldn't have blamed her if she'd given him some shit. *I know you wanted to make dinner, Nick. Just like you want to find a job. But you don't ever seem to find a job, do you, Nick? And who's out here in the kitchen making dinner tonight, Nick? Me, that's who. Because I've learned the hard way that if I want to get anything done around here I'd damn well better do it myself.*

She could have said something like that to him, and he wouldn't have had much to offer in his defense. It had been over two weeks now, and he hadn't done anything about finding a job.

But she hadn't said that. And what had he done to repay her? Gone and slept with the first bimbo who had come his way.

Though he kind of resented the way Anna acted, as if all he did was drink beer and watch sports shows. Like she just assumed that that's what he'd do while she made dinner. There were other things he could be doing. When he'd been working, when he'd had his life together, he'd been lucky to catch much TV at all. Maybe had one beer a night and a few on the weekend.

Wait a minute, Nick thought, looking up at the TV. What did he just say? This guy thought the Steelers were going to win on Sunday? Was he nuts? No way were the Steelers going to win on Sunday. Their defense always tanked in the fourth quarter.

"Nick?" Anna called out from the kitchen. "Dinner's ready."

"In a second," he called back. "I want to hear what this guy has to say. He actually thinks the Steelers are going to win on Sunday."

Anna was quiet during dinner. She didn't look mad, Nick thought, but she was definitely acting distant. Especially considering that he'd made most of the salad.

"Everything all right?" Nick finally asked. "You're kind of quiet."

"Just a little tired."

Nick winced. Anna wasn't looking at him, and it didn't sound like a dig. But he felt guilty.

"I know," he said after a minute. "Why don't I take you out for dessert? We'll go to the Cheesecake Factory."

"You don't have to do that."

"I want to."

"To tell you the truth, Nick, I really don't feel like going out tonight. I'm tired and . . . I kind of wanted to talk after dinner."

"Oh?" Nick asked nervously. "Anything in particular you wanted to talk about?" Nick asked after Anna didn't reply.

She couldn't know. No way she'd be sitting there that calmly if she knew. *Unless she's just been waiting until I let my guard down, acting nice so she can really whammy me with the Tina thing after dinner and I won't see it coming.*

Why couldn't women understand it wasn't any big deal? A guy just needed variety, that's all. Something new once in a while. It didn't have anything to do with *them*. It was like the male version of shopping. Anna didn't really need all those shoes, she just wanted something new to spice things up.

Could he help it if women got their kicks out of shoes and men got their kicks out of sex? That's just the way it was. Biology. Evolution had built it into his DNA. He'd read that somewhere. That meant it was beyond his control. Science said so.

But how could Anna know? He'd taken a long, hot shower and washed his hair twice, even though he'd worried that over-shampooing might make more of his hair fall out. Could someone have seen him going inside Tina's place? No. There hadn't been anyone around. Could Tina have told her? Kept a lookout for Anna, and run down and told her when she'd seen her coming home? No, Tina was at work. At least that's what she'd *said.* That she had to work tonight.

"Let's wait until we finish eating," Anna said.

But Nick wanted to get it over with. He couldn't stand the suspense.

"I'm pretty much done," he replied, even though he'd only eaten a few bites of his dinner.

Anna set her fork down and looked at Nick. She smiled at him affectionately. He didn't like the look of that smile. It wasn't an angry smile, but there was something about it that made him nervous.

"All right," Anna said. "Nick, I have two things to say to you."

Nick braced himself.

"The first thing is that I love you."

"Huh?"

"Loving you has been the best experience of my life. You're the first man I've said 'I love you' to before he said it to me. I don't even need you to say it back. That's one of the gifts you've given me, helping me get past my own fears. I'm a different person because I love you. I used to spend so much time worrying about what I got out of a relationship. But with you, the feeling I get by loving you is enough. And because of that I wouldn't give up one single minute of the time I've had with you. Not even having to listen to those stupid sports shows."

Anna paused. Nick thought he should say something. Usually women expected him to say something after they told him they loved him. But Nick didn't know what to say. For one thing, the way she'd put it had been different from the way it had been put by other women he'd known. More like a statement of fact than a statement that ended with a question mark. And for another, sports shows were *not* stupid.

Nick was still trying to figure out how to respond to the first thing Anna had said when she told him the second thing.

"And the second thing I have to say is that I want you to move out. As soon as possible."

"Huh?"

Which is exactly how I reacted. I'd been half listening, not paying much attention. Anna loves Nick. It doesn't matter whether or not he loves her. Blah, blah, blah. On and on and on it went. She was getting to be a broken record. I had my own troubles to worry about, and it wasn't as if this was new ground. Hold the presses! Anna loves Nick!

But then she told him to move out.

Huh? I thought, snapping out of my doldrums.

Had I missed something? Was this a trick? What in the hell was Anna up to now?

twenty-five

Nick stared at Anna with his mouth open. Move out? She couldn't be serious. Hadn't she specifically told him that he could stay as long as he liked? What had he done? What had changed? True, he'd slept with Tina, but she didn't know he'd slept with Tina, so that couldn't be it. Or did she know? And simply decided she wasn't going to give him the satisfaction of letting him see that she knew?

It couldn't be about the dinner, could it? Hell, he hadn't made dinner in the entire time he'd lived here. And today he'd at least started dinner. Maybe the tuna had gotten ruined, but he'd finished the salad. The salad they had in front of them-selves at this very minute. She'd had to boil some eggs, and slice the cheese, and throw it all together with the dressing. But he'd done the hard part, cutting up the vegetables. Didn't he get some credit for that? For making an effort, in spite of all the stress he was under?

Or had the tuna been the last straw? Had she stood there throwing the tuna away and just snapped? *I pay the rent and utilities, I'm out at work all day while he does nothing about getting a job. I come home to a dirty house; he's got his crap all over the place. And now I have to throw eight dollars and fifty cents' worth of tuna down the drain because he's too damn lazy to get out of bed from his nap! That's it! I've had it!*

And what was that bit about loving him so much? Did she just throw that in there to twist the knife a little? *I love you, that's not the problem, but I can't take any more. It's not me; it's you. God knows I love you and God knows I tried, but you make it impossible, Nick.* Make sure she acted sweet and nice and loving right before she threw him out on his ass? Make it hurt that much more?

Because it hurt. Nick couldn't believe how much it hurt. I could and did, and right then, I didn't have any pity for him at all. I've seen all the troubles your bodies cause you. I've never wanted to try one out for size the way some of the other spirits do. But I wished I had one then. I wanted to whoop it up. Kick my heels. Do a little jig. Shake my fist in the air and shout, "Glory hallelujah!"

I'd looked into Anna's heart, and I knew why she'd asked Nick to leave. She still loved him with all her heart, loved him today more than she had yesterday. She was doing this because she thought it was the best thing for *him*.

But that didn't matter. She'd asked him to leave, and she'd

meant it. She wasn't going to back down, no matter what he said. They would separate. I had my solution. True love, by its very nature, means two people will do anything to be together. Since Anna was choosing to separate from Nick not because of circumstances beyond her control but by her own choice—no matter how pure her motives—then, technically speaking, it no longer qualified as true love. It was a loophole, but it would work, dammit, it would work!

I loved Anna Munson so much at that moment that I decided I was going to do it. Give her some time to get over Nick, and then find her someone new, someone worthy of true love, and submit her name to the front office for approval.

A great guy this time. Someone loyal and kind and faithful, someone she could trust, not like that jerk Nick Wells. And he'd be hot, too. And bring her soup and ice cream when she was sick. Have a good sense of humor, a great career, like kids—all the things she was looking for. She'd earned it.

Nick didn't understand how she could be kicking him out if she really loved him. All he knew was that the thought of leaving filled him with dread and panic. Where would he go? What would he do? How was he supposed to find a new job when he was going to have to be scrambling around trying to find somewhere to stay? How could she do this to him? Didn't she realize the *stress* he was under?

"Move out?" Nick finally said.

"Yes," Anna said firmly, looking him straight in the eyes. "As soon as you can."

He heard the firmness in her voice. She was looking right at him, not flinching at all. This called for desperate measures.

"Anna," he said, getting up out of his chair, "I know things haven't been all that great the last few weeks."

Nick walked over to Anna's chair, and knelt down beside her. He took her hands in his. She didn't pull her hands away, which he saw as a good sign.

"I know I don't show you enough appreciation. It probably seems as if I take it all for granted, everything you do for me. But I don't. I'm just not myself lately. Not having a job has really done a number on me."

Anna looked at him and smiled. "I know," she said.

Good, Nick thought. She's starting to back down a little.

"And I know I haven't done everything I should have been doing. Maybe I needed a little time to get my head together. And I'm sorry about not helping out around here, letting you do everything. And I'm sorry I fell asleep and ruined the tuna."

"It's not about the tuna."

"I know. But maybe the tuna was like the last straw for you or something. I wanted to make you dinner tonight, as a way to thank you for all you've done. But I was so tired. I'm always so tired lately."

Anna nodded her head. She was still smiling at him, and her eyes were soft. He was almost home. But he needed to say one more thing. He knew he needed to say it. He'd said it before when he hadn't meant it. And it was what she wanted to hear. It was what they all wanted to hear. It was the one thing a guy could say to get himself out of just about any jam with a woman. No matter how mad they were, you just said it and they'd melt.

He started to say it, but he couldn't. He didn't know why he couldn't. Something about the look in her eyes. Something about the way she just let her hands rest in his, not grasping at them. Something about how she'd taken him in, cooked for him, hadn't bugged him every day about how he was spending his time, let him watch his stupid sports shows (Okay, sometimes they were stupid. Calm down, guys; it's just a game).

And he couldn't say it.

"Anna," he said instead, "I like you more than any other woman I've ever known. I don't want to lose you. If you'll give me another chance, let me stay, I'll show you how I can be. I won't lie around the couch. I'll be up every morning at six, hit the ground running. I'll find a job. Hell, I'll fry burgers if I have to. I'll help out. Cook dinner. Unless I'm on the night shift at McDonald's," he added with a hopeful grin. "Just give me another chance."

Anna squeezed his hands. Nick sighed with relief.

"I can't do that," Anna said.

Nick let go of her hands.

"Why not? I *said* I was sorry. I *said* I'd do better. And you told me I could stay as long as I wanted."

"Because I know something now that I didn't know then."

Here it comes, Nick thought. I can't believe I fell for this. She knew about Tina and she wanted to hear me beg. She wanted me to grovel. They always know. And now she's going to give it to me. Give it to me good while I'm down here on

247

my knees, after I've begged her to let me stay. Scream and call me every name in the book. And then demand that I pack my stuff up right now and get the hell out of here before she throws me out.

"I know that I'm not good for you."

"Huh?"

"I'm not good for you," Anna repeated.

Nick let out a deep breath. He felt like he'd just been given a new lease on life.

"Baby," he said, squeezing her hands, "are you kidding? You're the best thing that's ever happened to me. Sometimes I wonder what I've done to deserve you."

"No, Nick," Anna said, "I'm just a nice place to lay your hat for a while. And this isn't about you not loving me the way I love you. I'd be happy to love you for the rest of my life no matter what you felt for me. This is about me finally realizing that me loving you doesn't make your life better. Or you better. I'm not the person you should be with. You need to be with someone who makes you bigger, not smaller."

"That's not true," Nick insisted. "I'd be a mess right now if you weren't in my life."

"Or maybe you'd have another job by now."

"I'll get a job."

"No, Nick, you'll get up tomorrow morning with the best of intentions. You might even look at the want ads or make a few calls. Maybe you'll even really work at it. I don't know. But I do know that there's nothing about being with me that fills you with a desire to expand yourself. See, that's what I feel with you. It's like I forget all about myself, but in this weird way, I become bigger and better than I ever thought I could be.

"And, Nick, it's the best feeling. I want you to have that feeling. I want you to find someone who gives you that feeling. I want you to know what it's like. That's why I can't let you stay. You need to go out and do what you need to do. I know it's safe here with me, but you deserve a hell of a lot more in life than just safety. And I think, when it's all said and done, that's all you really get from me. Safety. That's why we can't live together anymore, or even see each other anymore."

Anna smiled sadly at Nick and looked at him with complete love. Nick looked away.

"How long do I have?" he asked, gazing down at the ground.

"A week?" Anna asked. "Will that give you enough time to find another place?"

"Whatever."

"If you need some money for a deposit or anything—"

"I don't want your damn money," Nick snapped, standing up.

He needed to get out of here. Screw her. He didn't need her. And he certainly didn't need her stupid speeches about love. He should thank her. This was just the kick in the pants he'd needed to get off his lazy ass and get his act together.

He'd get a job. A damn good job. He'd be back and better than ever. And find someone hot, really hot, who didn't blab at him all the time with her stupid theories of love, trying to make him feel guilty and weird. Which was how he felt. Guilty and weird. He didn't need this shit. Not from her, not from anybody. He never should have moved in with her in the first place.

Nick left without saying a word. Anna didn't ask him where he was going. It wasn't any of her business anymore. She got up, cleared the table, did the dishes, and sat down to do some work. She felt sad, but calm. And good. Good on the inside, without any of the anger and regret she usually felt when one of her relationships ended. Because really, she was lucky. Even if she never met anyone else again, she was one of the lucky ones. She'd truly loved someone.

She'd cry when Nick left for good, but she'd be okay. She honestly didn't know if she'd ever love someone again the way she'd loved Nick, and she didn't think she could settle for anything less. There was a good chance she'd never marry, even though she wanted kids. She could always adopt. There were a lot of kids out there who needed a good home. And when she was an old lady, she wouldn't be bitter or have any regrets. She'd have this really great memory. She'd loved someone.

I watched her for the next hour as she sat calmly doing her work, and I read her heart. It all still seemed too good to be true. I had to make sure she wasn't having second thoughts. She wasn't. Her decision was firm. It was final. I don't get very impressed with you people very often, certainly nowhere near as often as *some* of you get with yourselves, but I was kind of impressed with Anna.

Feeling secure that Anna wasn't going to screw things up for me again, I checked in on the not-very-promising girl to see how she was coming along. I found her writing in her journal. I read her heart. It was calm, and just a little bit more peaceful than it had been the last time I'd checked. Things were looking up all over the place.

Then I ran off to tell Herb the good news. I found him sitting glum and morose, the way he always got when he thought over the day's events on planet Earth. Good old Herb. He was a guy you could count on.

"Herb," I almost shouted, "I'm off the hook!"

"Glad to hear it."

"You should have seen it. It was a thing of beauty, and I never even saw it coming. Anna dumped him. She broke it off with Nick Wells!"

"You're Cupid. How could you not know she was going to dump him?"

"That's not important." I didn't want Herb to know I'd left Anna alone all day. I'd already broken enough rules. "The important thing is that they won't be together. And it was her own choice. She did it because she thought it was the best thing for him, but that doesn't matter. Technically speaking, it isn't true love. I'm off the hook." Herb didn't respond.

"Aren't you even going to congratulate me?" I asked. This was Herb; I didn't expect him to clap his hands—if he'd had hands—with delight. But I expected some kind of acknowledgment. How many times had I sat here and listened to him whine about getting turned down again for a transfer?

"I think there's something fishy going on," Herb said, sounding more downcast than I'd ever heard him. "And I think it involves me and you."

"What do you mean?" I asked, my good mood evaporating.

"Well . . . ," Herb said hesitantly.

"What is it? You're making me a nervous wreck."

"I kind of broke a rule, too. And no one from the office has said a word. What I did wasn't a big thing, like what you did. She had it coming. Maybe they just forgot to give me the orders. But then I got to thinking about it. How you and I both broke a rule. And how we're both working a couple of the same cases and—"

"What do you mean?" I interrupted. "What cases are you talking about?"

"I told you I had orders about Nick."

"And you said it wasn't anything out of the ordinary."

"It wasn't. But then I got another case. And maybe I should have said something before. But you had enough on your mind, and I wasn't sure. And we're really not supposed to talk about our cases with each other. And I'm still not sure. It's more like an intuition."

"An intuition about what?"

But before Herb could answer me, we both heard that unmistakable sound you never forget, hope you'll never hear again, and always dread.

We were being summoned to the front office.

twenty-six

"Have a seat, gentlemen," Barney (not his real name) told me and Herb when we arrived at the front office.

I was shaking, but seeing that it was Barney we'd be dealing with, I felt a little less terrified. (If you'd seen the things I'd seen, knew the power and capabilities the front office had, you'd have been terrified, too.) But Barney was only second in command. Not that he wasn't terrifying, but at least he wasn't Harold. Brrrr! Harold sent a chill of dread through my entire being. Harold ran the front office with an iron fist.

But he'd sent Barney to deal with us. Maybe I still had a chance.

"Tell me, Cupid," Barney said, "do you know the story of Jonah and the whale?"

"Yes, sir," I answered.

"Why don't you tell it to me? Briefly. Highlight the important parts."

"Yes, sir. Well, to put it as briefly as I can, God wanted Jonah to do something, which Jonah didn't want to do. So Jonah tried to hide from God so he could try to avoid doing the task God had assigned him. Jonah ends up getting swallowed by a whale, and while he's not too thrilled about living inside a big fish—"

"Mammal," Herb interjected.

"Right. Mammal. Anyway, Jonah figures he's safe from God in there. But in the end, God finds him and Jonah realizes he has to complete his mission whether he wants to or not."

"Well put, Cupid, well put. And what do you think the lesson is we're supposed to learn from the story of Jonah and the whale?"

"That you can run but you can't hide?"

"Correct. Is there anything you'd care to tell me?"

"I guess you already know," I said lamely.

"Did you really think we wouldn't?" Barney asked.

"I'm sorry, sir. I just lost control for a minute and then it was too late. The damage had already been done. It will never happen again. I hope you can forgive me."

How had I ever been foolish enough to think they wouldn't find out?

"And you, Herb, is there anything you'd care to tell me?"

"I guess you already know that, too," Herb said, sounding as lame as I had.

"Yes, Herb, we know all about the Martha Stewart incident.

Very clever. And while we understand how you feel about people who seem like they should have crap happen to them but don't, taking it out on Martha Stewart was not your prerogative. Our decisions are not made lightly, and there's always more to the picture than you spirits, with your limited powers, can see. Your actions showed an appalling lack of trust in the basic harmony of the universe."

"Yes, sir," Herb replied.

"However," Barney went on, "the incident with the arrow and the incident with Martha Stewart, while regrettable, aren't the real issue. The real issue is your lack of compassion. Both of you. No compassion for humanity whatsoever. Yes, they are a frustrating people. And yes, I've had similar feelings myself. There are some days I want to hurl a giant comet at Planet Thirty-Seven and be done with it."

I chuckled.

"This is no laughing matter!" Barney thundered. "After all your years of dealing with them, you still don't understand a damn thing! Have either one of you ever thought what it must be like to be born on Planet Thirty-Seven? You live inside a body that will eventually decay and die. You're essentially alone. No one, no matter how long they know you or how much they love you, can ever know what it's like to be you. You have no idea why you're there or if there's a reason for any of it. You hope, you guess, you might even have faith. But you never know for sure. And yet, in spite of all that, you keep on going.

"Cupid! Imagine what it's like to try to love someone under those circumstances. Throw in all the sexual complications, and it's a miracle they ever pull it off. And yet they do. And you, Herb. Imagine what it's like to have to wake up every single day without knowing what kind of crap might happen to you. Crap you have no control over. And yet they do! They get up every single day, most of them, and come out swinging. Or at least coping. Maybe they don't live up to their full potential. Maybe they screw up time and time again. But they still get up.

"The two of you love to sit around and talk about how they're always whining and complaining. Oh yes, we've heard you. All the little jokes. We've seen the little parties where you spirits all get together and take turns imitating them.

"You all think you're so amusing, and you should all be ashamed of yourselves. Look how frustrated you get, and you're spirits! You know there's a purpose and a reason for everything. You know the universe is infinite! You don't have to deal with having a body! And look how you've behaved! You have the nerve to look down on *them?* I'd like to put both of you down there for one day in human form and see how well you'd do."

I hung my head—metaphorically speaking—in shame. So did Herb.

"Knock it off!" Barney roared. "I didn't call you up here just to see you pout."

"Yes, sir," Herb and I mumbled.

"And that's another thing. Where did you two get the idea that if you screwed up we'd come up with some hideous punishment?"

"Well," I said, "there was the whole Garden of Eden thing."

"And the flood," Herb added.

"And the plagues and locusts."

"And the Red Sea incident."

"And—"

"Oh, for Pete's sake!" Barney interrupted. "They were brand-new life-forms. We had to get their attention, didn't we? And you should know better than anyone how hard that can be with them. When was the last time you saw us pull a stunt like that?"

"Well," Herb said, "there's the earthquakes. And the tidal waves."

"The wars," I added.

"Use your heads. Earthquakes and tidal waves are natural phenomena, part of the fabric of design. And the wars they cause themselves. Our job, which I would think you'd know by now, is to provide an environment where everyone can learn what they need to learn. And you two still have a lot to learn. You were assigned the planet you were assigned for a reason. And you've given us many centuries of dedicated service. We're not going to punish you or banish you."

"You're just going to retire us?" I asked hopefully.

"No. You're a long way off from retirement. You haven't learned what you need to learn. So this is what's going to happen. From here on in, we're taking over the Nick Wells and Anna Munson cases. Fortunately, the universe provided us with the principle of redemption, so we're going to redeem the situation. And you two will watch and see if you can learn something."

"What about Martha Stewart?" Herb asked.

"Well, actually," Barney admitted, "Harold found that rather amusing."

"Wait a minute," I said, looking at Herb as I put two and two together. "Was Anna one of your assignments, too? Why didn't you tell me?"

"I tried to tell you today that I thought there was something fishy going on."

"Enough!" Barney shouted. "What who told whom and what they told them isn't relevant here. And there's no reason for you two to discuss your cases with each other anyway. Now get back to your posts, before I change my mind and reassign the both of you to Planet Sixty-Five!"

Herb and I shuddered and beat a hasty retreat. Planet Sixty-Five is the cesspool of the universe. Planet Earth is a *cakewalk* compared to Planet Sixty-Five.

"Something fishy, my ass," I muttered as Herb and I raced back to our posts.

I was a little irritated with Herb, but I'd get over it. Things could have gone worse. Just ask Zeus. You wouldn't even recognize him now. Poor guy hasn't been the same since they revoked his thunderbolt privileges.

twenty-seven

Herb and I did as Barney ordered, and for the next few weeks we watched Anna and we watched Nick, trying to figure out what we were supposed to learn.

Nick stayed out late the night Anna asked him to move. He went to a bar, forgetting his vow never to become *that guy,* and found some other guys to hang out with. They drank beer, played pool, rated the varying degrees of hotness of the women that walked by, and in between bitched about how unreasonable women were in general. When they ran out of stories to share about their various girlfriends, wives, ex-girlfriends, and ex-wives, they exchanged theories and ideas that proved conclusively that if one of them were running things, the country wouldn't be in such a hell of a mess. Opinion was evenly divided as to whether or not the Carolina Panthers would make it to the Super Bowl.

Nick slept on the couch when he got home, a little pissed that Anna had already gone to bed. Wasn't even worried about where he'd been.

Anna saw him on the couch the next morning, and she got ready for work as quietly as she could in order not to disturb him.

Nick woke up around ten feeling like crap. But he didn't go back to bed or head down to the pool. He forced himself to get up, have some juice, and go to the gym. Using the treadmill and lifting weights hurt like hell with so little sleep and too much beer the night before, but he didn't stop until he'd done his whole routine.

When Nick got home he read the classifieds, made a few calls, and actually got two people to agree to have him send them his résumé. When he was done making his calls, Nick cleaned the apartment and made dinner.

Anna got home around six forty-five to find Nick on the couch reading her copy of *The 7 Habits of Highly Effective People.* The place was spotless, the table was set for dinner, and she could smell a roast cooking.

"Hi," Nick said casually when she closed the door, keeping his eyes glued on chapter two of the book.

"Hi," Anna said. "The place looks great."

"There's a roast and potatoes in the oven and a salad in the refrigerator," Nick told her.

"That was nice of you, Nick. Thanks."

Anna went into the bedroom and changed her clothes. Nick waited for her to come back out. Half an hour went by.

She was still in the bedroom. He went in to check the roast. It looked done. Nick took the roasting pan out of the oven, tossed the salad, sliced the roast, and put everything on the table.

"Dinner's ready," he called out.

Anna came out to the table a few minutes later carrying a copy of *Vanity Fair*. She sat down and put the magazine next to her plate.

"Everything looks great," she said. "Thank you. I was starved. I didn't have time for lunch."

"You're welcome," Nick said. "It was the least I could do after all you've done for me."

But then, once she'd served herself, Anna picked up the magazine, opened it, and started reading.

Nick took a few bites of food, sneaking a peek at Anna every few seconds. She sat there calmly reading her magazine and eating her dinner, as if he weren't there.

"How was your day?" he finally asked.

"Fine," she said, giving him a smile, then returning to her magazine.

"So is this how it's going to be?" Nick asked. "You giving me the silent treatment until I leave?"

Anna looked up from her magazine.

"I'm not giving you the silent treatment, and I'm not mad. I just think it's best if we don't pretend. I appreciate the dinner, and I appreciate you cleaning the place, but nothing's changed. I'm not right for you, Nick, it's as simple as that. And I love you too much to want to give you any false hope that I'm going to change my mind about you moving out."

Anna resumed reading. Nick sat there a minute, fuming. That was a great little line she had. No matter what Anna did, he was supposed to be okay with it. Whatever she did, she did it because she loved him. He wished he'd thought of it. The next time some woman screamed at him for something he'd done, that's what he'd say. I did it because I love you.

Nick scooted back his chair, stood up, and left again. He went to the same bar, found a new group of guys, and stayed out until three.

For the next two days, Nick was gone when Anna got home. He stayed out late, slept late on the couch, and whenever he happened to get up, he wandered on down to the pool. He slept with Tina both days and hated himself for it.

On the fourth day after Anna asked him to leave, Nick woke up and realized he only had three days left to find a place to stay. And then he realized he didn't *have* a place to go and stay. Most of his so-called buddies were married. And the few who weren't who might have had the room might say yes, but they wouldn't want to. And after a few days, a week at the most, he'd start getting on their nerves. They'd want him out of there. Start dropping little hints. Bitch about him at work, talk about how annoying he was to live with.

Nick had a horrible insight sitting there on the couch. He didn't have any friends. Not real friends. Not the kind of friends you went to when you were down on your luck and needed a break. Someone who'd say don't even think twice about it. I've got a spare room. Stay as long as you need it. And mean it.

And then Nick had an even more awful realization. He did have a friend. He'd had a friend. Anna. Anna had been his friend. Anna had said exactly that, stay as long as you like. He hadn't even had to ask. She'd asked him to move in. "I want to do this," she'd said. "I'm happy to have you here."

Anna. Why was it only now, when she didn't want him around anymore, that he realized how much he wanted her? Now that it didn't do him any good?

Anna went to work each day, did the best job she could, then came home and took care of herself. She didn't wonder where Nick was or what he was doing. She just hoped that he was safe, and taking care of himself, too.

She made sure she ate well, bought a book on yoga and started doing stretches when she got up in the morning, wrote in her journal faithfully every day, took long baths, and got to bed early each night.

She had lunch with Joan, who listened in amazement when Anna told her that she'd never loved Nick more than she did at that very moment.

On the fifth day after Anna asked him to move out, Nick went to a temporary employment agency, found a position as a temporary accountant for a restaurant chain, and rented a cheap motel room. When Anna got home that night, all his stuff was gone.

Anna poured herself a glass of wine, drew a bath, and sat in the tub sipping her wine and having a good cry. When she went to bed that night, just before she turned off her light and went to sleep, Anna wished Nick a great life and all the best the world had to offer.

I watched Anna drift off to sleep, and then I looked at Herb.

"You getting anything yet from watching the two of them?" I asked.

"Not really. You?"

"Nope."

Herb and I kept watching Nick and Anna day and night, the way Herb had ordered us to.

Anna met a great guy. A *great* guy. And he was interested. They started out as friends, and then one day he asked her if they could take their relationship to another level.

"Oh, Scott," she said with regret, "you're such a great guy."

Scott frowned. Why did they always tell you what a great guy you were right before they told you they weren't interested?

"But I'm in love with someone else," Anna told him.

"Oh," Scott said. "I didn't know you were seeing anyone. You've never mentioned him."

"I'm not seeing him. I'll probably never see him again. And I shouldn't. I'm not right for him. But I still love him."

Scott said maybe they could take it slow, see what developed over time. But Anna turned him down.

"It just wouldn't be fair," she said.

If I hadn't been ordered not to, I'd have shot a "pretty good" love arrow at Anna right there and then. She could have had a great transitional relationship with Scott. But I had my orders.

"I still don't get it," Herb said.

"Me either," I replied.

We kept watching.

Nick worked steadily at his temporary job, and they offered him a permanent position. Nowhere near the salary he'd earned before, and none of the perks he'd been accustomed to, but Nick wasn't complaining. He was happy to have a job.

Nick found a studio apartment he could afford and moved in. He still needed the rent money coming in from his condo. He sold his Lexus and bought a used Toyota Camry. He couldn't swing his gym membership anymore, and his apartment complex didn't have a pool, so he started running in the mornings. He had to give up cable—his credit card payments were killing him, and every penny counted—so he missed all his favorite sports shows. But he didn't have much free time to watch TV.

One day he ran into Matt Robbins, one of his old pals, at the video store, and they got to talking. It turned out Matt had felt so bad for Nick that he'd been afraid to call. He didn't know what to say and didn't have the heart to tell him there weren't any openings at his company in Nick's field.

"Sorry, buddy," Matt said. "I should have kept in touch more. Hey, let me call Jeannine and tell her I'm bringing you home for dinner."

Nick turned him down. He didn't feel like being around a family that night. But he and Matt got together later in the week with some of their other buddies to play poker. One of them still worked at Nick's old company, and he took Nick aside at one point to tell him that Mark had taken the money. Nick didn't feel much of anything on hearing that. It seemed like a lifetime ago.

And every day Nick missed Anna. And every day he knew it would be pointless to call her.

"I'm still confused," Herb told me after a month had gone by. "I don't see what it is the front office thinks we're supposed to be learning by watching the two of them."

"Me either," I said.

"She loves him and he feels something for her. I'm not sure it's love."

"It isn't. Not quite."

"But he misses her. Only it wouldn't work out, so they can't be together. It's not like I haven't seen this before."

"I've seen it a million times."

"Hey," Herb said, "maybe it's about survival. You know. How they keep on going even when it's hard for them? Maybe that's what we're supposed to learn."

I thought about it for a minute. It didn't feel right.

"No," I said with conviction, "that's not it."

We kept watching. More weeks went by, and it was all pretty much the same. Except Anna and Scott didn't have lunch together anymore.

And then one day Nick went into a sandwich shop to get a chicken salad sandwich and a cup of soup. And who should he see sitting there but the not-particularly-promising girl.

"Oh, boy," I told Herb. "This should be interesting."

"You're not kidding," Herb agreed. During our many te-dious hours of watching Nick and Anna, I'd filled him in about the not-particularly-promising girl.

Nick's first response was to get the hell out of there before she saw him. She was reading a book and hadn't noticed him yet.

But Nick looked at her again. He'd thought he'd want to kill her if he ever saw her again. If it hadn't been for her, he might not have lost his job. But he didn't feel angry seeing her sitting there; he felt guilty. And a little sad. Sad for her *and* him. And he suddenly got this impulse. No. It was crazy. What was he thinking? She'd probably go berserk if she saw him, let alone if he tried talking to her.

He turned to walk out of the sandwich shop, but he saw Anna's face in his mind, and the impulse grew stronger. Sud-denly, it was something he had to do. Not for Anna exactly, but because of her.

As Herb and I watched, Nick walked over to the not-par-ticularly-promising girl and stopped in front of her table. She was engrossed in her book and didn't notice him.

"Hi," he said hesitantly.

The not-particularly-promising girl glanced up from her book. She looked startled, and then embarrassed.

"Hi," she said, blushing.

"Could I sit down with you for a minute?" Nick asked.

The not-particularly-promising girl shook her head.

"Look, I'm sorry about what I did," she said, stumbling

over her words a little. "But if you've come here to yell at me, I really don't think I could take it today. I'm in therapy, thanks to you. No, that's wrong. I can't blame you for my problems—that's one of the things I'm learning. But I just had a bad session, and I'm hanging on by a thread here, and I'm sorry and all that, but I couldn't take getting yelled at right now. I really couldn't."

"I don't want to yell at you. I want to apologize."

Nick sat down at the table. The not-particularly-promising girl looked at him warily.

"I mean it. I'm sorry for the way I treated you."

"You mean like I didn't exist?" she asked. "Like I didn't have any feelings?"

"Yes."

"Do you even know what that's like? To be treated like you don't actually exist?"

Nick nodded. "I didn't before, but when I lost my job, that's how they treated me. As if I didn't really exist."

The not-particularly-promising girl looked down at the table. "I'm sorry about that. And the car, too. I thought it would feel great, but it didn't. It felt crappy."

"Yeah," Nick said, smiling. "It felt pretty crappy to me, too."

The not-particularly-promising girl looked up at him.

"You're not mad? You don't hate me?"

"I was. But I probably had it coming. You weren't the first woman I used. I'm probably lucky one of them didn't kill me. And you weren't the only reason I got fired."

"I hated you, you know," she said.

"Yeah. I guess you would."

"But I don't hate you anymore. I don't know if you even care, but you turned out to be exactly what I needed. The day that detective came to question me? God, I was so embarrassed and so humiliated. He was actually really nice to me, considering. He didn't just act like a cop; he acted like a person. Told me I was ruining my life. That I needed to get some help. And I saw myself through his eyes, what he must have thought of me, how I must have looked to him, and I wanted to die. I might have ended up doing something really horrible if he hadn't talked some sense into me and I'd kept on the way I was."

"I'm glad."

She looked at him.

"Glad you're feeling better, I mean. God, I don't know what I mean. I'm an idiot."

"I know what you meant. Can I ask you something?"

"Sure."

"The only reason I'm asking is so that you'll maybe understand just a little bit why I did what I did. I'm not trying to excuse it, but maybe explain it a little. I'd convinced myself I was in love with you. How pathetic is that? Some guy I'd met at a bar, and I thought I was in love. I wasn't, obviously—I just needed someone. Anyone. What a mess I was. Not like I've got it all together now, but I'm working on it.

"But do you know what it's like to really want someone? And to know you can never have them? To feel like you've been sliced right down the middle and you're never going to feel like a real person again?"

She looked back down at the table. "You probably don't. Someone like you, how would you know?"

"That's not true," Nick said quietly.

Me and Herb and the not-particularly-promising girl all watched with various degrees of shock as tears began streaming down Nick's face. I was the most shocked of all, I'm sure, because I'd just felt Nick's heart break.

"I think I get it now," I told Herb.

"Yeah," Herb replied. "I think I get it, too."

But before we could say anything else, or confirm that we'd both learned the same lesson, we heard that unmistakable sound again.

We'd been summoned back to the front office.

twenty-eight

"Okay, you two knuckleheads," Barney said as Herb and I stood before him in the front office. "What is it you think you've learned?"

"It's all about love," I said.

"Yep," Herb agreed, "it's all about love."

"Go on," Barney ordered. "You first, Herb."

"Well, Anna had all this crap happen to her because of Nick, but she didn't complain about it. She was happy just to love him, even if that meant dealing with a lot of crap. Love was the important thing. Like it was greater than the crap."

"What about Nick?"

"He didn't love her, or anybody else, for that matter. And he never stopped complaining."

"So what does that tell you?" Barney asked Herb.

"That human beings will endure a lot of crap for the sake of love?"

"And?"

"And, uh, since they really, really hate having crap happen to them, that love is more powerful than crap? And that maybe I should be a little more patient about all their whining, because most of them haven't learned how to really love yet and that makes it hard to deal with all the crap?"

"Good enough. What about you?" Barney asked, looking in my direction.

"Love changed them. Nick and Anna."

"Changed them how?"

"Well, Anna found out she could be bigger than herself. That she could transcend herself."

"Because?"

"Because of the power of love?"

"Correct. And Nick?"

"Nick was able to tell someone he was sorry for how he treated her. Before Anna, Nick not only wouldn't have been able to do that, he wouldn't have been able to even admit he'd treated someone badly."

"And?" Barney prodded.

"And he cried. Nick hasn't cried since he was five years old."

"And he cried because?" Barney urged.

"Because he loves Anna. Not in the same way she loves him, but he loves her at the level he's capable of loving someone, which is a lot higher than it used to be. He cried the tears he never let himself cry when he lost Lauren. And he cried because he saw how badly the not-particularly-promising girl must have felt when he treated her that way. Nick has never been able to put himself in someone else's shoes, let alone have an idea what they're feeling."

"And what was your opinion of Nick only a few short months ago?"

"That he was pretty hopeless."

"Could you have even imagined him doing what he did just now?"

"No," I admitted.

"And what does that mean to you?"

"Kind of what Herb said about how powerful love can be. And maybe I should be more patient, because deep down inside, the people of Planet Thirty-Seven want to love. They're just not very good at it yet. But they could be better at it than they realize. And when they do get better at it, everything will change, because they'll change.

"Good," Barney said, sounding pleased.

"But . . ." I hesitated. The next part was a little tricky, and I wasn't sure I could even put it into words.

"Yes, Cupid?"

"There's kind of a paradox."

"Isn't there always when it comes to Planet Thirty-Seven?"

"It's . . . well, you know I have the power to read human hearts."

"We know," Herb and Barney said, rolling their eyes. I wasn't bragging. I simply felt it had an important bearing on what I was about to say next.

"Anyway," I went on, ignoring their expressions, "when I was reading Anna's heart as she said good-bye to Nick, there wasn't any anger or bitterness. Just some sadness. But the love hadn't died. The kind of love she had didn't depend on anyone outside herself. No one, not even Nick, could take it away from her. The very thing she'd been afraid of—losing her heart completely—was the very thing that set her free."

"We call that the great paradox of unconditional love. Excellent work, Cupid. You've learned well."

"But I'm still confused about one thing. I've watched Anna for a long time. And her capacity for love wasn't bad. She had a good heart. But it wasn't exceptional. And I know my arrows are powerful, but at some point it's the people themselves who do the work. So I don't understand how all of a sudden Anna learned how to love for love's sake."

"I know you think you understand everything that goes on in a human heart, Cupid, but it just isn't so. The human heart is as infinite with possibilities as the universe is. And as mysterious. I'd have thought you'd have learned that by now."

"Sorry, sir," I said, shamefaced.

"For reasons you don't need to concern yourself with, that arrow you sent Anna wasn't an arrow of true love. It was an arrow of something even more powerful: pure love. It was only a taste, because that's all any of them can handle at this stage in their development. But just a taste of it changed her completely."

"You mean you did it?" I asked, flabbergasted and a little upset, considering what I'd put myself through these last months trying to fix the situation.

"No, Cupid, you did it. However, we knew it was only a matter of time before you cracked. So that arrow was placed in your bag of tricks knowing you'd use it sooner or later."

"So it could have been anyone who got that arrow?" I asked, feeling completely confused now. "The fact that it happened to Anna was just random chance?"

"There's no such thing as random chance, you idiot," Herb hissed under his breath, giving me a nudge. "You're gonna get us in trouble all over again."

"I can hear you, Herb," Barney said impatiently. "Anna was where she needed to be, Nick was where he needed to be, Herb was where he needed to be, and you were where you needed to be. And everyone learned what they needed to learn."

"I know I learned a lot," Herb said, like you weren't ever going to hear another bad word out of *him* about Planet Thirty-Seven, no, sir. "You guys here in the front office sure know what you're doing." He's such an ass kisser.

"Now I want to give you both a little refresher course," Barney said. "You aren't the first spirits I've had to call up here because you've forgotten what it's all about. Believe it or not, the front office understands the toll it takes on you dealing with human beings day after day. Even I get fed up at times. I love the little bastards, but sometimes I could just . . ."

Barney didn't have to finish the thought. I knew exactly how he felt.

"However, you must try and remember what this whole enterprise is about. When we say the universe is infinite, we don't mean it's really big. This isn't Texas we're talking about. We mean it has infinite love and infinite possibilities. I know a hell of a lot more than you two, but even all I know is just a drop in the ocean.

"And all these little dramas you deal with, all these human stories, no matter how pointless or frustrating or heartbreaking they appear, have a purpose to them.

"The universe does know what it's doing, it will all work out in the end, and your job is just to keep doing your job. And never forget that those human beings down there have a heavy burden. If you don't see them through eyes of compassion, then you're not seeing them at all. Got it?"

"Got it," Herb and I answered in unison.

"Now get out of here, you dopes, and get back on down there and see how this one little story turns out. Dismissed."

"Yes, sir," we replied, and flew out of there as fast as we could go.

And when we returned to Planet Thirty-Seven, we found Nick knocking on Anna's door.

Anna pushed her remote to turn off *Sports Buzz* (she still didn't watch the actual games, but these guys could be kind of entertaining), stood up from the couch, and walked to her front door, wondering who'd be coming by at this hour.

Anna peered out through her peephole. She saw Nick standing there, looking nervous. Anna felt her heart leap, then she got hold of herself. No matter how much she missed him, wanted him, loved him, she couldn't take Nick back. Not if she really loved him. She didn't want him settling just because he was lonely or feeling desperate.

And besides, in all likelihood Nick wasn't there to ask her back. He'd probably left something behind (she hadn't found anything of his when he'd left, but she might have missed something). Or maybe he needed some money. Maybe he still hadn't been able to find a job. Anna wasn't sure what her response would be to that. She didn't mind lending him some money if he needed it. That wasn't the issue. But she didn't want to do it for the wrong reasons.

I guess the best thing I can do, she thought, is listen to what he has to say first.

Anna opened the door. God, he looked good. Was he doing something different with his hair?

"Hello, Nick," she said.

"Hello, Anna," Nick said. God. She took his breath away. How had he never seen that she was the most beautiful woman in the world?

"Would it be okay if I came in?" Nick asked.

"Sure," Anna said.

Nick walked into Anna's apartment. Looking around, he couldn't believe he'd spent most of his time here lying on the couch watching TV. All that time he'd wasted, time he could have spent being with Anna. He was the biggest idiot that had ever lived.

"Have a seat," Anna told him.

Nick sat down on one end of the couch; Anna sat down on the other. She felt her heart beating rapidly, wondering what he was going to say. She'd stick to her resolve, but that didn't mean it wasn't hard having him this close, knowing she couldn't touch him.

Nick got off to a slow start, but he told her everything. The kind of guy he'd been when she'd first met him. Even admitted how he'd told that stupid football story to every single woman he'd dated, knowing how it had affected them.

He told her about Lauren, and how he had never let himself feel how hurt he'd been when she'd left him for someone else.

He told her about the not-particularly-promising girl. How he'd slept with her knowing full well he'd had no intention of seeing her again but that he'd said whatever she'd wanted to hear in order to get her into bed. And that, on some level, he'd known she'd been one of the walking wounded and he'd used that to his advantage.

He told Anna he hadn't looked for a job the entire time he'd lived with her.

And he told her about Tina.

Anna listened without interrupting him. He couldn't read the expression on her face.

He went on. He told her about running into the not-particularly-promising girl that afternoon. How at first his only thought had been to get the hell away from her. But that he'd forced himself to go over and apologize. He repeated their conversation almost word for word, since he'd actually paid attention to what the not-particularly-promising girl had said.

He told Anna that he'd cried when he'd realized he'd completely blown it with the one person he loved most in the world, but hadn't realized he loved her until it was too late. And how the not-particularly-promising girl had given him a Kleenex out of her purse and he'd ended up telling her all about Anna.

He told her that when they'd left the sandwich shop he'd told the not-particularly-promising girl again how sorry he was, and that if she ever needed someone to talk to, she could give him a call.

She'd smiled and told him no. "Let's not ruin a perfect ending," she'd said.

"And the reason I'm telling you all this, Anna," Nick said, finishing up what he had come to say, "is that when I first turned to leave the sandwich shop today, I saw something. You. Your face. And that's what made me turn around and go back inside to apologize. That's what gave me the strength to face her. And you. To come here tonight and tell you every stupid, shitty thing about myself. You were so right about everything, except one. And about that you were completely wrong. You don't keep me small, Anna, you make me big."

Nick was done. Anna sat perfectly still. Nick gave her a minute, and then he couldn't stand it.

"Aren't you going to say anything?" he asked, filled with dread and hope, knowing that whatever she said next would change the course of his life.

"I guess there's only one thing *to* say," Anna replied.

Nick literally stopped breathing.

"Do you want to catch the end of *Sports Buzz*?"

And then Anna Munson kissed Nick Wells with all her heart and soul, and for the first time in his life, Nick Wells did the same.

Herb and I smiled at each other. It had been a long time since we'd smiled. We kind of hated to leave. But you know what you humans are like—sex, sex, sex—and we made our exit.

Nick and Anna married, had children, grew old together, and moved to Des Moines after they retired to be near the grandkids. Their oldest son had been transferred there with his ozone layer repair company. (Fixing the ozone layer ended up costing you all *trillions,* by the way. The whole planet had to chip in. I won't even mention how much you had to spend on the simulated rain forests.)

None of the details about Nick and Anna's life together was out of the ordinary. But they were kind to animals, raised their children with the right mixture of love, discipline, and mutual respect, tipped well at restaurants, avoided gossip, never went to bed angry, always said hello to their neighbors, told each other, "I love you," every day, took turns holding the remote, and never used other people for their own gain. They were absolutely devoted to one another, and everyone who knew them envied their relationship.

In other words, they lived happily ever after.

epilogue

a note regarding publication of this book.

Normally the front office has a very strict policy about any of us revealing ourselves to you. In the early days they sometimes resorted to a burning bush or a voice booming out of the clouds or something of that nature, but the prevailing wisdom these days is that you're far enough along now not to need any more personal visitations or concrete evidence of our existence. At some point, you gotta take it on faith.

But shortly after Nick and Anna reunited, I was summoned once again to the front office. Wondering what I'd done wrong this time—it apparently never occurs to management that a little praise once every century or so might improve a spirit's morale—I reported immediately and found Barney waiting to see me.

"Cupid," Barney said, "in order to help humanity better understand the nature of love, and for other reasons that I can't go into, Harold has ordered me to order *you* to write the story of Nick and Anna and get it published."

"Published?"

"Yes."

"You mean on Planet Thirty-Seven?"

"That's exactly what I mean."

"But I thought we weren't supposed to contact them directly."

"Are you questioning my orders, Cupid?"

"No, sir. It just took me by surprise."

"It took me by surprise, too, but Harold figures that no one will believe you wrote it anyway. You know how those people are once they grow up. They think that since they buy their own presents, Santa Claus doesn't exist. You're just some cute little cherub on a Valentine's Day card as far as they're concerned."

"Who *will* they think wrote it?"

"We've got that covered. Human beings think they're the smartest creatures in all the universe and love to give themselves credit for everything. One of these days they'll probably convince themselves they invented gravity."

Barney paused while I chuckled. When he wasn't busy being such a know-it-all, sometimes Barney could be a funny guy.

"Once you're done with the book," Barney continued, "we'll get some human writer to think they thought up the story all on their own."

"Oh. You mean like we did with that Shakespeare guy?"

"Exactly."

"But didn't it take something like five or six lifetimes to get his ego humbled back down to normal size?"

"I hardly think your little book is going to be on the same level as *Hamlet*. Now quit asking me so many questions and go write the damn thing."

Writing the damn thing wasn't as easy as I thought it would be. It gave me a whole new respect for authors, and I began to understand why they're so temperamental. You should have heard me the day Herb barged in just when I'd figured out how to end chapter five.

But after a lot of sweat and toil, I got the book finished and took it up to Barney.

He made some suggestions and some revisions, and I did the rewrites. Then he made another set of revisions and suggestions—everyone's a critic—and we went through this many more times than I care to remember. To be an artist is to suffer. But finally Barney said it was ready for publication.

I didn't have to worry about getting an agent the way most first-time authors do. Barney handled everything. But after he got it sold to a publisher—I don't know how, and I knew better than to ask—and we went through *more* suggestions and revisions, my editor thought it might be nice to end the book with some handy tips from Cupid. She thought it would be cute. Cute? I'm not cute! Why do people persist in believing that I'm cute?

And she thought it would be clever to start off the suggestions with a note from Cupid, as if he'd actually written the book. And then, on top of that, write it as if Cupid came out and revealed that the human author was a fraud, knowing that no one would believe it anyway.

It was bad enough that someone else would get all the credit for my creation, a creation born of blood, sweat, and tears. But to have my work tampered with like this! As an artist, I was outraged.

"Barney, this editor is a Philistine!" I shouted when he told me the news. "She's ruining my work! She understands nothing! The reader knows that Cupid doesn't really exist, and yet she lets herself believe. That suspension of disbelief is what makes the story work! And then, at the end, to take away the fictional identity of Cupid? To reveal that all of this actually happened?"

"It did actually happen."

"You make it sound as if all I did was simply write down everything as it actually occurred. If it were that easy, any poor slob could be a writer! I shaped the material. I took a mass of details and made critical decisions as to what to keep in and what to leave out. I made those boring, ordinary characters come alive. I took their hours and hours of tedious conversations and thoughts and made them interesting. I took that whole gigantic mess and turned it into a compelling story.

"And what you're asking me to do ruins the integrity of the story, to say nothing of my integrity as an artist! I simply can't go along with it! And I won't! I refuse!"

Suddenly, it grew very quiet in the front office.

"What did you just say?" Barney asked, ominously.

"What I meant, sir," I stammered, "and I'm very sorry for shouting, I don't know what got into me. But what I meant was that, um . . . I guess for reasons that I don't need to know and probably wouldn't understand anyway—a lowly mid-level spirit such as myself—you want me to add on that last chapter, don't you?"

"That would be correct," Barney said, and I got out of there while I was still in one piece. I did as I was told, even though the front office was obviously nothing more than a bunch of bean-counting, paper-pushing bureaucrats who knew nothing about literature.

So here it is—for all the good they'll do: my list of tips and suggestions regarding love, transmitted through the mind of the human author.

CUPID'S HANDY TIPS
AND SUGGESTIONS REGARDING LOVE

1. Be careful what you ask for. If you ask for true love, be very sure that's what you really want. Take a careful look at yourself, evaluate your strengths and weaknesses, and ask yourself if it might not be better to ask for pretty good love. Or simple companionship.

2. If you honestly think you're ready for true love, ask yourself the following questions:
   a. If my true love developed a hideously disfiguring disease for which there was no known cure, would I

still want to stay with him (or her) for the rest of my life?

b. If my true love became incapacitated in some way, wasn't able to work for some reason, and I had to take care of her (or him) for the rest of her (or his) life, would I want to stay with her (or him) for the rest of *my* life?

c. Do I see true love as the opportunity to be truly loved or the opportunity to truly love someone else?

d. List the qualities that you think true love consists of, such as patience, endurance, generosity, sensitivity, etc. And then try to determine, as honestly as you can, if you actually possess any of these qualities yourself.

e. Ask yourself, Am I really far enough along in my development to be able to find my best self by forgetting myself? Or does the mere thought of that fill me with terror and dread?

3. If you know you're not ready for true love but think you could use some advice about love in general, I have the following suggestions:

a. Don't get too caught up in bodies. The best of them will, one day, if the person is lucky enough to live that long, become (and there's no nice way to put this) pretty hideous. Bodies wear out, run down, make funny noises, and they're disposable.

b. Be friends first.

c. Learn new stuff. No matter how interesting you are now, in fifty years the same you would be pretty dull to come home to.

d. Girls: Save yourself a lot of aggravation and buy your own razors, don't make him go shopping with you, and understand that feelings that are talked to death can eventually die. And if he doesn't talk about his feelings much when you're dating, he's not going to suddenly start when you get married.

e. Guys: Save yourself a lot of aggravation and remember to put down the toilet seat, buy some extra razor blades, don't drink the milk or orange juice out of the carton, and understand that feelings that are never talked about can eventually die. And if she asks you a lot of questions about your feelings when you're dating, she's not going to suddenly stop when you get married.

4. And, finally, remember that love comes in many varieties. It's the very foundation of the universe. And it doesn't necessarily have to come with kisses.

Maybe you haven't found it because you aren't ready yet. Start small and work from there. Get a goldfish. Love that goldfish for the way it keeps swimming around the bowl like it's going to find a way out if it keeps looking hard enough.

Love the sky at dawn, the sound of the ocean, the smell of freshly cut grass, the way aspen leaves shimmer when the wind blows. Love your friends, your relatives (I know, I know, but no one said this was going to be easy), your cat or dog.

Find work you love. A hobby you love. A painting or a piece of music you love. Learn to love knowledge for its own sake. Learn to bake bread. Plant a garden and love the first little shoots that make their way out of the soil. Love life.

And when all that fails—when it's two in the morning, and you're by yourself, and you can't sleep, and you hear the couple that lives next door come home from wherever they've been—and you feel all alone in the world, try to remember this: You're not. *We* love you. We must. We wouldn't have put up with all your crap for these many long and painful centuries unless we did.

up close and personal
with the author

THE PREMISE OF *I'M WITH CUPID* IS THAT IT'S ACTUALLY WRITTEN BY CUPID HIMSELF, AND THAT HE'S FED UP WITH ALL THE MISTAKES PEOPLE MAKE IN THEIR ROMANTIC RELATIONSHIPS. HOW DID YOU COME UP WITH THAT IDEA?

It was really strange. I had no intention of writing the book in Cupid's voice. In fact, I had a completely different idea of what this book was going to be about. And then one day, it was like I just had this inspiration out of the blue.

WAS IT HARDER TO WRITE THIS BOOK THAN YOUR FIRST NOVEL, *DRESS YOU UP IN MY LOVE*?

That was strange, too. It took me four years to finish *Dress You Up in My Love*. I made a lot of mistakes and learned as I went along. And I had less free time than I do now. I thought doing the second book was going to be easier. But since I'd spent so much time with my original characters, it was hard to let go of them. I made a lot of false starts trying to get the second book going, and felt blocked. Once I found the voice of Cupid though, it was almost like he took over the writing and it just flowed. I've heard other writers talk about that, how a character will seem to be talking through you, but I'd never experienced it the way I did with this book.

NOT EVEN WITH SAMANTHA STONE FROM *DRESS YOU UP IN MY LOVE*?

With *Dress You Up in My Love* I felt as if Samantha and I got to know each other as the writing progressed. I kept finding new layers. This time it seemed as if Cupid came fully formed and all I really had to do was let him guide my fingers over the keyboard.

IS THAT WHERE YOU GOT THE IDEA TO REVEAL AT THE END OF THE BOOK THAT CUPID WAS THE REAL WRITER BEHIND YOUR STORY?

I kind of threw that in at the last minute thinking it would make a nice twist. I didn't have any intention of including it. In fact, I thought the book was done. And then the night I was getting ready to print out the final version, I got the idea out of the blue and decided to throw it in.

SO YOU DREW ON YOUR OWN PERSONAL EXPERIENCE YOU HAD WRITING THE BOOK AND ACTUALLY TURNED IT INTO A PLOT TWIST?

Exactly. I mean, it's not as if Cupid actually exists. (Author chuckles.)

OF COURSE, THAT'S WHAT HE SAYS IN THE BOOK. THAT IT'S OKAY TO ADMIT HE'S THE REAL WRITER BECAUSE NO ONE WILL BELIEVE IT ANYWAY.

He doesn't say it. I do. I came up with all of this.

ACTUALLY, NOW THAT I REMEMBER IT, CUPID DOESN'T WANT TO WRITE THOSE TIPS TO FINDING TRUE LOVE. WASN'T THAT YOUR EDITOR'S IDEA?

No! That was another twist I threw in! I made it all up! I wrote those tips on true love. Me! From my imagination. That's what writers do! It was like a little inside joke because writers are always complaining about how their editors end up ruining their work.

YOU THINK YOUR EDITOR RUINS YOUR WORK?

No. Not me! I love my editor! Really. We have a great relationship! When I showed her my original draft, she helped me see that

Cupid's voice was a little too overpowering in the first few chapters, and once I rewrote them I saw how right she was.

ALTHOUGH THAT WOULD BE FAIRLY COMMON FOR A FIRST-TIME WRITER, WOULDN'T IT? TO HAVE THEIR OWN VOICE DETRACT FROM THE STORY?

This is my *second* novel. My first one, *Dress You Up in My Love*, received some very nice reviews. And all my friends said they really liked it.

RIGHT. IT'S GOOD YOUR EDITOR CAUGHT THAT, THEN. HOW DID YOU GET THE IDEA TO MAKE IT SEEM AS THOUGH TIPS FROM CUPID WERE HER SUGGESTION?

Writers don't always know where they get their ideas.

THAT REMINDS ME OF A BIT YOU HAVE IN THE BOOK ABOUT HOW SHAKESPEARE DIDN'T REALLY WRITE ALL HIS OWN PLAYS. SOME HISTORIANS AND LITERARY EXPERTS HAVE WONDERED THE SAME THING. HOW ONE SEEMINGLY ORDINARY MAN COULD PRODUCE SO MANY WORKS OF GENIUS.

That's where I got the joke from.

REMEMBER THAT PART IN THE BOOK WHERE CUPID'S BOSS REMINDS CUPID HOW HARD IT IS TO BE HUMAN BECAUSE UNLIKE HIM, WE DON'T *KNOW* THERE'S LIFE AFTER DEATH?

Yeah. I mean, I wrote it. I think I would remember it.

WOULDN'T IT BE GREAT IF CUPID REALLY DID WRITE THE BOOK? AS A WAY OF LETTING HUMANITY KNOW THAT THERE REALLY IS A PLAN AND PURPOSE FOR EVERYTHING? AND THAT WE DO HAVE THE ABILITY TO LOVE UNCONDITIONALLY IF ONLY—

Those were fictional characters! I wrote the book! There is no Cupid! There is no Cupid's boss!

OF COURSE THEY WERE. HOW WERE YOU ABLE TO WRITE ABOUT ANNA'S EXPERIENCE OF TRUE LOVE? FROM PERSONAL EXPERIENCE?

Well . . . I mean, it's an *ideal*. Part of the humor of the book comes from realizing how much we all fall short in our relationships.

I SEE.

And it's also a continuation of what Samantha Stone learned in *Dress You Up in My Love*. That just because she and Greg weren't going to be together didn't mean she had to stop loving him. That you can choose to keep loving someone even when they let you down.

WHATEVER YOU SAY.

That's something I learned from an experience I had when—

I'M SORRY. WE'RE OUT OF TIME.

And part of it comes from a more spiritual idea of what love means. For example, if you read—

THANK YOU, DIANE. IT'S BEEN A PLEASURE TALKING TO YOU.

Be the Next Downtown Girl
Contest Rules

NO PURCHASE NECESSARY TO ENTER.

1) ENTRY REQUIREMENTS:

Register to enter the contest on www.simonsaysthespot.com. Enter by submitting your story as specified below.

2) CONTEST ELIGIBILITY:

This contest is open to nonprofessional writers who are legal residents of the United States and Canada (excluding Quebec) over the age of 18 as of December 7, 2004. Entrant must not have published any more than two short stories on a professional basis or in paid professional venues. Employees (or relatives of employees living in the same household) of Simon & Schuster, VIACOM, or any of their affiliates are not eligible. This contest is void in Puerto Rico, Quebec, and wherever prohibited or restricted by law.

3) FORMAT:

Entries must not be more than 7,500 words long and must not have been previously published. Entries must be typed or printed by word processor, double spaced, on one side of noncorrasable paper. Do not justify right-side margins. Along with a cover letter, the author's name, address, email address, and phone number must appear on the first page of the entry. The author's name, the story title, and the page number should appear on every page. Electronic submissions will be accepted and must be sent to downtowngirl@simonandschuster.com. All electronic submissions must be sent as an attachment in a Microsoft Word document. All entries must be original and the sole work of the Entrant and the sole property of the Entrant.

All submissions must be in English. Entries are void if they are in whole or in part illegible, incomplete, or damaged or if they do not conform to any of the requirements specified herein. Sponsor reserves the right, in its absolute and sole discretion, to reject any entries for any reason, including but not limited to based on sexual content, vulgarity, and/or promotion of violence.

4) ADDRESS:

Entries submitted by mail must be postmarked by July 31, 2005 and sent to:

Be The Next Downtown Girl
Author Search

Downtown Press Editorial Department
Pocket Books
1230 Sixth Avenue, 13th floor
New York, NY 10020

Or Emailed By July 31, 2005
at 11:59 PM EST as a
Microsoft Word document to:

downtowngirl@simonandschuster.com

Each entry may be submitted only once. Please retain a copy of your submission. You may submit more than one story, but each submission must be mailed or emailed, as applicable, separately. Entries must be received by July 31, 2005. Not responsible for lost, late, stolen, illegible, mutilated, postage due, garbled, or misdirected mail/entries.

5) PRIZES:

One Grand Prize winner will receive:

Simon & Schuster's Downtown Press Publishing Contract for Publication of Winning Entry in a future Downtown Press Anthology, Five Hundred U.S. Dollars ($500.00), and

Downtown Press Library
(20 books valued at $260.00)

Grand Prize winner must sign the Publishing contract which contains additional terms and conditions in order to be published in the anthology.

Ten Second Prize winners will receive:

A Downtown Press Collection
(10 books valued at $130.00)

No contestant can win more than one prize.

6) STORY THEME

We are not restricting stories to any specific topic, however they should embody what all of our Downtown Press authors encompass—they should be smart, savvy, sexy stories that any Downtown Girl can relate to. We all know what uptown girls are like, but girls of the new millennium prefer the Downtown Scene. That's where it happens. The music, the shopping, the sex, the dating, the heartbreak, the family squabbles, the marriage, and the divorce. You name it. Downtown Girls have done it. Twice. We encourage you to register for the contest at www.simonsaysthespot.com in order to receive our monthly emails and updates from our authors and read about our titles on www.downtownpress.com to give you a better idea of what types of books we publish.

7) JUDGING:

Submissions will be judged on the equally weighted criteria of (a) basis of writing ability and (b) the originality of the story (which can be set in any time frame or location). Judging will take place on or about October 1, 2005. The judges will include a freelance editor, the editor of the future Anthology, and 5 employees of Sponsor. The decisions of the judges shall be final.

8) NOTIFICATION:

The winners will be notified by mail or phone on or about October 1, 2005. The Grand Prize Winner must sign the publishing contract in order to be awarded the prize. All federal, local, and state taxes are the responsibility of the winner. A list of the winners will be available after October 20, 2005 on:

http://www.downtownpress.com

http://www.simonsaysthespot.com

The winners' list can also be obtained by sending a stamped self-addressed envelope to:

Be The Next Downtown Girl
Author Search
Downtown Press Editorial Department
Pocket Books
1230 Sixth Avenue, 13th floor
New York, NY 10020

9) PUBLICITY:

Each Winner grants to Sponsor the right to use his or her name, likeness, and entry for any advertising, promotion, and publicity purposes without further compensation to or permission from such winner, except where prohibited by law.

10) INTERNET:

If for any reason this Contest is not capable of running as planned due to an infection by a computer virus, bugs, tampering, unauthorized intervention, fraud, technical failures, or any other causes beyond the control of the Sponsor which corrupt or affect the administration, security, fairness, integrity, or proper conduct of this Contest, the Sponsor reserves the right in its sole discretion, to disqualify any individual who tampers with the entry process; and to cancel, terminate, modify, or suspend the Contest. The Sponsor assumes no responsibility for any error, omission, interruption, deletion, defect, delay in operation or transmission, communications line failure, theft or destruction or unauthorized access to, or alteration of, entries. The Sponsor is not responsible for any problems or technical malfunctions of any telephone network or telephone lines, computer on-line systems, servers, or providers, computer equipment, software, failure of any email or entry to be received by the Sponsor due to technical problems, human error or traffic congestion on the Internet or at any website, or any combination thereof, including any injury or damage to participant's or any other person's computer relating to or resulting from participating in this Contest or downloading any materials in this Contest. CAUTION: ANY ATTEMPT TO DELIBERATELY DAMAGE ANY WEBSITE OR UNDERMINE THE LEGITIMATE OPERATION OF THE CONTEST IS A VIOLATION OF CRIMINAL AND CIVIL LAWS. AND SHOULD SUCH AN ATTEMPT BE MADE, THE SPONSOR RESERVES THE RIGHT TO SEEK DAMAGES OR OTHER REMEDIES FROM ANY SUCH PERSON(S) RESPONSIBLE FOR THE ATTEMPT TO THE FULLEST EXTENT PERMITTED BY LAW. In the event of a dispute as to the identity or eligibility of a winner based on an email address, the winning entry will be declared made by the "Authorized Account Holder" of the email address submitted at time of entry. "Authorized Account Holder" is defined as the natural person 18 years of age or older who is assigned to an email address by an Internet access provider, online service provider, or other organization (e.g., business, education institution, etc.) that is responsible for assigning email addresses for the domain associated with the submitted email address. Use of automated devices are not valid for entry.

11) LEGAL Information:

All submissions become sole property of Sponsor and will not be acknowledged or returned. By submitting an entry, all entrants grant Sponsor the absolute and unconditional right and authority to copy, edit, publish, promote, broadcast, or otherwise use, in whole or in part, their entries, in perpetuity, in any manner without further permission, notice or compensation. Entries that contain copyrighted material must include a release from the copyright holder. Prizes are nontransferable. No substitutions or cash redemptions, except by Sponsor in the event of prize unavailability. Sponsor reserves the right at its sole discretion to not publish the winning entry for any reason whatsoever.

In the event that there is an insufficient number of entries received that meet the minimum standards determined by the judges, all prizes will not be awarded. Void in Quebec, Puerto Rico, and wherever prohibited or restricted by law. Winners will be required to complete and return an affidavit of eligibility and a liability/publicity release, within 15 days of winning notification, or an alternate winner will be selected. In the event any winner is considered a minor in his/her state of residence, such winner's parent/legal guardian will be required to sign and return all necessary paperwork.

By entering, entrants release the judges and Sponsor, and its parent company, subsidiaries, affiliates, divisions, advertising, production, and promotion agencies from any and all liability for any loss, harm, damages, costs, or expenses, including without limitation property damages, personal injury, and/or death arising out of participation in this contest, the acceptance, possession, use or misuse of any prize, claims based on publicity rights, defamation or invasion of privacy, merchandise delivery, or the violation of any intellectual property rights, including but not limited to copyright infringement and/or trademark infringement.

Sponsor:
Pocket Books,
an imprint of Simon & Schuster, Inc.
1230 Avenue of the Americas,
New York, NY 10020